DYING DAY

ALSO BY STEPHEN EDGER

Dead to Me

STEPHEN EDGER

A Detective Kate Matthews novel

DYING DAY

bookouture

Published by Bookouture in 2017

An imprint of StoryFire Ltd.
Carmelite House
50 Victoria Embankment
London EC4Y 0DZ
www.bookouture.com

ISBN: 978-1-78681-270-4
eBook ISBN: 978-1-78681-269-8

For my wife and children.

PROLOGUE

FRIDAY, 15 JANUARY 2016, 10.45 P.M.

I push him away with all my might, and he topples from the bed. This was a huge mistake. I never should have asked him to come into the bedroom. I should have seen him watching me. I should have recognised the look of lust. But I thought he was just being friendly.

I dive off the bed, keen to put distance between us, but he's on his feet again and chasing me. He grabs my arm, spinning me round. He's still aroused, and that look is still in his eyes, but I don't want him here anymore. I try to push him away, but he squeezes my arms tighter, pulling me closer.

'Don't fight me, Amy,' he growls, and I can smell the wine on his breath.

I need to get away, so I charge at him, and we slam into the shelving units by the wall. I scream, but this only spurs him on. I have no other choice; I drive my knee into his groin and he doubles over in pain.

Now is my chance.

I have to escape.

I turn to run, but he lunges forwards, and grabs my ankle with an outstretched hand. I lose my footing, and my body twists in the air as I fall to one side. There's a sharp pain in the back of my neck as I crash into the corner of the table. I land on the carpet and everything goes black.

CHAPTER ONE

WEDNESDAY

The Audi bounced out of the industrial estate as Kate took the speed bump without slowing. Two hundred yards in front of her she could see her suspect hightailing it along the slip road leading to the M3.

She held the radio to her face. 'This is Charlie-Victor-Two-Zero-Zero-Five in high-speed pursuit of suspect Niall Renshaw. He's driving a 2012 red Porsche Boxster, registration is Kilo-Yankee-Six-Two-Mike-Romeo-Kilo. I am pursuing in a grey Audi TT, registration Hotel-November-One-Five-Hotel-Papa-Papa. I need backup to intercept him. Over.'

The Boxster joined the motorway and cut across two lanes, disappearing from view behind a supermarket lorry. Kate dumped the radio into her lap, dropped a gear, and shot down the hard shoulder of the slip road, cutting back onto the motorway and almost clipping a caravan crawling along the inside lane. The blue lights built into the grille at the front of the car were all the warning she could offer.

Her radio burst back into life. 'Charlie-Victor-Two-Zero-Zero-Five received. I have two units joining you at junction 11, ma'am. Over.'

Kate lifted the radio, almost losing control of the wheel. 'Received.'

The dashboard display flashed with the supe's ID and she tapped her Bluetooth.

'Matthews, what the *hell* is going on?'

'He deserted the scene and I'm on his tail.'

'Where?'

Kate pulled around a supermarket lorry, and could just make out the Boxster a quarter of a mile ahead. He had to be doing over a hundred to be pulling away from her that fast. She darted into the outside lane and floored the accelerator.

'M3, sir. Joined at Eastleigh, heading East towards—'

'Jesus! On whose authority?'

'Sir, there wasn't time to—'

'Pull over now! There's too much at stake here. I don't want him panicked into doing something stupid. There'll be other chances.'

'But sir—'

'I don't want you causing an incident. End the pursuit.'

She flashed her lights at the Range Rover directly in front and gesticulated for him to move as she charged up behind him.

'Sir, I wouldn't do anything to risk—'

'Desist, Matthews. That's an order. You can't keep pushing yourself like this.'

The Porsche was still eating up road, but she was finally gaining on him, her hands clammy against the leather strapping of the wheel. 'Sir, I've got two support vehicles on the way. I need to keep him in sight until they can intercept.'

There was a pause. 'Where will they join?'

'At Winchester. I still have eyes on him.'

She was still gaining.

'I want you to leave the pursuit when the patrol cars join. We need you back at the crime scene straight away, they need the SIO on-site.'

There was no point in arguing with him. 'Understood, sir,' she said through gritted teeth.

'Do not engage with him, Matthews. I mean it. I want to hear you say it.'

They'd now passed the next junction, and the signs at the side of the road showed there was a mile until the Winchester turn-off.

'Matthews? I want you to respond,' he repeated, louder this time.

'I'll leave at Winchester, sir.' She cut the call, and pushed the speedometer on. Now she was only four car lengths behind Renshaw.

Suddenly he jerked into the middle lane to the sound of blaring horns. Kate couldn't copy the move as an SUV was blocking her path. She forged forwards, cutting in front of the SUV and then over again as she saw the Porsche dart up the slip road. He must have spotted the patrol cars on the road ahead.

'Shit!' she shouted, before jabbering into the radio. 'This is Charlie-Victor-Two-Zero-Zero-Five, the suspect has left the motorway at junction 12. Are there any other cars in the area?'

'Negative, Charlie-Victor-Two-Zero-Zero-Five.'

'He's heading north towards Winchester. I'm in pursuit, but I need backup. Over.'

'Received. Over.'

She hadn't lied; the supe had told her to exit at Winchester, to maintain eye contact until backup could intercept, which is exactly what she was doing.

The Porsche raced through a red light, narrowly avoiding a collision with a double-decker bus. The light went amber as Kate mounted the kerb, shot across the grass and back onto the road, only two car lengths behind him now.

'I've got you, you son-of-a-bitch,' she yelled at the windscreen.

She followed him onto the single carriageway and thumped the steering wheel in elation as she saw a tractor pull into view just beyond the bend in the road. With the stream of traffic coming the opposite way, there was no way he was overtaking.

But she was wrong. Suddenly, he shot out and accelerated into an opening. It was an insane move, but if she didn't replicate it, she'd lose him. She pulled the wheel right and tucked in behind him, praying that he would hurry so they could both get past the tractor before the bend that was hurtling towards them.

As the nose of her Audi crept past the tractor, Renshaw slowed, trapping her in. She pressed harder on the accelerator, nudging his bumper. She saw him glance up into the rear-view mirror and give her a sickening grin. She bumped him again, but he remained where he was. What was he playing at?

He swung left.

The breath caught in Kate's throat as sunlight reflected off the windscreen of the 4x4 approaching. A second later, she was flying through the air.

CHAPTER TWO

The glare of bright light. Incessant pounding behind her eyes. And then suddenly, the sensation of tumbling; her body held fast by the sheets that swaddled her as her head rolled through the darkness.

Kate fought the urge to retch as she tried to focus on a single thought: *where am I?* But the synapses of memory were singed in the heat of the headache that raged behind her eyes. Opening her mouth to call for help released little more than a whimper.

Somewhere in the distance a banging sound, followed by beeping horns and scraping metal. A flashback of her car flying through the air.

The accident.

Glimpses of foliage and a chainsaw. Then the dense fog returned.

'Matthews? You awake?'

The supe's voice. Had he come to save her?

A cool hand was grabbing at her arm and shaking her.

'Matthews? Wake up. I need to talk to you.'

Kate strained her eyelids apart, suddenly aware of the pillow behind her head and the firm mattress pressing against her aching body.

'Sir?' she choked, her voice little more than a whisper. She cleared her throat, the taste of blood clinging to the roof of her mouth.

She heard movement, the clatter of blinds being pulled closed. 'Is that better?'

It was. Opening her eyes wider, Kate's surroundings came into focus; a private room; her bed against one wall; machinery beeping and whirring behind her; to the left a door was ajar, revealing a small bathroom.

'Hospital?' she croaked.

The supe passed her a beaker and straw, and she sucked the warm water in.

'I should have brought some grapes,' he muttered dismissively.

She cleared her throat. 'I'd prefer wine.'

Some of the tautness in his face evaporated as he smiled, but his smile was short-lived. 'How are you feeling?'

'Like I've been in a car accident.'

'You're lucky to be alive.'

'Renshaw, sir… did we—'

'He's in a room down the hall, with a police guard.'

She sighed, some of her tension easing. 'We got him.'

The chair screeched against the floor as he leaned in. She could smell the tang of coffee on his breath. 'But at what cost, Matthews? Your car is a write-off and you… what if he'd driven into someone? A family? Would that have been enough?'

'Enough?'

'Enough for you to stop this one-woman campaign to put away every criminal who crosses your path? You think I haven't noticed all the extra hours you've been putting in? First in, last out, you're in danger of burning yourself out. I thought you were smarter than that.'

She bristled as the pain in her head intensified. 'We caught him. It's over.'

He stood, aggravated. 'But for how long? Until the next case? I gave you a team for a reason. You don't have to do *everything* on your own.'

'Sir, I give Patel and Laura plenty to do.'

He raised a cynical eyebrow, but didn't break pace. 'You are supposed to lead by example. But your relentless determination to put yourself in the line of fire is going to bring nothing but pain to you, and those around you. You're out of control and it's dangerous.'

'I wouldn't do anything to endanger the lives of my team, or the public,' Kate said, meaning it.

He continued, unconvinced. 'I'm not the only one who's worried about how hard you've been pushing yourself.'

'I learned my lesson in London.' She gritted her teeth against the pain, against the memory.

'I hope you did… Don't think I haven't realised that this weekend marks the anniversary of DC Spencer's murder. There's nothing you can do about that. It happened, and you need to move on.'

The memory of Amy's lifeless face assaulted her; that cold stare from the gutter, her bruised and lacerated body abandoned like yesterday's rubbish. Kate fought to clear her mind as her head dissolved further into the pillow.

Not now. Not now.

The supe's eyes trailed across the end of the bed where her foot poked out from beneath the sheets, bandaged and elevated slightly. 'Have they said how long you'll be out of action for?'

She frowned, registering her injured foot for the first time and not daring to move it. 'It's fine. I'll get some painkillers, maybe some crutches.'

He looked at her sceptically. 'You have holiday. I suggest you take it now, before you make me do something we might both regret.'

'But, sir, the case. We need to secure the evidence against—'

'Underhill will take control in your absence.'

She groaned.

'I know the two of you don't see eye to eye, but he is one of the best and it's time for you to take a step back.'

She fought against the rising emotion in her throat. 'Don't do this, sir. Please.'

'It's out of my hands. Professional Standards will have questions for you; if you're lucky, you'll come out the other side unscathed, but you'll benefit from being out of the light for a bit. We all will.'

There was a pause as Kate considered pushing back, but it wouldn't help her cause.

'They've reopened the case into DC Spencer's murder. I presume you know that?'

She winced. So this was why he really wanted her to take a break. Ben had been urging her to take a holiday too. Why did they all think she couldn't cope? She'd lived through it once, she could do it again.

'I'd heard a rumour.'

'Yes, well, given what is likely to be dragged up, a few weeks away from the office is exactly what you need.'

'But what if they want me to discuss the case?'

'They don't want you anywhere near it.' He said it so matter-of-factly it must have been an order.

'That's ridiculous. I was the SIO; I know that case better than anyone—'

'They want fresh eyes on it, and that's that. You've been instructed to stay away.' He glanced back at the door. He'd said his bit. 'I'll be in touch when I've heard from Professional Standards. Go home, Matthews, and rest.' He turned and disappeared out the door.

CHAPTER THREE

THURSDAY

Kate handed the taxi driver a ten-pound note, and pushed the rear door open, before shuffling around so she could rest her bandaged foot on the damp pavement. The doctor had confirmed there was no fracture and that the cause of the swelling was a sprain. She'd taken the offer of crutches but didn't intend to use them for too long. The symptoms of her concussion could last a few days and she'd been prescribed painkillers for when the pain got too much. She'd dry-swallowed two pills the moment she left the hospital.

'You want change?' the driver asked.

Spotting a photo hanging from the visor of the driver with two young children, she waved her hand in resignation. 'Keep it.'

She closed the door, regained her balance on the crutches and stared up at the seven-storey structure of the city's police headquarters. She stifled a yawn, promising herself an enormous cup of coffee when she made it up to the third floor.

Tottering forwards, she felt the strain of the crutch handles digging into her palms as she followed the wheelchair ramp up to the main entrance, deciding it was the quickest way into the building, rather than entering from below as she was supposed to. She waved her badge at the PC behind the front desk and he buzzed her through with a disapproving look.

The lift deposited her on the third floor and she made her way slowly along the corridor, until she arrived, panting, at the door to her department, only to find it deserted.

She rested against the edge of her desk until her breathing steadied, and then pushed herself onwards, heading out of the office and further along the corridor. The blinds were pulled shut in Major Incident Room One. Peering through the tiny vertical strip of glass in the door, Kate could see the room was packed as DI Underhill pointed urgently to the words scribbled on the whiteboard behind him. Something big had happened and she hadn't been called.

Pressing her nose against the strip of glass as she strained to see more, Kate spotted Laura at the back of the room. Laura caught her gaze, her eyes widening with concern, shaking her head in warning. Whatever was going on inside, interrupting was not an option.

The supe's door opened behind her.

'Matthews? I told you to stay at home. Get in here.'

Taking one last look, Kate circled back around and followed him into his office. The fish in the bowl on top of the filing cabinet gave her a slow, cold stare.

'I thought I made myself abundantly clear. You are on leave until further notice.'

'I know that, sir, but I thought if I could show you how mobile I am, you'd realise I can continue working. It's just a sprain, and I'll only need these things for a couple of days.'

'Your leave has nothing to do with your mobility and you know it, Matthews.'

'Sir, please. I know what you said, and I take that all on board, but I am fine. I really am.'

He sat. 'Go home, Matthews.'

'What's going on in MIR-1?'

He fired her a warning look. 'It's not your concern.'

'You've called the entire team in there. It must be something major. There's been a murder, hasn't there?' The supe's head shot up, the same look of unease in his eyes. 'I knew it! You *need* me, sir. I've got the experience. After last time—'

'We're not discussing this, Matthews.'

'Let me in, just for support and then I'll take leave, I promise.'

'Goodbye, Matthews.'

He wasn't usually this stubborn. There was only one reason he wouldn't want her involved.

'Is this… is this about Amy Spencer, sir?'

He looked at her, exasperated. 'This is *exactly* why you need some time away. A woman's body turns up, and your first thought is it's somehow related to what happened in London. It has absolutely *nothing* to do with any of that.' He closed his eyes and steadied his breathing. 'Clearly you're feeling the strain of the anniversary of DC Spencer's death. You've been pushing yourself too hard for weeks, and if I don't force you to take a break, you're going to run yourself into the ground. I'm telling you this as a friend now: this is an intervention. You need to go home and rest. I don't want to see you anywhere near this office for at least a fortnight. Go abroad somewhere while her story is raked through the press again. You don't need that stress.' He pointed at the door. 'Go home, Matthews. I won't tell you again.'

Kate made it back to the lift and pressed the down button. She would follow the supe's instructions and leave the building, but she wasn't going to go home. If he wouldn't tell her what was going on, she knew someone who would, and she could guess exactly where that person might be within the next twenty minutes.

CHAPTER FOUR

Opting for a seat with a view of the counter, but out of sight of the front door, Kate waited for the waitress to bring the tray of drinks over, placing it on the small table between Kate and the vacant chair. If she was right, the first thing Laura would do after escaping the incident room would be to come here and order her regular takeaway coffee.

Kate tilted a cardboard cup towards her as she entered. 'A skinny mocha latte with an extra shot of espresso, right?'

Laura looked surprised but approached the table and accepted the cup. 'Spot on, ma'am, thank you. So, I didn't imagine seeing you outside the Incident Room then?'

'Please, take a seat. Did I miss anything interesting?'

Laura eyed the spare chair pulled up close to Kate's table, and reluctantly sat. 'I can't stay long. How's the ankle?'

'Inconvenient. How's your coffee?'

Laura took a sip and nodded enthusiastically, but kept her mouth shut and glanced back at the door.

'Are you all right, Laura?'

'Fine, ma'am. I really ought to be getting to the crime scene.'

'What can you tell me about the body that was found?'

Laura eyed her cautiously. 'I'm not supposed to discuss it with you... Supe's orders.'

'He specifically told you not to discuss your case with me?'

'Well, he told the whole unit we're not to discuss any ongoing investigations with you while you're recuperating. But, yes, he was looking specifically at Patel and me as he spoke. I'm sorry, ma'am, he'd have me in a disciplinary if he knew I was here with you now.'

'Relax, Laura. Nobody knows we're here, and nobody from the office is going to stop by and catch us here. They all get their drinks from the local Starbucks. I know this is where you like to get your coffee from, because you fancy the handsome barista.'

Laura blushed, and forced herself not to look round at him. 'I never told you that.'

Kate winked. 'You didn't have to. The coffee isn't anything special, so I figured there had to be some reason you kept coming back.'

Laura's cheeks reddened further, but she kept her eyes on the paper cup.

Kate reached for her hand. 'You don't need to be embarrassed. He's cute.'

Laura glimpsed back at the door to check the coast was clear. Kate could see the tension in her face, but touched her hand again reassuringly. 'I promise I won't tell a soul what you say.'

Laura looked like she'd rather be anywhere else, but they both knew she would cave eventually. 'Okay, fine… They found a body. A girl in her twenties discovered around three this morning in the boot of an abandoned BMW. The owner of the car reported it had gone missing two nights ago, and it was located by a passing patrol car this morning. All we know so far is that she was badly beaten. The body is with the pathologist now to establish cause of death.'

'And what do we know about the owner of the car?'

'He's a businessman, married with a son. The car was stolen from his driveway in the night, he thinks the thief fished the car keys through his letterbox.'

'Has the victim been identified yet?'

'We're waiting for confirmation from SSD.'

'And Underhill's running it?'

Laura nodded. 'In your absence, there really was no other choice.'

Kate kept her emotions in check.

'I'm sorry, ma'am, but I should be going.'

Kate smiled warmly. 'Of course, of course, I understand. I appreciate you sharing with me. And don't worry, I won't mention our chat to anyone.'

Laura stood and held the coffee cup in Kate's direction. 'Thanks for the drink.'

But Kate didn't answer, her gaze already focused on a point in the distance as her mind whirred into motion. Why wouldn't the supe want her involved in a fresh murder investigation? Given her experience, she was the ideal candidate to act as SIO. There had to be something about this case he didn't want her to know.

CHAPTER FIVE

136 DAYS UNTIL I DIE

The stench of his cologne hangs in the air as a permanent reminder of the line we've just crossed. Even though I know it's still early, there is already sunlight pouring through the thin curtains. I haven't slept much, but I put that down to the never-ending stream of planes passing over the hotel. Of all the places he could have brought me, he couldn't have made this feel any cheaper than in a cheap hotel by the airport.

I should have turned on my heel as soon as I saw the place. I wasn't expecting the Ritz, but something better than a room where I can see the previous residents' hair on the patchy carpet. I'd lied to myself and said it would all be okay.

I turn my head and watch the rise and fall of his bare chest. I'm sure he must shave or wax it, not that I mind a guy who takes pride in his appearance. He certainly knew what he was doing as we tore each other's clothes off and dived beneath the sheets. But the thought of his hands on me now makes my stomach turn, and I push the sheet back and race to the bathroom, barely making it before I bring up last night's dinner. Prawns.

'Are you okay?' he asks as I reappear in the small bedroom. He already has his underpants and socks on, and is busy buttoning up his shirt.

'I'll be fine,' I say, catching an unsightly glimpse of my face in the mirror; last night's eyeliner and lipstick are smudged. As I perch

on the edge of the bed, I can see traces of the make-up on my pillow, where he pressed my face into it while he did me from behind.

My stomach turns again, but this time I'm able to swallow down the reflex.

'Can you hang back an hour before heading in?' he asks. 'I don't want anyone to see us arriving at the same time.'

I nod my understanding.

Why do I suddenly feel like a naughty schoolchild? He wasn't so formal when he drove me here last night.

'Have you got much on today?' I ask to break the awkward silence that descends.

He is now tying his tie. 'Meeting the DSI for coffee and croissants at eight, then off to the Media Relations team for a briefing before heading to the television studio to prepare for tonight's show.'

I forgot I'd just slept with a minor celebrity. Not that he'd admit it, but I saw the glint in his eye when he mentioned the show. He loves his quarterly appearances on Crimewatch*; lives for them, in fact. Maybe it was his ambition that first attracted me to him.*

Or my desperation.

It's not easy meeting good men when all you do each day is hunt the wicked. I suppose it was inevitable I would fall into bed with another cop.

'Can I call you later?' I ask, surprised by the desperation in my own voice. I'm really not fussed whether we hook up again or not.

'You know the rules, Amy: I'll call you. I don't want my wife to suspect anything.'

And there it is, the two words I was dreading he'd mention: his wife. A fresh wave of nausea sweeps from head to toe.

He fastens his belt, and leans in to kiss my forehead, as he grabs his suit jacket and briefcase and flees out the door. 'The room's paid for until ten,' he adds before closing the door.

And then he's gone, leaving me alone on the dishevelled bed. He might as well have left cash on the nightstand for how I'm feeling right now.

What would my father say if he could see me?

He'd tell me that fornicating with a senior officer is disrespectful to the badge we wear and the service we honour. He'd tell me I'm about to fuck up my detective-in-training assignment if the truth ever gets out. He'd tell me I need to be better than that. Better than everyone else if I'm ever to live up to his memory.

I miss him more than ever, but I refuse to cry.

Not here.

Not now.

I will do better, even if it kills me.

CHAPTER SIX

The clink of Kate's crutches echoed along the narrow corridor in the belly of the hospital. Overhead, the fluorescent light whirred and flickered, heightening the hostile atmosphere of the mortuary. Reaching the entrance to the lab, she used the end of her crutch to push the heavy swing doors open. Ben looked up from the far side of the lab. Dressed in green scrubs, only the dark skin around his eyes was visible above his face mask.

He raised a hand to wave; a gesture made sinister by the bone saw he was holding. Realising, he lowered the tool and his mask, and strode over. 'Christ! What's happened to you?'

She looked down at her foot, tucking it away behind her. 'Nothing, really. I had a little accident.'

Ben's look of surprise slipped into concern. 'Are you okay? Why didn't you call me?'

She knew he'd overreact. 'Listen, I'm fine. The Audi's a write-off, but I'll survive.'

Despite the rules she'd clearly laid down before agreeing to let him into her life, he could never uphold the routine of detective and pathologist for long when they were alone. She'd told him she didn't want any relationship to undermine her position within the unit, for her fondness to ever be seen as weakness. The police had strict rules about internal relationships, and she wasn't ready to have *that* conversation with the supe.

He removed his vinyl gloves and disposed of them in a waste bin. 'You should have called me. I'd have collected you. Do you need a lift home now? Is that why you're here?'

'What? No, I've come to see what you can tell me about the girl found in the boot of the car.'

He couldn't hide the disappointment in his voice. 'Oh, that. I thought maybe you wanted to talk after what happened on Sund—'

'No, this is about work. Right?'

'Please, Kate, there's nobody else around. Can we just…' He trailed off, defeated.

Being with Ben confused things for Kate. Her sharp senses – her emotions – were what made her so good at her job, but she had learned to keep her personal and professional lives in separate boxes. The passion and determination that drove her to push every boundary, to challenge every rule and never give up, couldn't be flicked on and off like a light switch. They spilled into her personal life and now her personal life was pushing back.

Resilient as ever, Ben tried a different tack. 'How about tonight? Maybe we could go for a drink?'

She didn't want to push him away. He had an amazing ability to get under her skin, and he was kind and caring, with a good heart. She needed that. But not tonight. Tonight was the *Crimewatch* reconstruction of Amy's final moments and Kate needed to be alone.

'I can't tonight. But tomorrow?'

A smile crept back on to his face and she couldn't help but give a little glimmer back. Catching herself, she pushed up onto her crutches and hobbled forwards. 'Have you finished the autopsy on her yet?'

He looked like he wanted to continue their conversation, but knew better than to start it again. 'Not yet, but I have a provisional cause of death. Wait here, I'll get you some scrubs.'

She watched him walk out of the lab, before finding a vacant slab to rest against. Allowing the crutches to balance against her legs, she massaged her palms, which glowed red from the pressure of the plastic handles. She'd had them less than a day, but knew they couldn't hold her back much longer.

Her head snapped round as she heard the sound of a door opening, followed by footsteps growing steadily closer and an unmistakeable voice: DI Underhill.

Kate had no choice but to hide.

CHAPTER SEVEN

From behind the cupboard door, Kate heard the approaching voices grow louder. 'It's not that I don't appreciate your faith in me, Guv, but I thought you wanted me watching the security feed.'

The lab doors swung open as Underhill breezed in with Laura in tow. 'I've pulled in a uniform to do that shit. You're better than that, Trotter, and I thought it would be good for you to work alongside an experienced detective like me, so you can learn a thing or two.'

'With respect, Guv, I'm learning a lot with DI Matthews.'

He paused and Kate could just imagine the frown lines crinkling around his eyes. 'What you don't understand is that all the time you're thinking she's helping you, she isn't. This job can be… political. You understand? She's a maverick, not a role model. Am I making myself clear?'

Opening the door a fraction, she glanced through the small gap, just about able to see them waiting by the slab at the far end of the room.

'I think I understand, Guv,' Laura said, unconvincingly.

'So, while she's out of action, you've got the opportunity to work with someone who knows how to get the job done the right way. Leading a team requires more than just acting on gut instinct. You need to give clear direction too, but I haven't seen her doing that with you, Trotter.'

'Sir, actually, I think you'll find—'

'It's admirable that you stick up for her, but it's time to face facts: you won't realise your full potential with DI Matthews holding you back.'

Kate shifted her position, causing a small box to clatter to the floor. She held her breath as Laura and Underhill looked in her direction. Kate had never been so relieved to hear Ben whistling as he returned to the lab.

'I found some,' he called out. 'Sorry, I had to go to the storeroom to get…' He halted when he saw the two new visitors. 'Oh… you're not…'

Laura was the first to speak, obviously sensing something wasn't quite right and covering capably. 'Sorry, the Guv asked me to tag along. Do you think you could fetch me a pair too?'

Ben returned a moment later, tossing a second packet of scrubs to Underhill. 'I take it you're here about—'

Underhill tore open the cellophane packet. 'The victim from the boot. Have you finished the post-mortem yet?'

'Uh… so *you're* heading this one up then?' Ben asked, his voice thick with realisation.

Underhill cracked his knuckles. 'Yeah, I'm SIO.'

'I was just about to stitch her up when I heard you coming. If you slip those on and come with me, I can talk you through my preliminary findings.'

Kate heard Ben snap on vinyl gloves. 'Our victim is in her early twenties, hair colour is peroxide blonde, though originally much darker judging by her body hair. She's five feet four, weighing 120 lbs, which is healthy for her age. A non-smoker. There are scars on her arms – historic drug use – but nothing recent. I also found a tattoo of Chinese symbols on her shoulder.' He lifted the body slightly so they could see.

'Copy those down,' Underhill instructed Laura. 'Any idea what the symbols mean?'

'No clue, I'm afraid,' Ben confirmed solemnly. 'I can tell you that they were inked at least a year before death, judging by the penetration of the skin.'

'Thanks, I'll follow up on it, Guv,' Laura confirmed.

Through the gap, Kate saw Ben raise the body higher. 'She suffered a blow at the base of the head, but that isn't what killed her. I'd say you're looking for an object with a large flat surface. Something like a cricket bat, perhaps. You can see the bruising around the neck and shoulders, but it was delivered pre-death.'

Kate heard Underhill take a step backwards, and she suppressed a small laugh. Underhill's weak stomach was notorious in the unit, and she could imagine how green he'd be looking about now.

Ben returned the body to the slab and lowered the white sheet. 'I've sent her bloods off for testing, but at this stage I believe cause of death was suffocation. The pupils were dilated and bloodshot.' He raised one of the victim's eyelids for them to see.

Underhill shuffled further backwards.

'I didn't find anything trapped in her airway to confirm the cause of the suffocation, but there was sufficient strain on the lungs to indicate this was the likely cause. I also found markings around the neck, consistent with something being pressed hard or pulled against the skin.' He pointed at the marks with his finger. 'The skin isn't broken, so she wasn't strangled or garrotted. Until the bloods come back, I'd presume a bag of some kind was pulled or held over her face.'

Laura asked the question on Kate's mind. 'Were there any signs of struggle?'

'I didn't find anything significant beneath the nails, but I've sent cuttings for analysis regardless. Due to the nature of the blow to the back of the head, it's possible she wasn't fully conscious when the bag was pulled over her.'

Underhill cleared his throat. 'That's great, doc. Thanks. Trotter, shall we go?'

Ben raised his hand. 'Hold on, I haven't finished yet. There's more.'

He pulled back the sheet to expose the victim's legs and lower body. 'There is significant bruising around the abdomen consistent with beating. I found a slight imprint of a boot, which I've photographed and forwarded to SSD. It's not a full print unfortunately, but they may be able to narrow down the make from the tread.'

'It looks like he went to town on her,' Laura remarked.

Ben was nodding as he spoke. 'There was internal haemorrhaging, which suggests a pretty brutal attack.'

'Crime of passion?'

'Possibly. It was definitely aggressive.'

'And the person who delivered the beating was also our killer?'

'The two attacks occurred very close time-wise, so that's a fair assumption, but not to be presumed.'

Kate was relieved Laura didn't avoid the next question. She had trained her well. 'Any sign of sexual assault?'

'Interestingly, no. There is partial bruising at the top of the thighs, suggesting the victim was curled in a ball when the beating was initiated, but there's no evidence of penetrative intercourse.'

'And time of death?'

'Rigor was still present when she arrived, but was in the latter stages. I would estimate TOD as late Tuesday night or early Wednesday morning.'

Laura was still scribbling notes in her pad as Underhill made towards the swing doors, stopping by the air-conditioning unit in the ceiling to take several deep breaths before turning to face the others.

'Trotter, I want you to find out what her tattoo means and chase up SSD about her fingerprints and DNA. I don't want us wasting time trying to identify her. I want to know who her boyfriend, husband or partner was. I want to know who had it in for her, and why they decided to leave her locked in a boot.'

Laura jotted his requests down as he quickly removed his scrubs. She looked up. 'I just want to check something else with the pathologist. Shall I meet you in the car park?'

He nodded, pushing the doors open and charging out.

Laura walked purposefully over to the cupboard and pulled the door open. 'Ma'am?'

Kate squeezed herself forward, relieved to be out of the narrow space but embarrassed to be caught out. She avoided eye contact with Ben, speaking directly to Laura. 'How did you know I was in there?'

Laura pressed her foot up to the handbag that rested against one of the other slabs. 'I recognised it as soon as we arrived. You're lucky it's me who caught you and not Underhill.'

'Yes, well, I appreciate your discretion.'

'Discretion? Ma'am, I can't keep covering for you. The supe gave strict instructions that we weren't to discuss any part of this case with you, and you've collared me twice in as many hours. I can't risk losing my job.'

Ben's mouth opened and closed, nonplussed.

Kate did her best to give him a look that said, I'll explain later. She touched his arm gently for reassurance.

Laura turned back to face him. 'Dr Temple? I had one more question for you. Was any jewellery discovered on the victim's body when she arrived?'

Momentarily moving his eyes from Kate, he replied. 'Um, as a matter of fact, yes. There was a diamond ring – low carat, but a diamond nonetheless – which I sent to SSD.'

She turned back to Kate. 'Go home, ma'am – please,' she said, turning on her heel and marching out of the lab before she had chance to respond.

Kate could feel Ben's eyes on her as she leaned against a pillar. 'Ben, I'm sor—'

'I thought you said you were SIO on this case?'

'I just asked for an update.'

All good humour was gone from his voice. 'Cut the crap, Kate. What's going on?'

'All right,' she finally sighed. 'The truth is, the supe told me he doesn't want me in the office until my ankle is healed.'

'What else is going on, Kate?'

'Nothing.'

He pointed an accusatory finger. 'You're not authorised to be in here. You'll jeopardise the evidence. If anyone found out, the case would be kicked out of court.'

'That's not going to happen… Please, Ben, I just need to know. Let me see the body.'

He gave her a look that said she better be right. She reached out for him to say thank you, but he'd already turned and moved back to the slab. Picking up her crutches, she followed him over.

He pulled back the sheet and for a few cold heartbeats Kate was back in the South London mortuary, and she was staring down at the body of Amy Spencer. She shook her head, and the new victim's face returned to the table. The pale skin clung to her slender frame, save for the patches of yellow and purple bruising around her torso. She couldn't have been much older than twenty-two; such a tragic waste of life. 'Do you think he meant to kill her?'

His mood was sullen. 'I just deliver the facts, you have to piece them together.'

'Please, Ben, help me get this clear in my mind. Walk me through the timing of the attacks. Do you think the blow to the head occurred before or after the abdominal beating?'

He sighed heavily. 'I can't say for certain which happened first. For the blow to be delivered and cause that kind of bruising, I'd say the victim was on her feet when he struck her. I just don't think the angle and severity of the blow would be the same if she was already on the floor. I found slight abrasions on her hands, consistent with scraping on a hard surface, maybe in an effort to break a fall.' He lowered himself to his hands and knees. 'I think when she was down like this, he delivered a kick, as there was moderate bruising at the base of the ribcage.' He mimicked falling, having been kicked. 'This would leave her in a foetal-type position, allowing the subsequent kicking and punching to ensue.'

'You mentioned a boot print?'

He pointed at his hip. 'That was here, and was part of the attack.'

'She would have been in agony about now, right?'

'Absolutely, but the blow to the head may have dulled the senses.'

'Tell me, had she not suffocated, would she have survived the other assaults?'

He considered her question. 'Mmm… the blow to the head was significant. I found some trauma when I examined the brain. I can't say for certain that the haemorrhage would have killed her straight away, but it may have led to a loss of consciousness as it developed. Had she been left with just the two beatings, it is possible that she may have died after several days, but it's also possible that she might have survived. I really can't say for certain.'

'Is there any way to identify what type of bag was used?'

'I can examine her skin beneath an ultraviolet light to see if any ink may have passed from the bag to her face, but if it was a plain polythene bag, there won't be any way to identify it as far as I know. Maybe I could try speaking to SSD and see what they suggest.'

Kate paused, taking it all in. 'Thanks, Ben. I really mean it, I know I don't make things easy for you, but it means a lot.' She looked at her watch, a little shocked by her own admission. 'I better go call a taxi.'

'If you give me half an hour, I can give you a lift home?'

'Thanks, you're sweet, but I'm not going home… Actually, what are you doing this afternoon? There's somewhere I need to go and I could do with a little company.'

'I'm done as soon as she's back in the fridge. Where are you going?'

If she told him the truth he probably wouldn't agree to take her. 'I'll tell you when we get there.'

CHAPTER EIGHT

79 DAYS UNTIL I DIE

Her dark skin looks almost grey; the effect of the elements and death's touch. It has been raining overnight, and the grass is slippery, with surface puddles where it hasn't drained away properly. The flesh where her throat has been slit is crusty where the blade has snagged the upper layers. And then the final indignity: left naked and pressed against a wire fence like an unwanted sofa.

I've not seen a dead body up close before. The closest I've come is standing at the cordoned perimeter, protecting the scene. I'm swallowing my nausea, as we move closer so the DI can examine her. A bitter wind cuts me in two, as I stand there like a statue, waiting to be put in my place. I'm several feet from the body, but I know I don't want to be any closer, in case death grips me too.

The DI asked me to come along. My body tingles with nervous excitement at the prospect of showing her what I can do. If I can impress her, then I'm sure she'll agree to mentor me. I would never admit it to her face, but she inspires me so much. Nobody has a record that compares to hers. She's unconventional, but she stays until she gets the job done. It's like she can read the minds of the criminals she hunts.

My dad wouldn't approve of her methods, but he would admire the results.

From behind, I can see the cellulite on the victim's buttocks and large black thighs. There is no sign of her clothes. Nor is there any sign of a struggle. It is likely that she was killed elsewhere and then dumped here in this park for all to see.

The DI is hunched over the body, examining the position. I find myself watching her in awe. She looks up, sees me watching and calls me over.

'Amy, can you get SOCOs down here straight away? And the pathologist. Also, we could do with a tent to enclose the victim while the work is carried out. Enough people will have gawked by now. Let's preserve what dignity remains.'

I jot these notes down with eagerness. It isn't a lot of work, but she has specifically asked me to do it, and I won't let her down.

She calls the DS over and tells him she wants to know what security cameras are in the area, so he can start requesting access to the footage. It amazes me how calm she is under pressure. Someone chose to kill this woman and DI Matthews is now responsible for finding out who. But where does she begin? We don't know who this victim is, where she lived or what she could have done to drive someone to murder her.

As I hang up my call to the SOCOs she calls me over again. 'The victim's throat has been slashed by some kind of blade. I want you to find it before some kid or passer-by does. Look in every bin and flower bed until you find it. Check each of the exits too. At the very least, finding it will tell us something about the monster who did this.'

I nod my understanding, heading off along the path, my eyes darting left and right as I scour the ground. I take a final glance back at the Jane Doe, grateful that her eyes can't watch me. I make her a silent promise that I will do everything I can to catch the person who did this to her.

CHAPTER NINE

'I think it's time you tell me what we're doing here,' Ben said, as he pulled the car into an empty space in the cemetery car park.

Kate gazed out of the window at the rolling green hills stretching to the horizon. White frost still dusted the grass around the small stone chapel behind them, where the sun had failed to reach. This was the first time she'd been back to Sunbury in the last year.

Ben killed the engine. 'Well?'

Kate's eyes lingered on the landscape a moment longer, before turning to face him. 'How much do you know about why I left London?'

His eyes narrowed. 'You've never wanted to discuss it, and I figured it was best not to push you. Is that why we're here? Is this where… is this where that young DC is buried?'

Kate nodded. 'Her mother owns a place nearby.' She took a deep breath. 'It's my fault she's dead.'

She could see Ben wanted to offer reassurance, but he kept his lips tight and allowed her to speak, knowing she would only tell him as much as she wanted to.

'We were hunting for a killer: a monster who had already assaulted and butchered three women across London. I was leading the investigation, but in the months since the first victim had been discovered, we were no closer to identifying who it was… I was under so much pressure to find a breakthrough. The tabloids were phoning our comms team hourly for updates. The story was everywhere; people were terrified. All we knew was single women were being targeted.'

Kate stared out of the window, trying to distance herself from the memory. 'It wasn't until the third victim that we found a connection: they'd all had profiles on online dating sites – never the same one – but each had uploaded a profile in the three months prior to their deaths. We subpoenaed each site's records trying to find the one person who'd been in contact with each of them, but there were no matches. We didn't tell the public about the connection, as we didn't want to cause more hysteria. Instead, we… *I* decided to put one of our officers undercover as a singleton looking for love. It was like casting bait into the sea, hunting for a rare breed of fish.

'She was such… a bright and brave detective. I recognised her passion and fight to prove herself. I never really expected we'd snare him, but…' Kate pulled her hands across her face, conscious that she'd shared more than she'd intended. 'Anyway, that was a year ago, the least I can do is pay my respects to her.' She opened the car door and eased her swollen foot out.

Ben touched her arm tenderly. 'Do you want me to come with you?'

She couldn't face him; he'd already done too much. 'No – thank you. I need to do this alone.'

Kate forced herself up, closing the door with her crutch, shivering against the wind and tucking the small bunch of petrol-station flowers under her arm, before making her way up past the chapel.

She hadn't been welcome at the official ceremony, her bosses at the Met warning her to keep away 'for the sake of the family'. They'd made her the scapegoat in a situation that had grown beyond her control as Senior Investigating Officer. Amy's family had wanted someone to blame, and her colleagues at the Met had thrown her under the bus, making false promises about how a more experienced SIO would bring about justice for their daughter. Twelve months on, and the investigation hadn't progressed. Despite everything that had happened, she desperately hoped that tonight's *Crimewatch* reconstruction would shed fresh light on the murders. Even if she wasn't the one to catch the killer herself, at least knowing that he'd been found would bring some peace to her.

She reached the summit of the hill, and rested the blooms she'd bought against the gravestone. Saturday was the official anniversary date, and she anticipated there would be more mourners here then, but she didn't want to cause further pain by paying her respects then.

Reading the inscription on the stone, Kate bowed her head. 'I think about you every day,' she said quietly. 'I replay the events of that night over and over in my mind, and I still don't know what I could have done differently. I'm so sorry... I won't ever stop until I catch him.'

A sudden gust of wind caused the bunch of flowers to topple. Balancing on one of the crutches, Kate stooped to pick them up again and didn't hear the woman approaching from behind until she spoke.

'You're not welcome here.'

It was said so matter-of-factly, without a trace of emotion, but Kate recognised the rich Belfast accent immediately.

She straightened and turned. 'Mrs Delaney, I didn't think—'

'Be gone now, you hear.'

'I understand your—'

'I don't want your sympathy, or your pity. I don't want anything from you.'

'I – I just came to pay my respects.'

'Will you just go?'

Kate pressed her crutches into the grass, but the right one slipped on the mud, and before she could correct her balance, she crumpled to the ground. She looked up at the woman dressed head-to-toe in black to see if she would at least offer her a hand, but Erin Delaney couldn't even look at her.

Kate rested on her elbow to catch her breath. 'I would do anything to trade places with her. You must realise that I never meant for Amy to get hurt? I didn't want her to go undercover, but she was so keen to prove herself, and to honour her father's name. *She* volunteered. I know I should have been stronger and rejected her request, but that wouldn't have been fair on her. You will never know how sorry I am for what happened.'

Erin bent down and looked Kate in the eye. 'You allowed that bastard to take my little girl. If you want forgiveness, you're looking in the wrong place.' She picked up the bunch of flowers and threw them at Kate's feet. 'You're not welcome here, Detective Inspector Matthews. Leave my family to mourn in peace. Don't come back.'

A figure appeared by Erin's side. Kate recognised him as Amy's stepdad. He nodded towards Kate, but made no effort to help her up. 'I think you should go, detective,' he said, no resentment in his voice, just a statement.

Kate watched the woman kiss her palm and rub the tombstone before the couple made their way further into the graveyard. The wind blew against the bitter sting of tears, but Kate willed herself not to crack. She would save her mourning for later, for when she was alone; her heartache wasn't welcome here, and she owed them that much at least.

CHAPTER TEN

Ben had offered to help her up to the flat, but she'd refused. She wanted to be alone to watch the *Crimewatch* re-enactment.

Letting herself into the block, she leaned on the bannister as she tentatively put weight on her foot. The jolt of pain shooting up her leg was strong, but manageable. She dropped two more painkillers onto her hand, threw them into her mouth and made for her front door.

Turning on the television in the sitting room she set the PVR to record just as the anchor finished summarising what was coming up in the programme; an image of Amy Spencer's sweet smiling face filled the screen over his shoulder. It was her Hendon graduation photograph, the metal buttons of her full-dress uniform gleaming as brightly as her eyes. Kate could hardly breathe.

The narrator's voice echoed around the small living room. 'It was on a cold and wet January evening one year ago that London police officer Amy Spencer was walking home to her flat when she was attacked, assaulted and stabbed to death. It was a brutal slaying that sent shockwaves across the nation's capital.'

Kate didn't need reminding. The day had started like any other, but nothing could have prepared her for how much would change by the time Big Ben struck midnight. Kate was working every hour of every day at that time. They were under pressure. *She* was under pressure. Those moments where Amy would share horror stories of some of the men she'd met through the dating site over a glass of wine, seemed all too brief. Somehow, even though Amy was really the one with her neck on the line, she managed to keep the team's spirits high. Kate knew she would go far.

The screen faded to a shot of two paramedics in green tending to a young woman in a dark, wet gutter. The word 'RECONSTRUCTION' appeared in the bottom corner of the screen as a male voice – one of the paramedics – provided commentary.

'We were called to the scene in the early hours of Saturday morning, and found Amy Spencer dead from heavy blood loss. There was no pulse and it was clear she'd been dead for some time before we arrived.'

Kate could remember running towards the ambulance's flashing lights. She'd nearly slipped on the wet ground several times, but she needed to see the scene for herself to believe it. One of the uniforms at the perimeter had tried to restrain her, but she'd fought him off and dived under the cordon just as the body was just being lifted by the coroner. *It had to be a mistake. It couldn't be Amy, she wasn't working that night. It had to be someone else.*

She'd screamed and shouted for the medics not to give up. Amy was young; a fighter like Kate. She wouldn't pass away without a battle. But as Amy's lifeless emerald eyes stared blankly back at her, a spear of ice lodged itself in her heart. It would remain there until she caught the monster that did this.

The scene on the TV cut away to the redheaded actress playing Amy, now dressed in a shirt and trousers, walking towards their old office. A new voice took over the narration, explaining that Amy wasn't just a vulnerable young woman cut down in her prime, but a serving police officer.

Kate paused the screen, her cheeks burning with anger; furious thoughts raced through her mind. *She looks nothing like her! How is this supposed to jog people's memories? Why is her hair down? Amy always had it tied in a ponytail… Who put this shit together?*

She cursed the Met for not consulting her. It had been her investigation for months; she'd lived and breathed every second of it. Kate knew Amy and the case better than anyone.

Erin Delaney appeared on screen, her accent unmistakeable. 'Amy didn't deserve to die like this… she was my little baby…' She paused to dab her eyes. 'She never should have been left alone out there… She was a good girl, and nothing was ever too much for her. Amy needed protecting, but where were her colleagues when she needed them most? Where was her backup?'

Kate thought back to the last time she'd seen Amy alive. She'd said she was going to stay with her family for the weekend. Kate teasingly told her not to have too much fun. Amy replied that she should take the weekend off too, but despite promising that she would, she'd planned to spend both days reviewing everything they knew about the killer, trying to find that one additional link to help identify him. Amy wasn't due to return to her cover until Monday, the night of her next date. There was nothing in the books for Friday night.

Amy's step-brother Finn Delaney was next on screen. Wearing a jumper and jeans, he spoke with the anguish that only a sibling could convey. With a rugged handsomeness, he looked much older than when she'd first met him in the days following the discovery of Amy's body. The strain of a year of not knowing who had torn his family apart had clearly taken its toll.

He'd been the only one who defended Kate when the press vultures tore apart her investigation, and her personal life. Finn had demanded that she stay on the case, even if she was replaced as SIO. He understood that she was the best person to find the killer, but his demands had fallen on deaf ears, particularly when Erin Delaney had spoken out so strongly against her. The Met had had little choice but to remove her from the line of fire.

The screen flicked back to the reconstruction; it was night-time and the actress playing Amy was dressed in a tight miniskirt, heels and a low-cut top. It was a good match for Amy's outfit in the security-camera footage they'd traced from that evening at Waterloo station.

The voice of DCI Trevor Armitage picked up the narration, explaining that Amy had been working undercover in the hunt for the man suspected of slaying three other women in the capital in the previous six months. The images of the three other victims emerged on the screen, followed by a map of London, pinpointing the seemingly random locations where their bodies were discovered.

Kate paused the screen and studied the map. Even looking at it with fresh eyes, there was no obvious pattern in where he'd struck. That was until he'd killed Amy: her body had been discovered just outside her flat, not far from where they'd found the second victim. Was that a clue? Or was it just coincidence?

Limping to the kitchen, Kate opened the freezer and pulled out the half bottle of vodka she kept there. Back on the sofa, she threw two more pills into her mouth and washed them down with a long pull on the bottle, anticipating the moment when the pain would ease.

She un-paused the programme and Armitage continued. 'We know Amy caught a tube to Waterloo, arriving just before seven, but where she went from there is still unknown. Despite extensive CCTV coverage of the area, the last image we have of her is the one of her leaving the station and heading in a north-westerly direction up the Waterloo Road.'

Kate knew where she'd been heading. The voicemail Amy had left said she was meeting someone at the National Theatre. Kate had given the recorded messages to the new SIO who'd taken her place, but the team had been unable to locate Amy on footage around the theatre, so the lead couldn't be corroborated.

'Amy didn't own a car,' Armitage continued, 'and neither her Oyster card or debit card were used on the underground after her appearance at Waterloo, so we're appealing to anyone who may have spotted her on her way back to her flat in Battersea. It's possible that her killer gave her a lift home from Waterloo, but we don't have any witnesses who saw her climbing into a car.'

Kate had managed to get her hands on a copy of the pathologist's post-mortem report before she was benched. Defensive wounds on Amy's body suggested she'd put up a struggle, but had been unable to prevent the stabbing. Another officer suggested that Amy could have been killed by someone new, unconnected to the previous murders, but Kate knew this wasn't the case. He'd taken the bait, but he'd slipped through their fingers.

Through *her* fingers.

'It'll do you good to spend some time out of the limelight,' her DSI had advised.

'But, sir, he's still out there. He *will* strike again. I need to finish this case. I owe it to Amy—'

'You screwed up, Matthews!' His outburst caught her off-guard. 'We can't have you anywhere near this going forward. I'm not prepared to lose anyone else.'

She'd stared him down as she had so many times before. 'Nobody knows as much about the killer as I do. I've been tracking him for months, and I know I'm getting closer.'

But this time he didn't back down. 'Closer? How close are you, Matthews? Do you have a name? A photograph? An address?'

'We have descriptions of him from witnesses—'

His tone had been mocking. 'Remind me, no wait, I remember: he's between five feet eight and six feet two, of medium build, with either light- or dark-brown hair. That was it, right? I mean, that describes a third of the male population of London. Christ! I match that description too. Do you think I'm the killer?' He'd scowled at her. 'An interagency task force is being put together to catch this bastard before he kills again.'

'That's precisely what I need, sir. More detectives mean—'

'I want you nowhere near the task force. You're finished here, Matthews. If you've got any sense you'll tender your resignation.'

Kate paused the picture again as the paramedics hovered over the body on the screen. Something else was off. She'd looked at the scene-of-crime photos dozens of times in the aftermath and post-op enquiry, but no matter how hard she concentrated now, she couldn't put her finger on what wasn't right. She closed her eyes to recall the scene-of-crime photographs, but her head was feeling fuzzy. She took another sip of vodka and narrowed her eyes to cover every pixel, but she still couldn't see it. She sat back and restarted the programme.

It ended with Armitage staring into the camera making a heartfelt appeal to anyone who had been in the area at the time of Amy's death and might be able to offer an eyewitness account. Kate rewound the programme to the beginning, finishing off the vodka in one long and wonderfully agonising drink. Placing the empty bottle on the floor, she promised herself again not to rest until the killer was behind bars.

CHAPTER ELEVEN

FRIDAY

The sound of the phone persistently ringing finally dragged Kate out of a deep sleep that had taken her by surprise. After crashing out on the sofa, something had woken her in the middle of the night, and the sharp blade of her hangover cutting through her every thought prevented her returning to sleep. She'd tossed and turned, tried reading, and in the end only another dose of her painkillers allowed her to settle. Clearly, they had worked.

She had no idea what time it was, and she reached out for the phone and put it to her ear without even checking who was calling.

'Matthews? I need you to come in for a chat.'

Was she dreaming? Whilst she'd anticipated such a call, she hadn't expected it to come so soon. She lowered the phone and checked the display.

'Sir?'

'Matthews? Are you there?'

She forced herself to sit up, and squinting through the glare of the light flooding through the gap in her curtains, she tried to snap out of her haze. 'I can be in within the hour, sir. Why the change of heart?'

He muttered something incomprehensible, and when he spoke again, he was terse. 'Professional Standards have advised that you should be placed on restrictive duty until they complete their investigation.'

She allowed herself a small smile. He was backtracking, and they both knew it. They needed her.

'Will Laura be there to bring me up to speed on the investigation?'

'Absolutely not. Restrictive duty means exactly that. You are not to be involved in any major investigative work. Underhill has the case. For you, I have something rather different planned.' His tone suddenly lifted. 'You're to review our archive of unsolved cases until you're cleared to return to your position.'

Kate thumped the mattress beneath her. 'Is there nothing more relevant I—'

'What's more relevant than cases where we have yet to deliver justice for those victims? You can start from cases going back five years and work forwards until you're cleared. How's that foot?'

She rotated her ankle with a grimace. 'It's absolutely fine, sir. Like new.'

'Good. Well there's no urgency for you to return. Take the weekend and report to me first thing on Monday.'

He hung up.

If he thought she was going to wait for Monday, he had another think coming. Pushing back the duvet, she tentatively stood up. Pain coursed through her body, from her throbbing head to her swollen ankle. With a deep breath, Kate pushed herself on, straight past the crutches propped against her dresser, and out into the corridor. If she was going to be ready, she needed a cold shower and a strong coffee.

An hour later, the cool breeze against Kate's face blew the final cobwebs from her sleep-addled brain. She tipped the taxi driver, and limped to the railings outside the police station, straightening up as she passed any familiar faces.

Leaning over she could just make out Laura and DC Olly Quinlan heading to one of the patrol cars in the underground car park. She called down to them.

'Ma'am?' Laura asked, shielding her eyes as she strained to make out the face directly above them. 'I thought you weren't coming back until Monday?'

'The supe said I could take the weekend, but I feel well enough to come straight back. Where are you headed?'

'SSD have ID'd our vic. We're on our way to break the news to her family.'

'Drive up and collect me. I'll go with you.'

Laura glanced at Olly before focusing upwards again. 'Aren't you on restrictive duty?'

'That's just because he doesn't want Underhill to feel undermined. I'm back, and that's an order. Quinlan, three's too many for a home visit, head back in and follow up on the background. Hurry up, or I'll die of cold up here.'

CHAPTER TWELVE

'The woman found in the BMW's boot was Helen Jackson,' Laura said once Kate was belted in. 'Last known address is her mum's flat in Thornhill. I printed her file from the PNC database. There's a copy in the glove box.'

Kate leaned forward and pulled the file out, flipping it open and devouring the details. 'Born December 1993. Bloody hell, I was fourteen then.'

Laura chuckled. 'It's a good thing Patel isn't here. You know how he feels about swearing.'

'Where is he, anyway?'

'The supe asked him to oversee the collection of evidence from the raid on Wednesday.'

Kate couldn't think of a better person for the job. 'Who is Helen's next-of-kin?'

'File lists it as Angie Jackson, her mother. You'll see Helen had a number of small run-ins: shoplifting, possession of marijuana, antisocial behaviour. She never served more than a month inside, but there are no reported arrests in more than two years, so maybe she cleaned up her act?'

'Or maybe she was killed for her habit.'

They fell into a comfortable silence as they moved out of the city, over the Northam Bridge and towards the high-rise towers dominating the skyline of Thornhill.

'Jeez, this place doesn't get any better, does it?' Laura said, as she stared out of the window at the towers.

'You sound worse than Underhill,' Kate mocked. 'Thornhill isn't all that bad.'

Laura gave her a surprised look. 'Are you joking?'

Kate looked out of her own window. Sure the tower blocks were covered in grime and graffiti, and the bus shelters were missing glass, but in her experience appearances could be deceptive. She'd seen enough horror in more affluent areas to ever make assumptions.

'I know it's got a bad reputation, but it's the minority who cause that. Most people who live here aren't troublemakers.'

Laura located the address and pulled up at the kerbside. 'Yeah, bet you wouldn't move here though.'

Kate ignored the jibe, knowing, deep down, she was right; not with her daughter Chloe visiting more and more these days. She unbuckled her seatbelt, the grey clouds overhead closing in. 'Which block are they in?'

Laura climbed out and pointed to the middle of three stacks. 'That one, I think. Tenner says we'll have a broken window by the time we get back.' She grinned to show she meant no offence.

Kate stepped out of the car onto the muddy grass, and Laura followed her to the entrance doors and up to the sixth floor. Kate steadied herself against the wall as the movement tugged at the last traces of her hangover, or perhaps her concussion.

'Are you all right, ma'am?' Laura asked.

Kate opened the blister pack she'd stashed in her pocket and popped two more Oxycodone. 'I'll be fine,' she said, willing it.

The door to flat six was beaten, weathered and in a terrible state, just like all the others on the row. There was no doorbell, so Laura thumped the palm of her hand against it and it was opened a moment later.

Laura raised her ID. 'I'm DC Trotter, this is DI Matthews. Is Mrs Angie Jackson home?'

The man, who clutched the door like a shield, had a shaved head and a snake's head tattoo on his neck. 'Wha' you want?'

'Is Mrs Jackson home?'

He wiped his nose with the back of his hand. 'Nah, she's at work.'

Laura stepped forward. 'And who are you?'

'I'm 'er 'usband, innit.'

'You're Mr Jackson?'

He puffed his chest out. 'Tha' s'what I said.'

Laura forced a thin smile. 'Mr Jackson, would you mind if we came in?'

He looked from Laura to Kate and then back to Laura, before stepping aside and opening the door for them to enter. The hallway beyond was dark, the doors to the kitchen and bedrooms closed so the only light was coming from the open door, which Jackson swiftly closed behind them. A haze of stale marijuana smoke hung in the air and got stronger as he opened the door to his left into the living room. He pointed at a two-seater sofa for them to sit on. He sat in the single armchair, and reclined it. To the left of the armchair, a small table was topped by a glass ashtray overflowing with squashed, hand-rolled butts.

He caught Laura eyeing the butts. 'They're not mine.'

Laura waved her hand passively, before sitting. 'We're not here about that… is your wife due home any time soon?'

He glanced up at the wall above her head. 'Not likely… she's working late.'

Laura turned and spotted the clock on the wall. 'Mr Jackson, I'm afraid there's no easy way for me to say this… it's about your daughter, Helen—'

'Oh wha's the silly cow gone and done now?'

Laura flattened her hands on her knees and looked at him solemnly. 'I'm afraid we found Helen's body in the early hours of yesterday morning. I'm so sorry, Mr Jackson.'

His forehead furrowed. 'You what?'

Laura's expression remained sincere. 'We identified her via fingerprints. Is there anybody you'd like us to call to be with you?'

He blinked several times, and looked from Laura to Kate as if he was waiting for one of them to break and explain the joke. 'Wait… this must be some… Helen? As in my Helen… no, it's not… I mean, she can't be…'

It never got easier. All the training and guidance provided for handling these situations, none of it really helped. Kate's heart went out to him. She'd wanted to be the one to break the news of Amy's death to her parents, but the DSI had forced her to remain at the station during the post-incident analysis. At times like this, the bereaved needed the support and understanding of friends.

The two women remained quiet, allowing him to digest the news. Jackson shifted uncomfortably in the armchair, not knowing where to look as his gaze darted around the room, finally resting on a silver photo frame on the wall above the television stand.

He launched out of his chair and grabbed the frame from the wall, thrusting it towards Kate. 'You mean 'er? Is this who you mean? Are you sure?'

Kate leaned back, studying the image in the frame. She recognised Jackson sitting at the head of the table, a juicy-looking roast in front of him. To his right was a woman who looked like an older version of Helen – clearly her mother. And then to his left, holding the camera for the selfie was Helen herself: full of life, a large smile spread across her face.

Kate stood, and gently rehung the frame. 'I'm afraid so, Mr Jackson.'

She'd lost count of the number of times she'd had to deliver this kind of news, and no two occasions had been the same;

everyone acted differently. She glanced down at Laura, who was focusing on a point on the opposite wall, either not prepared to let her own emotions show, or unable to.

Jackson wiped his cheeks, before settling back into the armchair. Laura stood and offered to make him some tea.

He declined. 'Wha' 'appened to 'er, like?'

'We are still investigating that at this time. What I can tell you is that we're treating her death as suspicious.'

'Wha' does tha' mean?'

Laura glanced back at Kate for support, but she was focusing back on the photograph. 'It means we have reason to believe that she didn't die of natural causes. As soon as we know more, we will—'

'You think someone killed 'er?'

It was always tricky to know how a relative will respond to the news that their loved one was murdered. Some cried, some shouted, some refused to believe it. *Everybody* asked questions.

'We believe that may be a possibility. As my colleague said, we are investigating the cause of her death. Can I ask when you last saw her?'

'She had her own place, like. But she was here last weekend... for my birthday.'

'And how did she seem? Was she troubled about anything?'

'No, she were jus' herself.' His brow furrowed. 'Was it tha' Rhys?'

Kate's eyes narrowed. 'Rhys?'

'Tha' lowlife, shitbag of a boyfriend of 'ers.'

She looked to Laura, who took the cue and pulled out her notebook.

Kate turned back to Jackson, her pulse quickening at the prospect of an early lead. 'What can you tell me about Rhys, Mr Jackson?'

'Where do I start? I never liked the bastard.'

'Can you tell me his full name?'

'Rhys Leonard. He's known to your lot. I told 'er he was trouble. I warned 'er. I told 'er mother only last week tha' he was trouble. But would either of 'em listen to me? No, but I told 'em.'

'What made you suspect he was trouble?'

'Blokes like tha' always are, aren't they? You know the type: flash a bit of cash, but nothin' 'angin' between their legs where it matters, like. Mark my words: if someone killed 'er, it was probably him.'

CHAPTER THIRTEEN

Laura had been jabbering away since they'd left Helen's parents' flat in Thornhill, but Kate failed to follow the thread of what she was saying, her headache thumping despite the pills.

Laura glanced over at her. 'You don't look well, ma'am. Is everything okay?'

Kate grimaced. She'd had her eyes closed since she'd got in the car, sensitive to the bright sky hanging over the city.

'Do you need me to stop so you can get something for the pain?'

Kate shook her head as she reached into her pocket, one more wouldn't hurt.

'I'll be right as rain in a bit.'

Laura watched her, silently. 'Well, if you need me to stop, just let me know.'

Kate nodded, without opening her eyes.

'Ma'am, tell me to mind my own business, but why are you so keen to be involved in this investigation?'

For a moment it looked like Kate wasn't going to answer, but then she replied in a distant voice. 'Twelve months ago I was hunting a man targeting women just like Helen, and I let him get away. I'm not making that same mistake again. Ever.'

'This is the place,' Laura confirmed as she pulled into the industrial estate and pointed towards the large iron shutter. 'Leonard's record was linked to Helen's, so we know he's done time for theft and assault. *If* he's in work today, he might run when he sees us.'

'Let's break the news to him gently, and see how he reacts. Just because Helen's dad pointed the finger at him, we can't make any assumptions.'

They exited the car and crossed the estate, ducking beneath the shutter. Somewhere in the large workshop, a radio was playing '80s music. Three men were leaning over the bonnet of a Land Rover at the front of the garage, while two others worked beneath another vehicle raised on a platform. Tools littered the worktops at the sides, and a wall of tyres was barely visible at the far end.

'We're looking for Rhys Leonard,' Kate called out.

The sound of something heavy clanging to the concrete floor echoed around the large brick unit and an overweight man in grimy dungarees and a T-shirt, leaning nearest the Land Rover, reached for a rag and wiped his hands. His thick, greying beard hung low enough to hide his entire neck, making him resemble a grubby garden gnome.

'He's around 'ere somewhere,' the man said. 'What d'you want with him?'

Kate nodded for Laura to show her identification before sending her off towards the back of the garage to have a look around. 'It's a private matter. Who are you?'

The mechanic threw the rag onto a counter to his right. 'I'm Duggan. I own this place.'

The lighting towards the back of the unit wasn't good, and Laura had all but disappeared into the shadows.

She raised her eyebrows nonchalantly. 'It's a nice place.'

Laura returned a moment later with a man in his twenties; he was bony, wearing a sleeveless vest layered with dirt and grime, like his boss's. His skinny arms were covered in tattoos, and his head was bent low.

Kate nodded towards Duggan. 'Have you got somewhere private we can chat to him?'

Duggan eyed her cautiously. 'Use the office in the back, but don't touch anything. I know my rights.'

Laura ushered Rhys towards the plastic enclosure at the opposite side of the garage. The room contained a small desk and three chairs. The desk was covered with various papers, and a black-and-white monitor in one corner flashed up security-camera images every few seconds. Kate took Duggan's seat behind the desk, allowing Rhys to take the seat opposite while Laura remained on her feet, standing guard at the door to ensure they wouldn't be interrupted.

Kate rested her hands on a stack of papers on the desk. 'I'm DI Kate Matthews, and this is my colleague DC Laura Trotter.'

Rhys nodded at them both, the anxiety in his eyes hard to miss.

Kate watched him carefully. 'Do you know a woman by the name of Helen Jackson?'

His head snapped up. 'She's my missus.'

'Can you tell me the last time you saw her?'

He looked anxiously at Laura, before turning back to Kate. 'Wha's this about?'

'Just answer the question, please. When did you last see her?'

His eyes wandered towards the ceiling. 'Must be… I don't know… What day is it today?'

'Friday.'

'I don't remember… maybe Monday night?'

'Monday night? And where were you when you saw her?'

He chewed at a nail on his right hand, and Kate noticed the grazes on his knuckles. 'We was at her place.'

'And where was that?'

'At her flat, like.' He glanced back at Laura again, as if she might pounce at any moment. 'Wha's all this about? Wha's she done?'

'I'm sorry, Rhys, but Helen's body was discovered in the boot of a car yesterday morning.'

He blinked several times as if he didn't understand what she'd said. 'What? Is this a wind-up?'

'I'm afraid not, Mr Leonard. We're treating this as a serious murder enquiry.'

He buried his head in his hands.

'I'm afraid, I have to ask, where were you on Tuesday night, Rhys?'

His head snapped up. 'You think I could… I loved her, for fuck's sake!'

Kate spotted the small red needle marks in the skin in the bend of both his elbows. 'Nobody is accusing you of anything. I just need to know where you were and what you were doing, so we can make headway with our investigation.'

He opened his mouth, but the words wouldn't come out. He looked from her to Laura and then back again. 'Well, I was nowhere near wherever this 'appened. What d'you take me for?'

'So where were you then? It's easier if you just tell us so we can focus on arresting the real person responsible.'

He shuffled in his seat, sweat now clinging to the top of his head. 'I was out.'

'Out where?'

He was staring down at his hands. 'At a mate's, that's all.'

'Which mate?'

'Gibbo.'

Kate tried to control her growing frustration. 'What's Gibbo's full name?'

'I don't know. Everyone just calls him Gibbo.'

'Do you have his phone number, or can you tell me where I can find him?'

He screwed up his face and raised his voice. 'He don't like phones. Look, why does it matter? I didn't kill her. I loved her.'

Kate leaned in towards him. 'Someone hit the woman you love over the back of the head and then smothered her with a carrier bag, and we need to find them before they do it again. Tell me where you were on Tuesday night, or so help me I'm going to drag you down to the station and leave you in a cell for twenty-four hours while you come down off whatever shit it is you're on.'

Laura's eyes widened.

Rhys cowered against the side of the chair. 'All right, all right… I was at Dave Gibson's flat. He lives in Millbrook, near the KFC.'

Kate sat back, taking several breaths, while a look of concern grew on Laura's face. 'And will Gibson corroborate you were there?'

'Yeah, of course, but you can't go asking 'im. If he knows I sent you lot to his door, he'll fucking kill me. Can't you just take my word for it?'

'Write his address down.'

His eyes were pleading. 'No, please, you can't go there. Listen, I swear to you I was there.'

Kate was all too aware of who Dave Gibson was, and his reputation. Against her better judgement, she relented; Leonard was a petty criminal and junkie, probably not even capable of inflicting that kind of physical attack on Helen. 'Was anyone else there who can confirm your presence?'

Rhys desperately scanned the wall, trying to remember. His eyes widened. 'Yeah. My parole officer phoned me while I was there. Check with him. He'll tell you he spoke to me for over an hour on my mobile. You can do one of them phone signal tracking things, can't you? You'll see I was with my phone all night round Gibbo's.'

'Can you think of anyone who might have wanted to see Helen dead?'

His expression softened for the first time. 'Nah, she was an angel.'

'You said you haven't seen her since Monday. It's now Friday. Weren't you concerned about where she might be?'

A look of disappointment fell across his face. 'She told me she didn't want to see me anymore. I figured that's why she wasn't answering my texts.'

'But when we arrived you said she was your girlfriend.'

His knees jiggled up and down. 'She is, I mean, was… she told me she couldn't be around me now that she was clean. But I figured she was just saying it and that she'd be back again. It wasn't the first time she'd tried going clean.'

'She broke up with you on Monday night? That sounds like a motive to me.'

'I told you, I didn't think she meant it. We had our rows, but we always patched things up. But now she's…'

'How long had she been clean?' Kate interrupted.

'Must be three months since I saw her using – around Halloween. She was determined to get her life on track. She got a job at a grocer's near her place. I've never seen her looking so good.' He rubbed his eyes, trying to focus, trying to take it all in.

'She was found wearing a ring. Was that from you?'

He nodded, a fresh wave of agony stealing across his face. 'It was my mother's. I gave it to Helen for her birthday. I told her it was a stopgap until I could afford a proper engagement ring. That's why I knew she didn't really want to split up, 'cause she didn't give me the ring back. She – she loved me.'

Kate pushed her seat back. 'I want you to write down your mobile number so we can trace it. If I think you've lied to us, I *will* visit Gibson and tell him you sent me, so if there's anything else you'd like to say before I go, now's your chance.'

He gulped, but shook his head.

Kate watched him as she spoke. 'There's just one more thing. I'd like you to provide a voluntary DNA sample, so we can compare it against what was found at the scene.'

'What if I don't want to?'

'That's your choice, Rhys, but tell me why you wouldn't want to help us rule you out as a suspect?'

He turned away dismissively. 'I know my rights.'

Back at the car, Laura turned to Kate. 'Why'd you ask for a DNA sample? I thought the pathologist didn't find the killer's DNA there.'

'He didn't. I just wanted to see what he'd do when I asked for it.'

CHAPTER FOURTEEN

75 DAYS UNTIL I DIE

It's been five days since we found Steph Graham's body in Finsbury Park, and we're no closer to finding a suspect. The tension in the office is palpable. Everyone is tired from the extra hours and activity we've all volunteered to put in. But the lack of progress is beginning to impact even the most confident.

The DI has gathered us around, and I can't help but hope for some kind of breakthrough. Anything to encourage the direction of the enquiry. Nobody is prepared for what she says next.

'Steph is one of three victims that have recently been killed and left exposed in public areas around London.'

There are gasps of breath and murmurings. I remain silent, holding my own breath to strain to hear every word.

The DI sticks an image of a woman, who can't be much younger than me, to the wall. 'His first victim – Willow Daniels – was discovered in Watford, attacked on her way home from a night out with friends and choked to death by someone wearing gloves.'

A second photo is stuck up. This time the woman is much older, older than the DI even. Her face is round, her hair a deep auburn. She reminds me of a teacher I used to have.

'His second victim – Roxie O'Brien – was discovered in a park in Lewisham. Again she was attacked late at night, but this time her head was caved in by a hammer.'

I know the next words are coming, but I'm desperately hoping the DI won't say them.

'We believe we have a serial killer on our hands, hunting vulnerable women and leaving them in public so they'll be found. We have to catch him before he strikes again.'

I look around the room, and I'm amazed that the rest of the team are stony-faced. Didn't they hear what she said? There is some psycho out there murdering women. Women like me. Why aren't they shocked? Why am I the only person struggling for air?

'Half of you will rework the Daniels case, and the other half the O'Brien one. We're looking for connections between our victims. Who are their friends? What are their common hobbies? Why were they targeted?'

The DI continues to shout questions at the team, but I can't take any of it in. I lean back against the desk behind me. I've never felt fear like it.

I hear my name being called, and when I look up I see the DI is waving for me to approach. I don't let her see my terror, taking a deep breath and pushing my shoulders back. She heads to the DCI's office, which she has taken temporary ownership of, and asks me to close the door.

'I spoke to Steph Graham's landlord this morning,' she tells me. 'Apparently she made a complaint against one of his other tenants. I want you to bring him in for a little chat.'

I watch as she describes what she expects me to do, and I can only begin to imagine what experiences have driven her to this peak in her career. Leading a triple homicide is not the kind of operation they give to just anybody. She is the role model I've always craved.

'What's that look for?' she asks, and I suddenly realise she's asked me a question. I can feel my cheeks reddening, but try to ignore it.

'I was just picturing Steph Graham's body in that park,' I lie, relieved when she doesn't pick up on it.

'We'll get him, Amy. I promise you. Come hell or high water, we will catch him.'

I don't doubt it. With Matthews as SIO, I believe anything is possible. And I'm ready to do anything she asks of me, and more.

CHAPTER FIFTEEN

'Where to now, ma'am? Back to the station?'

Kate shook her head. 'Not yet. If – and it's still a big if – but *if* Rhys Leonard killed Helen, we need to work out why he chose to do it in a car stolen from the other side of the city.'

In truth, Kate was keen to stay out of sight of the supe, who was bound to question what she was doing back before the weekend, and why she'd barged her way back into the investigation.

'What can you tell me about the guy whose car was taken?' Kate continued.

Laura thought for a moment. 'His name's Gavin Isbitt, and he reported the car missing on Wednesday morning, almost a day before the body was discovered.'

'Has anyone in the team spoken to him directly?'

'I'm not sure, ma'am. I know that uniform took a statement from him at the time, but I can't say if it's been followed up yet.'

'Then maybe that should be our next step.'

Laura couldn't help smiling. 'You have that look in your eye, ma'am.'

'Look?'

'You get it when things are slotting into place in your mind.'

Kate had no idea what look Laura was referring to, and pulled the visor down to check her expression in the mirror. She looked tired. She pushed the visor up and closed her eyes as Laura edged slowly through the traffic. 'What do we know about Leonard? He's a druggie, and how do most addicts fund their habit?'

'Theft.'

'And he works at a garage, a place where stolen cars could be stripped for parts, or repackaged and sold.'

'That's a bit of a leap, ma'am. We have no evidence that the garage isn't legit.'

'Just go with it for a moment. I got the impression that the owner wasn't totally on the level. You saw how he reacted when we went into his office.'

Laura's frown confirmed she wasn't buying the assumption.

'So, let's say Leonard needs a score. Maybe Duggan sends him out to steal a car – or maybe he goes of his own volition – either way, he's looking for something he can sell quickly to get his fix. For some reason – one we can't see yet – he is over that way and spots the BMW on the driveway. He decides it will do the trick, but how does he get in and drive it away without disturbing the owners?'

'Ah, Isbitt mentioned something about his keys being taken via his letterbox.'

'So, Leonard, being the opportunistic thief we know he is, uses a wire or stick or something to poke through the letterbox and pinch the keys. He gets in and drives off, either back to Duggan's garage, or maybe on to somewhere else.'

'Where does Helen fit in with this?'

'He said he hadn't seen her since Monday, but, as we know, it isn't uncommon for suspects to lie, so maybe she phoned him on Tuesday, or they'd already arranged to meet up. He turns up in the BMW, and for whatever reason a fight breaks out. Maybe she realised the car was stolen and didn't want him to drag her back down; or maybe they fought about her dumping him, who knows? But it ends in violence, and then he regrets what's happened. What does he do with her body? Her DNA could already be in the car, so he decides to get rid of both. He's been in enough times that he would know to wipe the car's surfaces down. He drives the car to a remote area, and abandons it before hot-footing it home.'

'Ah, but what about his alibi? He said he was speaking to his probation officer.'

'We can check that. I have no doubt that he knows Gibbs, and maybe it was Gibbs that put him up to the job, rather than Duggan. I don't know. There's nothing to say that that wasn't how things went.'

'True. It's a workable theory, with plenty of avenues we can explore to rule it in or out.'

'Let's go and speak with Isbitt and verify exactly when the vehicle was taken and confirm he didn't hear anything suspicious.'

'I'd better check in with Underhill, and let him know what Helen's dad told us about Leonard.'

'Of course. Probably best not to mention me by name, though; we don't want him to think that I'm trying to steal the investigation from him.'

Laura glanced at Kate with concern, but nodded her understanding.

CHAPTER SIXTEEN

Gavin Isbitt lived in a four-bedroom detached property in Valley Park, a suburb in Southampton's north-western outskirts. Kate noted the presence of another BMW on the large driveway. They'd called ahead to ensure Isbitt would be home, and he'd kicked up a fuss, but agreed to meet them there. Although the discovery of Helen Jackson's body in the boot of a car had been reported on the news, they'd managed to keep the make and model of the vehicle out of the headlines.

With her ID raised, Laura knocked on the door, and offered a warm smile to the woman who answered it, carrying a young boy.

'Yes?' the woman said abruptly, her expression softening as she realised who they were.

Introducing herself after Laura, Kate asked, 'Mrs Isbitt? Is your husband in, please?'

The woman slowly nodded and opened the door wider for them to enter. The child in her arms jiggled excitedly. She lowered him to the floor and he toddled off, disappearing into a room on the left. Mrs Isbitt closed the door, and indicated for them to head through to the second room on the left.

'I'll go and get him,' she offered. 'Can I make either of you a cup of tea or coffee?'

'We're fine.' Kate smiled reassuringly, as she stepped into the dining room, and took a seat at the far end of the long table.

They heard the woman call for her husband, who appeared a moment later, looking harried. 'Is this going to take long? I'm supposed to be in Newcastle by six tonight and traffic is always slow on the M1.'

He had to be in his forties, but he looked good for it. Dressed in an expensive-looking suit and shirt, with hardly an ounce of fat on him. His aftershave wafted into the room, and wasn't unpleasant.

'Take a seat, please, Mr Isbitt.' Kate said, passing him a business card, as she had yet to collect her warrant card from the supe. 'We're here about your stolen car.'

'Have you found it?'

'As a matter of fact, we have.'

He frowned. 'Is it still in one piece?'

She wasn't ready to tell him that every nook and cranny of the vehicle was currently being closely inspected by SSD, so she nodded.

'That should make things easier with the car company then. Do I need to come down and collect it, or can I send someone from the agency?'

'Agency?'

He checked his watch. 'Yeah… it was a leased vehicle for business. As soon as I gave them the theft reference number they sent a replacement.'

That explained the new BMW on the driveway. 'Can you talk me through the theft?'

He frowned. 'I don't know what you want me to say. I went to bed and it was there, and when I woke up it was gone. What more do you need to know?'

'We're trying to narrow down the window of where your vehicle was taken to before it was discovered. What time did you go to bed on Tuesday night?'

'I explained all this to the chap who was here two days ago.'

She kept her voice even. 'And now I'd like you to explain it to me.'

He looked at his watch again. 'I had been at a conference over the weekend, and must have got home around eight o'clock. I had a glass of wine and headed up around ten, as I was knackered from driving.'

'Where was the conference?'

'Penzance, in Cornwall.'

'How long was the drive? Five hours?'

'Closer to seven with traffic. I was exhausted.'

'What is it you do for a living, Mr Isbitt?'

He removed a business card from his wallet and passed it to Kate. In the top left corner, the company's logo – a bald eagle carrying a mobile phone and laptop – was emblazoned in gold. 'I'm the Commercial Director of a business I own with my brother.'

She feigned an impressed look. 'And what does a Commercial Director do?'

'I visit prospective clients and discuss our suite of products with them and make introductions to our sales team.'

'Ah, so you're a sales rep then?'

He glared at her. 'No, I'm a Commercial Director. My company made three million net last year.'

'What do you sell?'

'Network solutions for small- to mid-sized companies. We also rebuild personal computers when they go wrong. If you ever need anything fixing, give us a call. We're very competitive and service computers nationally.'

She frowned. 'You live in Southampton. Why would I call you if I was based somewhere up north?'

'We outsource work to areas where we don't have a presence.'

'And the conference you attended in Cornwall was…'

'A technology expo. There were clients there from all over the world.'

'So you got back here around eight, but when was the last time you saw the car? Did you check on it before you went to bed?'

'Of course not, why would I?'

'You told my colleague that the car was still on the driveway when you went to bed, but what you're telling me is you can't be sure it was still there. For all you know it could have been taken any time after eight, when you got home.'

He opened his mouth to speak. 'Well… I… when you put it like that… but then I'm sure I would have heard the engine start if it had been taken while I was still downstairs.'

'Are you sure? You didn't hear the engine start after you'd gone to bed.'

'Yeah, but I was in the lounge at the front of the house before I went to bed, whereas our bedroom is upstairs at the back of the house.'

'I'm not trying to trip you up, Mr Isbitt, I just want to make sure I have a clear understanding of what happened. You also told my colleague that you believed someone may have used a coat hanger to snatch your keys through the letterbox.'

'That's right. We have a small table for the telephone near the front door, and I usually leave my keys and wallet there so I see them before I leave in the morning. A couple of weeks ago, a car was stolen in a similar fashion in one of the other roads in the area. I reckon it was probably the same lot who stole mine.'

'What time did you notice the car was gone?'

'I got up around six and did half an hour's workout in our gym before jumping in the shower. I got dressed and ate breakfast, but then as I was about to leave for an appointment, I couldn't find my keys. That's when I looked outside and saw the car was gone.'

'You didn't lend the car to anyone? Or leave your keys somewhere?'

'What do you take me for? The car and the keys were here on Tuesday night, and gone on Wednesday morning. I don't think there's anything else I can tell you.'

'And you were home all night, Mr Isbitt? You didn't go back out after eight?'

'I was here all night.'

'Can anyone corroborate that?'

'My wife was here too.'

Kate nodded for Laura to go and speak with Mrs Isbitt. 'And you don't remember hearing any strange noises during the night? You didn't wake up at any point?'

'Slept like a baby; always do after a long drive.'

Kate watched him closely. 'Do you know a woman by the name of Helen Jackson?'

He frowned before shaking his head. 'Name doesn't ring a bell. Why?'

Kate pulled out a copy of the picture she'd taken from Helen's parents' house that morning, and slid it across the table. 'Do you recognise this woman's face?'

He lifted the image. 'No. Who is she?'

Kate returned the photograph to her pocket. 'Her body was discovered in the boot of your car yesterday morning. She'd been beaten and choked to death.'

The blood drained from his face. 'Jesus!'

'That's why I'm so keen to establish exactly when your car was taken as it may help us identify who carried out this terrible crime.'

A look of recognition crossed his eyes. 'Wait, the body in the boot… it was on the news… You're telling me it was *my* car she was found in? Christ!' His eyes widened as he realised the implication. 'I swear to you, I have no idea who she is, I mean *was*… I… I didn't do it. I was here all night. Ask my wife.'

'Calm down, Mr Isbitt, nobody is accusing you of anything. But given what you now know, can you think of anything else that might help our investigation? Any strange sounds or disturbances? *Anything* out of the ordinary at all?'

The earlier frustration was gone from his face. 'No, nothing, I'm sorry. I wish there was something I could tell you.'

'Are you prepared to give us a sample of your DNA so we can use it to identify foreign DNA within the vehicle? It is voluntary.'

The colour had yet to return to his cheeks. 'Of course, that's fine. Whatever you need.'

Back in the car, Kate watched Isbitt from her window as she reversed off the driveway. 'He looks like his whole world just collapsed.'

Laura glanced out of the window. 'Do you think he's telling the truth?'

'I think so. What did his wife say?'

'She backed up his story. She said they went up to bed around ten and neither of them left the room until he got up at six. What are you thinking?'

She mused. 'I'm not sure. It's just a bit odd. Why take this particular car? Helen lived nowhere near here and the body wasn't found in the vicinity. I still think our theory about Leonard is closest, but if the parole officer backs up his alibi, we have nothing. There's more to this than we're seeing, I'm certain of it. But we need to work out what, and fast; I don't think this will be the last murder we're called to this week.'

CHAPTER SEVENTEEN

Kate elevated her foot at the end of the bed and rested her head against a pillow, but despite her best efforts to clear her mind, her brain continued to fire. Closing her eyelids, she inhaled deeply through her nose, exhaling slowly though her mouth. She rolled onto her side to try and stem the throb of her ankle, but it didn't help. Amy's lifeless face filled her mind; it haunted her every thought.

Forcing herself up as frustration took its toll, she headed to the kitchen, picking up the bottle of painkillers. It had only been an hour since she'd last taken one of the pills, but it had done nothing to ease the ache in her ankle, head or heart. Opening the bottle, she dropped another pill onto her tongue, washing it down with a mouthful of tap water.

Not hungry, but wanting to be occupied, Kate searched the fridge for anything she could snack on. Nothing appealed. Reaching for the open bottle of wine, she tucked it under her arm as she slowly made her way to the living room. If her mind wouldn't still, maybe she could distract it with television. Dropping to the sofa, she stretched her body out on the cushions, and poured a glass of wine.

After five minutes of channel-hopping, she turned the television off, throwing the remote at the armchair. Enough was enough. She wouldn't be able to rest until she'd looked back through the evidence she couldn't forget.

Sliding the two boxes along the carpet from the spare room to the living room, she welcomed the musty smell as she lifted the lid of the first box. Before the move from London, she'd very carefully boxed up the paperwork in chronological order, knowing one day she'd feel compelled to re-examine it. Her hand hovered over the first file. Was she really ready to pick this scab? Not only was it the investigation which had ended her stint in the Met, it was the unsolved case she'd spent a year trying to block out of her memory.

Taking a large gulp of wine, she lifted the first folder out and opened it. The bright, smiling face of Willow Daniels stared back up at her. Kate delicately ran a finger over the contours of the face, remembering how much Willow had resembled Mrs Daniels.

She shuddered as she slid the photograph aside, staring down at the autopsy image, the yellow-purple bruising clearly evident around her neck and collarbone. Murdered only weeks after her twenty-first birthday, she'd had her whole life ahead of her before the Metropolitan Killer struck.

Kate read her summary notes. In late August 2015, Willow had been partying with friends in Watford town centre, visiting half a dozen pubs before ending up in the town's biggest nightclub. They'd been out celebrating one of the group's birthdays. Just the girls, no boyfriends allowed. Her body was discovered less than half a mile from her home, naked and dumped on a seat in a bus shelter. Kate removed the next photograph, a mugshot of a lad in his early twenties: Willow's ex-boyfriend. The original investigative team pegged him as their prime suspect, and arrested him within a week of the discovery of Willow's body. A bricklayer by trade, he was already known to the local uniform patrol for anti-social behaviour offences. Under interview he'd admitted to being in the town centre on the night in question, but claimed not to have seen Willow in the week leading up to the attack. The team had noted that he'd come across as cocksure and arrogant in their initial meeting.

When CCTV near the nightclub was reviewed, Willow could be seen in a heated argument with her ex on the night of the attack.

Under caution, the bricklayer admitted to seeing her at the club, but claimed their argument was born out of drunken jealousy on his part. He still loved her and wanted them to get back together, but she wasn't prepared to discuss their future there and then.

Kate lowered her notes. Rhys Leonard had said something similar about him and Helen today, hadn't he?

Parking the thought, she continued reading. Willow's ex claimed he'd gone straight home, a mile and a half's walk from the club, yet his car was later seen on a traffic camera close to Willow's parents' house, where she was living at the time. He was dragged back in and this time admitted that he'd got home, but had driven back to the club to try and find Willow, only to discover that she'd already headed home. Parking at her parents' house to await her return, he'd fallen asleep behind the wheel, and didn't wake until dawn, at which point he'd driven back to his flat.

Kate grabbed a packet of Blu-Tack and stuck the three images to her main wall, along with a printed map of Watford from the file. The club was in the heart of the town, and while Willow's parents' house was north of that, the suspect's house was to the west.

Willow's friends confirmed she'd left the club at 1.00 a.m. to make the mile-long journey home on foot, and should have cut through a children's playground on her way. She'd been a confident young woman who knew the streets around her home, and wasn't worried about being set upon. But she'd never made it. Although her body was found shortly before 6.00 a.m., the pathologist concluded she'd been killed between 1.00 a.m. and 2.00 a.m. Plenty of time for her ex to have carried out the deed.

Kate reached for her glass of wine as she studied the images on the wall. Her team had interviewed the ex-boyfriend after she'd taken over the investigation. Despite him having the motive and opportunity to commit the murder, there was insufficient evidence to bring charges. The nature of the bruising around the neck meant they were looking for a killer with larger than average hands and long fingers, and his were neither. Kate tacked each page of the pathologist's report to the wall, carefully reading each word, as they began to swirl on the page before her.

She lowered her glass and slumped back to the floor, removing the second file. Roxie O'Brien's profile stared back at her. Kate lifted the image and compared it to the one of Willow hanging from the wall. It was easy to see why the murders weren't originally connected. Facially, O'Brien and Willow bore little resemblance; Willow was petite and brunette, while O'Brien was slightly overweight with deep auburn hair. Then there was the gap of twenty-four years in their ages, the fact that they had no mutual friends and lived in different parts of the city. There was nothing obvious to connect them. O'Brien was a hairdresser and nail technician, running a salon with her best friend and housemate, while Willow worked in a local gym.

O'Brien's body was found in September 2015, beneath a tree in Hilly Fields Park, a wide expanse of green in Lewisham, with a view of Canary Wharf on the horizon. What made the discovery of the body more sinister was the presence of an all-girls secondary school on the south-east corner of the park. Many of the students walked across the grass as part of their daily route to school.

As with Willow, O'Brien's body was discovered within walking distance of her home, as if the killer had been following her when he'd struck. But what had motivated the attack? Had he chosen her at random, or was there something in particular that he'd been searching for? A claw hammer was used to cave in O'Brien's skull, though the lack of spatter on the area surrounding the body confirmed she'd been killed elsewhere.

In fact, the only similarity between the attacks was the fact that both victims were left naked, and in a public area. But it was enough for Kate to link them when a third victim was discovered a month later in Finsbury Park.

Kate's vision blurred as the memories of that chilly and damp October morning flooded her mind. The naked body left on its side, squashed up against a wire fence, robbing the victim of all dignity. She held the scene-of-crime photograph in her hands, running a finger along the slash in the victim's throat. Cut from ear to ear, she would have quickly bled out, choking on the blood as it filled her throat. Gasping for life would only have sped up the process. Did he watch as the life drained out of her body? Was that his thrill? Her final image would have been of his face.

Reaching for her glass again, Kate stretched her leg out, but unable to make herself comfortable, she sat on the floor; her blasted ankle still throbbed with pain. Dragging herself onto the armchair, she reached for the bottle of pills. He might as well have prescribed placebos for the effect they were having. She drained her glass before refilling it, and reached for her case notes.

Steph Graham was twenty-five, obese and lived in a flat above a takeaway on the Seven Sisters Road, a ten-minute walk from where her body was discovered. Born in the UK to Nigerian parents, Steph looked even less like Willow than O'Brien did. Graham's murder was the first major investigation DC Amy Spencer had been part of, and Kate had welcomed her youthful exuberance and eagerness to learn.

Kate let out an inaudible sigh as the memories of Amy's own murder on that cold January night tormented her mind. The anguish she felt was as strong now as the moment she'd received the phone call. *How could she be dead? How could he have found her without them realising? How could she have let this happen?*

Steph was Amy's first murder case and Kate should have picked up on the young detective's downward spiral behind her determination, but she'd been too caught up in her own private battles, maintaining control of the investigation against the invisible forces yearning for her to fail. If only she'd been more attentive. If only she'd heard Amy's messages that night.

If only…

The sound of rain pattering against the living room window caught Kate's attention and brought her back to the room. The night sky looked even darker, and although she'd switched on the electric radiator, the room felt icy.

Picking up the remote, she scrolled though her shows and started the *Crimewatch* recording again. This time she fast-forwarded the introduction and paused the screen when it reached the reconstructed crime scene outside Amy's flat. She compared her copy of the crime-scene photo to the image on-screen, but she still couldn't see what had alerted her subconscious mind on Thursday night. She was certain there was something she was missing, but as hard as she tried to focus, her brain just swam with wine, painkillers and guilt.

CHAPTER EIGHTEEN

Jolted into consciousness by the sound of her name being called out, Kate opened her eyes, feeling a heavy cloud hanging over her. For a moment, she couldn't remember where she was or what was going on.

Ben's face appeared through the door, and although she could see his lips moving, she couldn't quite understand what he was saying. She stared blankly back at him, blinking several times to try and focus on what he was saying and how long he'd been there.

His forehead wrinkled and a look of concern grew in his eyes. She saw him move forward and wave his fingers in front of her. It felt like she was lost in a bubble, like she was looking at the world from the inside of a fish bowl. She heard him say her name again, and as he clapped his hands together in front of her face, the bubble burst.

'Kate?' he repeated, louder this time. 'Can you hear me? Have you taken something? You don't look well.'

He clapped his hands in front of her face again. 'Kate? Stay with me? Did you take these?' He was holding an empty plastic bottle in the air.

She nodded, as best she could.

'How many did you take? How long ago, Kate?'

He blurred into two Bens until she blinked again. 'I don't… know.'

He left the room, returning a moment later with a glass of water, his phone pressed firmly to his ear. He put the glass to her lips and told her to drink. She retched at the bitter taste of salt and knocked the glass from his hand in a clumsy swoop. It bounced and rolled lazily across the carpet.

Ben leaned down – the phone suddenly gone – and hoisted her into the air, carrying her out of the room. His embrace was warm and firm, and she found herself nuzzling her head into his shoulder as her eyes grew heavy again.

Suddenly he was undressing her and lowering her into the bath. She clasped her hands around his neck, but he broke them free, and rested them by her sides.

'I'm really sorry about this,' she heard him mutter, 'but it's for your own good.'

The spray from the showerhead was cold, and shocked her into a scream.

'I'm sorry,' he repeated, but the spray didn't relent.

Kate tried to bat it away, but he moved it out of reach, focusing the spray primarily on her face and head. She tried to stand, but he had hold of her bandaged ankle, outside of the bathtub, and as the sides of the tub became slippery with water, she couldn't find purchase to shift her body weight.

The fog was lifting and her anger began to boil. 'Enough… of… this…' she pleaded between mouthfuls of spray.

He tilted his head to look at her properly. She folded her arms, no longer resisting the funnel of water. Shutting her eyes, she let the water wash over her.

Satisfied, Ben turned off the tap and lowered the showerhead into the bathtub. She wanted to call him every name under the sun, but the words just weren't there.

He left the room, returning with a large towel, which he held out for her, offering her his arm to lean on. If she hadn't been so cold, she would have remained there staring him down, but she relented, shivering into his arms.

Ben wrapped the thick towel around her torso, and then rested her dressing gown over her shoulders, tying it in the middle. He helped her hobble through to the living room, propped her up on the sofa and left the room.

'Wh— what are you doing here?' she stammered when he returned with a steaming mug of tea.

'Laura phoned me. She was worried about you. When you didn't answer the door, I asked your neighbour Trish to let me in.' He paused, studying her face again. 'How are you feeling?'

Her teeth chattered. 'Cold. And wet.'

'You're only supposed to take two of those painkillers every four hours. By my count, you've taken at least twelve today already.' His eyes fell on the empty bottle of wine on the carpet. 'You're lucky I turned up when I did. Drink your tea.'

She wanted to ignore his command, but the warmth of the mug was too tempting. She sipped the tea, and grumbled. 'You put sugar in it.'

'Yes, lots of it. It's good for shock.'

'I'm not in shock. I'm just cold.'

'You could have died, Kate!'

She shuffled, unnecessarily fussing the cushion beside her. 'I'll be more careful next time.'

'I'm *serious*, Kate. What if I hadn't stopped by? You could have slipped into a coma, or choked on you own… I need to know you can take care of yourself.'

She rested the mug on the coffee table nearest her seat, and tried to sit up, but her head felt woozy, and she collapsed back against the cushions.

Unable to look her in the eye, his voice strained. 'Just tell me one thing… was it deliberate?'

'Was *what* deliberate?'

He continued to stare at his feet. 'The overdose.'

She gritted her teeth. 'Ben, I didn't…'

He finally met her stare, the frown lines like crevices in his forehead. 'I'm worried about you, Kate. The doctor told you to rest. But I can see by the state of this room that that's the last thing you've been doing.' He glanced around, taking in the various papers stuck to the three walls opposite the sofa. 'What the hell is all this stuff, anyway?'

'Just a case I'm working on.'

He moved to the nearest wall and read one of the pages. 'This is a pathologist's report on someone called Roxie O'Brien. Why have you got a copy here? These reports are confidential, not wall-art.'

'I don't need a lecture on procedure. Besides, they're all copies.'

He stared wide-eyed. 'That makes it worse! You're breaking all kinds of rules having this sort of material here!'

'I'm not doing any harm. It's just an old case of mine.'

He started reading the next document. 'Willow Daniels… why does that name ring a…? Wait a minute, Daniels and O'Brien were victims of the man who killed…' He turned back and glared at her. '*Tell me* you're not interfering with an active investigation.'

'How is reading a few old notes *interfering*? Watching the reconstruction last night got me thinking, that's all. I just wanted to check a few things, read though my old notes from the case.'

Ben shook his head in disbelief. 'No, no, I'm not buying that for a second. I *know* you, Kate. You're like a dog with a bone when you get an idea in your mind. You're stubborn and you won't let anyone persuade you you're wrong. Remember that mess you got in with Danny Fenton six months ago?'

'I solved a triple homicide!'

His voice rose. 'And nearly lost your own life in the process. You seem to have conveniently forgotten that psycho who broke into this very flat, tied you up and threatened your life. Chloe's life!'

Now Kate's voice rose to match. 'I haven't forgotten what happened. He came after *me*, not the other way around. I learnt my lesson. I got an intruder alarm, for God's sake. Nobody is getting in here again without my knowledge.'

'*I* got in here without your knowledge just now. It really wasn't all that hard.'

'That's different and you know it is, Trish wouldn't let in some stranger she didn't know.'

'You're missing the point, Kate. You take these cases so personally.'

She could feel her eyes beginning to sting as she shouted. 'It was my fault! *I* put her undercover, *I* missed her call, and *I* let that sonofabitch get away with it. You know *nothing* about it.'

He moved to the door as if he was going to leave. 'That's because you won't let anyone in! Laura called me, begging me to check on you. Don't you see? We're *all* worried about you.'

She forced herself up, leaning against the edge of the sofa so they were almost back at eye-level. 'I know my mind and my strengths. *I* failed to protect Amy, but I will *never* make that mistake again.'

'Dammit, Kate, you're not listening to me! We all know how much pressure you've put yourself under these last few months, but surely even you can see what it's doing to you.'

'You don't know anything about the pressure I'm under.'

'Listen to yourself! You are putting *yourself* under this pressure, and if you don't do something about it, you're going to push away everyone who cares for you.'

She grabbed the mug of tea and hurled it at the wall nearest him. It crashed against the wall, spewing tea across the pale-blue paint, ceramic shards bursting out like a firework and dropping silently to the carpet. 'Get out of my flat!'

Ben looked from the patch of liquid on the wall back to her. He opened his mouth to speak but the words wouldn't come.

Kate's breathing came in quick, shallow breaths. She was shocked by her own actions.

He left the room, the front door clattering open and shut a moment later.

Hot tears streamed down Kate's face as she shivered, alone.

CHAPTER NINETEEN

65 DAYS UNTIL I DIE

I feel exhausted as I step into the office, and I freely allow a yawn to escape my jaw. All the lights are off, save for the lamp on my desk at the far end. Outside, the dark sky hugs the horizon like a deathly veil. I pause and move across to the window closest to me, staring out.

He is out there. Somewhere. Lurking, or waiting to pounce again.

And his next victim is out there too, with no idea she is on his list.

Two separate figures going about their daily activities, waiting for the moment when their paths will cross and fate will own them both. These aren't crimes of passion. He is methodically selecting each victim and deliberately extinguishing them. Liberals will argue that he is sick in the head and needs to be treated. But I disagree: that kind of sickness needs to be wiped free of the earth. Like a cancer, all traces of it must be expunged.

Maybe capital punishment would have deterred the scumbag who shot and killed my father in a botched armed robbery. But instead, he will spend the next fifteen years living off the taxpayers, and breathing the air he stole from my dad.

I feel Pop standing next to me, like a ghost wishing to console me, but as I glance at where his face should be reflected in the window, I see I am alone.

I need to pull myself together. It's this kind of self-pity and delusion that drove me into that DCI's bed in the first place. At least that chapter is now closed, even if the memory still haunts me.

Moving to my desk, I unlock the drawer and drop the files in. I'll sort them out and write up my notes in the morning. But right now, I need sleep. I won't be able to live up to my promise if my brain can't function.

I push the drawer closed with my foot and lock it, before switching off the computer. I'm about to pick up my bag and head out when I hear two raised voices approaching. I thought everyone else had gone home already. I'm frozen to the spot as I recognise the voice of the DCI arguing with Matthews.

Oh God, that's all I need. If there's any tension between me and Armitage, the DI will pick up on it immediately, and then she'll see through the positive image I've been projecting. I switch off the desk lamp, hoping that the darkness will shadow me from their sight. I am rooted to the spot as they enter the large room, and I'm relieved that neither reaches for a light switch until they are in his office at the far side.

'The only thing connecting these three murders is YOU, Matthews,' he shouts.

'You're wrong, sir.'

'Oh I'm wrong, am I? I'm so relieved you pointed that out! Explain to me how three different MOs in three different parts of the city suddenly mean we're hunting just one person.'

'He left them all naked in public places.'

'Hardly a conclusive link though, is it? Have your team found anything else to connect the three victims?'

The DI paused, and replied through gritted teeth. 'Not yet.'

'Well, maybe that should be your focus. But I'm warning you, Matthews, unless you can find something significant to corroborate your theory in the next few days, I will be shutting down your involvement in the first two murders, so you can focus on finding Steph Graham's killer. Don't think your previous reputation will protect you. You have a job to do, so bloody well go and do it.'

She storms from his office, but I remain where I am. I hadn't realised that her theory about the murders wasn't supported by the top brass. I have no right to question her, given my own limited experience, but what if the DI is wrong? What if I've backed the wrong horse in the race to find Steph's killer?

CHAPTER TWENTY

SATURDAY

'I really appreciate the lift, Trish,' Kate said, squeezing her friend's arm. 'I don't deserve you.'

Trish rolled her eyes, and waved away the praise. 'Give over; you're just lucky I happened to be driving to London to visit my sister.' She pushed the indicator down and pulled onto double yellow lines. 'Do you think you'll be long?'

Kate looked out of the window at the eight-storey, neoclassical building marked NEW SCOTLAND YARD. 'I don't know yet. Can I call and let you know?'

Trish nodded. 'But don't forget, okay? I know what you're like when you've got your head in a case. A text message is fine.'

Kate offered her a smile. 'Do you and your sister have exciting plans for today?'

'Nothing special. We'll do the shops in Oxford Street, maybe lunch at Covent Garden. I'm hoping to be on the road home before the football traffic gets in the way. Shall we say four?'

Kate was staring back at the new headquarters of the Metropolitan Police Service. The building was pleasant enough to look at, but even with the familiar revolving sign in place, it lacked the character of the old building down the road. Kate wondered how much of the sale price had been invested back into the service, as promised.

Trish brushed her arm. 'Kate? I said I want to be back on the road by four. Let me know when you're done; maybe you could meet me and my sister somewhere?'

Kate opened the car door, and lifted herself out. At least it wasn't raining here. Steadying herself on the single crutch, she closed the door, thanked Trish again and waved her off.

At the front desk, Kate showed her business card. 'I'm here to see DCI Trevor Armitage.'

The officer behind the desk studied her credentials and picked up the phone.

'DCI Armitage will be down in a few minutes,' the officer confirmed as he replaced the receiver. 'Please take a seat over there.'

She was relieved to sit and rest for a moment; she'd taken one of her painkillers before leaving home, and had promised herself not to take any more before she'd spoken to Armitage. She needed a clear head.

She looked up at the sound of her name, and recognised the tanned face and athletic build of DCI Trevor Armitage, wearing a winning smile that gave away very little. He remained behind the security barrier, but beckoned her over.

As she slowly made her way over, Armitage nodded at the officer behind the desk who clicked for the glass gate to open. He extended his hand to Kate and she shook it, trying not to react to the strength of his grip.

'To what do I owe this pleasure?' he asked, his Oxbridge education evident in his voice.

'I have some information about the Amy Spencer murder I thought I should share.'

He flashed the winning smile again. 'That's great. I have a room upstairs where we can discuss it.' He called the lift, and when it arrived ushered her inside.

The doors opened on the sixth floor, and Armitage held each of the three security doors open for Kate until they reached a small glass room with a circular table inside.

'Can I get you a tea or coffee?' he offered, as she sat and dropped the crutch to the floor.

'Coffee. Black, no sugar.'

He closed the door and returned a moment later with two plastic beakers of coffee, placing one on the table in front of her. 'Sorry, it's just the shit from the machine. I'm sure you're as used to it as me.'

'This'll be fine.'

He sat down and spread his fingers on the table. She noted he hadn't brought any paper or recording equipment with him. She tried not to let it get to her. 'Have you had much response to the *Crimewatch* appeal? I watched it. You came across well.'

'Thank you, but you know I can't discuss an ongoing enquiry outside of my team.'

'Come on, Trevor, it's me you're talking to.'

'With respect, Matthews, nobody invited you to come here today. Why don't you tell me why you're here?'

'I thought you might have been more pleased to see me. After all, it was me who helped you get here.'

The smile disappeared. 'I got to where I am on my own merit. Yes, you helped me secure my first posting, but a lot has happened since then.'

She sat forward. 'Why haven't you come to speak to me about the deaths of Willow Daniels, Roxie O'Brien and Steph Graham? I was SIO on those cases for nearly four months; nobody knows more about them than me.'

'I've studied the case notes from your time in charge. They've given me a good insight into what went on. If I do have any questions, I know where you are, and I'll get in touch. But for now, I'm comfortable with how we're progressing.'

Clearly Armitage wasn't going to make it easy for her, it was time to lay her cards on the table. 'I think I know why the killer stopped after Amy.'

CHAPTER TWENTY-ONE

Armitage's expression remained blank. 'I'm all ears.'

'I have watched and re-watched the *Crimewatch* reconstruction from Thursday night too many times to mention. And something has been niggling at my mind since the first time I saw it. I couldn't place what it was at first, and then last night, it suddenly hit me. I don't know how I didn't notice it before.'

He nodded for Kate to continue.

'All of the victims were found naked and in a public place, right? But his means of killing them varied each time. We also know that although they were left in public places, he didn't kill them where they were discovered.'

Armitage glanced at his watch.

'They were all found near their homes, with Amy discovered right outside her place in Battersea, but how did he know that was where she lived? Throughout her cover, we had her staying in a flat in Balham, working out of a local GP practice. If he found her through the online dating sites, he would have left her in Balham.'

His eyes darted back to his watch. 'Yes, we know all of this.'

'But can you explain it? Why did he leave her there and not in Balham?'

'Do you really need me to spell it out? DC Spencer was an inexperienced detective, who knew little about undercover work. She got sloppy and allowed him to follow her to her real home. For all we know, he was watching her for weeks, waiting to strike.'

'That's my point! He knew she was a detective, and he *still* chose to kill her. That's why he stopped. He knew we were close to finding him. He knew we'd worked out how he was targeting his victims. The heat was on him, and so I believe he left the country after he killed Amy.'

She paused, waiting for him to embrace what she was hinting at. 'That's your brilliant insight? He emigrated?'

'Reach out to Interpol, check whether any countries have unsolved murders where the victims were left naked in a public place. That's how to find where he is now. Let me back on the task force and you'll see that—'

He raised his hand to cut her off. 'Enough, Kate. You've wasted enough of my time already.'

'But, Trevor, please—'

He stood and buttoned his jacket. 'I'd prefer it if you'd address me as DCI Armitage.'

She grunted. 'I can't believe you'd throw your rank in my face like that. I still remember the naïve DC who came to me in tears because he'd fucked a witness in—'

'How dare you bring that up!'

'Don't forget I kept you out of the firing line, and *this* is how you repay—'

He banged his fist against the table. 'I agreed to see you out of professional courtesy. When the officer downstairs phoned to say you were here, the DSI told me to stay well clear. But I ignored his concerns and came to meet you anyway. Well, more fool me. Everyone around here knows how you screwed up the original investigation. You're bad news, Kate, and the sooner you realise that, the better!'

She offered her hands in a calming gesture, and softened her tone. 'Listen to me, okay? Just listen. I know what people around here think of me, and they're welcome to their opinions. But you know – deep down you know – that I'm a good detective. You need me on this task force; someone who can see what's hidden between the lines.'

He erupted into mocking laughter. 'You think I would allow you anywhere *near* my investigation? It was because you couldn't focus on what was important that this killer walked away.'

'That's just it – he walked away, but I don't think he stopped. That was what struck me last night. We ruffled him because we were getting too close. But someone like that can't just stop killing. I know he's still out there.'

He marched to the door and yanked it open. 'DC Jarrod, will you escort DI Matthews down to the front desk? We're done here.'

Kate watched him leave the room and head away down the office, without looking back. She'd never felt more sure of her instincts, but she'd been unable to convince him to listen. A young woman hovered at the door, waiting for Kate to stand and exit.

Kate followed her back through the security doors to the lifts. 'I can make my way from here,' she said, preferring to avoid the humiliation of being escorted from the building.

The young detective nodded and headed back towards her desk.

The lift doors opened and Kate stepped in. 'Ground floor, please,' she said to the man who stood nearest the controls.

'Well, this is a turn up for the books,' he said.

Kate looked up. 'Finn? What are you doing here?'

His face looked fresher than it had done on the television as he'd spoken about Amy and he looked genuinely pleased to see her. 'I could ask you the same question. Here, what's happened to you?' he asked, nodding at the crutch.

Kate brushed off his concern. 'It's nothing. Why are you here?'

'I just dropped Erin and my dad with the SIO. DCI Armitage, is it? They're just going over details before this afternoon's memorial service. You know Armitage, don't you?'

She nodded.

'He seems pretty confident they'll finally catch the killer,' Finn continued, as the doors opened and they exited the carriage. 'He's even planning to station undercover officers at the graveyard for tomorrow's memorial service, in case anyone suspicious decides to show up. Listen, I need to kill some time until they're ready for me to drive them home. Do you fancy going for a coffee somewhere?'

If anyone had an inside track on Armitage's investigation it would be Finn – at last Kate's luck was changing.

CHAPTER TWENTY-TWO

Finn and Kate opted for an Italian deli just down the road from New Scotland Yard because there appeared to be enough room to sit without being overheard by the people on the next table. She didn't like to guess how many of the other customers were somehow connected to the police.

He insisted on buying the drinks, and also ordered some biscotti to share. Once seated, Kate asked him how much Amy had told him about the undercover operation.

'Nothing really,' Finn responded. 'But we all suspected she was on the investigation for that serial killer, because every time the story was mentioned on the news, she'd insist we quieten down, and turn up the volume. She didn't like to talk about the job, I think, because she didn't want to worry her mum.'

Kate nodded. She'd also preferred to keep quiet about work when she first joined the force. But secrecy wasn't an issue now her mother's dementia had worsened. Now she couldn't even be relied on to remember Kate's name.

'I'll never forget the voicemail from my dad on that Saturday morning, saying something terrible had happened and that he wanted me to phone him immediately. I thought maybe Erin had been taken ill, but…'

'I'm sorry to make you relive it.'

He sipped his coffee. 'You don't have to apologise. I *want* you to find the bastard who did this.' He paused, taking a moment to look at her directly. 'What were you really doing upstairs this morning?'

'I asked DCI Armitage to add me to his task force—'

'That's great!'

She lowered her eyes. 'He said no.'

Finn's cheeks reddened. 'Oh.'

Kate shrugged apologetically. 'I'm sure he's got the situation in hand. They wouldn't have appointed him if they weren't confident he could draw a line under all this. But know this, *I* won't rest until I see Amy's killer behind bars.'

'I don't doubt it.'

'I heard you'd moved away,' Kate said, placing a biscuit in her mouth and brushing the crumbs from the table.

A sadness filled his eyes. 'Things weren't the same after... we needed a fresh start. My wife's family live in Devon and her dad was looking to retire from farming; he invited me to take over while he dealt with the business side of things.'

'You look well for it. All that fresh air suits you.'

He rubbed his hand over the thick stubble covering the lower half of his face. 'I'm not sure it has a lot to do with the fresh air. It's been tough trying to focus on the future while Amy's murder still hangs over us all. I wish there was something I could do to help.'

'So do I.'

'You're certain the man who killed Amy is the same man who killed these other women? Armitage suggested there could be more than one killer?'

'He's just trying to cover his own arse. Trust me, when he catches the sole person responsible for all four murders, he'll realise I was right all along.'

'You're very passionate. You're the only person I've ever really believed when they've said they were going to catch Amy's killer.'

'Good policing is what will finally catch him, not passion.'

'Listen, I don't want to cause offence – especially if Armitage is a friend of yours – but it seems like he's got his own agenda. I don't know what I'm trying to say… it just sometimes feels like he's heading up a PR campaign, rather than an investigation. I had confidence in you, but I'm just not convinced that he'll find Amy's killer.'

'That's kind of you to say, but I'm sure Armitage will do a good job,' she lied, dipping another biscotti into her coffee. 'Remind me, when was the last time you saw Amy?'

'The Saturday before it happened. She asked me to come over to be around while some engineer came to reformat her computer. It had contracted a virus and needed to be repaired. She was good at a lot of things, but not very tech-savvy, or house-proud; her place was a state! The guy showed up, stripped the hard drive back, and reinstalled the operating system and then the software she'd requested. It took a few hours. When Amy returned from work she offered to buy me dinner as a thank you.'

'You were close, weren't you?'

He looked away as he nodded, the pain almost unbearable. 'Yes. I felt protective towards her. I still feel like I failed.'

Kate reached out and took his hand. 'It wasn't your fault. Nobody could have predicted what happened.'

'When I was checking her browsing history I saw she'd signed up to several dating agencies, but it was only after the funeral that I realised they were work-related.'

Kate suddenly looked down at her coffee, conscious she'd said too much. 'We probably shouldn't be talking about this.'

'No, please, I want to know what happened. I mean, what *really* happened. I read what the papers printed, but there must be more to it than that.'

'Then you should ask Armitage.'

'We both know he won't share any information with me. Please, Kate? I'm desperate to know what really happened to my sister.'

Kate sighed. 'It was a theory of ours, a loose one but it was all we really had. Each of the three women he'd killed before had featured on one dating site or another. Never the same site, but I felt that was how he identified his victims.'

'Do you think he ever met any of his victims face-to-face?'

'He had to have, as he caught them close to their homes. We posted Amy's profile on several different sites to see what kind of attention she received. You won't be surprised to hear that she was very popular. We ran background checks on every client who made contact. We searched phone and bank records to see if any were in the locations of the murders at the right time, and ruled out most of them. Where there were those who warranted further investigation – either because we couldn't find out where they were previously, or they had a chequered past – we arranged for Amy to go on a date with them, while my team sat in a van outside, ready to pounce.'

'Couldn't you just demand the lists of clients from those sites the women had been on and try to find the person who had seen all of their profiles?'

'We tried that, but the problem with the digital age is that anyone can reinvent themselves at any time. We looked for patterns; for similar dates of birth, heights, locations, profile pictures, IP addresses, you name it, but the user numbers are so vast. If he used false information each time, and was logging on from different computers then we'd never find him. I know it's a cliché, but it was actually like looking for a needle in a haystack.'

'Can I be blunt?'

Kate finished her coffee. 'Of course.'

'Are you absolutely certain that the same man murdered each of those women *and* Amy? Is it not possible you're looking for two killers? Or three? Or even four, like Armitage thinks?'

'I'm *certain* it's the same person, and what's more, I don't think he stopped. Someone like that doesn't just stop.'

'Maybe he was arrested for something else and stopped because he wound up in prison?'

'The same thought has crossed my mind, but I'm sure the SIO who took over from me reviewed arrest records around the time of Amy's death, but couldn't find a viable suspect.'

He checked his watch. 'I've taken up enough of your time, I bet you've got a million and one better things to do than keep me company. Just promise me one thing: if there is *anything* I can do to help you catch him, please ask. I owe Amy that much.'

She offered him the last biscotti as a thought dawned on her. 'You really want to help?'

He threw the biscuit into his mouth. 'It would mean a lot.'

'Is your car nearby? I could do with a lift somewhere.'

CHAPTER TWENTY-THREE

One of the windows in the bus shelter was boarded up with plyboard, which someone had unimaginatively sprayed their name on, replacing the dot on the 'i' with a marijuana leaf.

'Some things never change,' Kate commented, as Finn studied the bus-route map plastered on the portal next to the boarding.

He nodded at the graffiti. 'Not a lover of urban art, then?'

She grunted. 'How anyone can call *that* art is beyond me!'

'Oh, I don't know,' he mused, 'some of this stuff goes for a ton. Banksy and all that.'

'It's vandalism. And it's ugly.'

'It's probably just kids acting out. It's harmless.'

'We'll have to agree to disagree on that I'm afraid.'

'Is this where…?'

Kate nodded, picturing the disturbing crime-scene photograph hanging in her living room. 'Yeah, Willow Daniels was slumped up against this corner here. The pathologist reckoned she'd only been dead for six hours when she was discovered.'

'Who found her?'

'The bus driver on the first stop of the morning. He'd pulled in thinking she was waiting for the bus, but when she didn't respond to him calling her, he got out and took a closer look. That's when he realised she was naked and spotted the bruising around her throat, and called for help.'

'Poor bastard.'

'He was traumatised for weeks from all accounts. Treated for PTSD, or so the rumour went.'

'And he was never a suspect?'

She shook her head. He had a cast-iron alibi, he'd been in central London watching a TV show being recorded. There were dozens of witnesses who corroborated he was there.'

Finn took a step back and surveyed the area. 'It's hard to imagine that someone was killed here. You'd never know looking at it. It looks like any number of grimy grey bus shelters across the country.'

'Assuming he killed her here… this road isn't busy during the night, but there would still have been cars travelling along it, so it's unlikely this is where he committed the crime. It would only take one alert driver to see him throttling her. No, he's smarter than that. Leaving her here was part of something bigger.'

'What?'

Kate crouched down and looked at the seat the body had been propped on. 'That's just it, I have no idea. It always struck me as odd that he left her at this particular shelter.'

'I don't follow.'

She straightened up and turned to face the road. 'Well, look at this place. Okay, it's a public road, but there isn't a property for a mile radius, right? So why did he choose to leave her here? If it was about displaying her in a public place, then there are far more public bus shelters up and down this road. But if it was about leaving her somewhere she wouldn't be found, why pick a bus shelter in the first place? We spoke to the bus company who run this route, and they estimated that more than two hundred people use this particular stop each day, either to join or leave the bus. Of all the stops on this particular route, it isn't the busiest stop, but it certainly isn't the quietest. So why here? There has to be a reason he chose this particular stop.'

Finn puffed out his cheeks. 'I don't know how you lot do it. I'd just assume he picked it at random and move on.'

'That's where you'd be wrong, though. Nothing is ever just random. Even when we think we're making a decision at random, our subconscious drives the decision. I'll prove it to you. Pick a number between one and five.'

He frowned sceptically. 'What will that prove?'

'Trust me. I bet I can guess which number you'll choose. In fact, your subconscious mind has already chosen. Go on.'

'Got one.'

'Four.'

'Wait, how did you…?'

'Simple. Whenever you give someone a range to choose from, they overthink it. They want to avoid the two named choices, so that rules out one and five in your so-called random selection. Now I'd say three is the obvious answer, but your sceptical outlook would want to prove me wrong, so you won't go for the middle option, and suddenly your choice is between two or four. You strike me as someone who is generally quite optimistic about life, so I guessed you would choose the higher of the two options. There you have it: four.'

He narrowed his eyes. 'What kind of witchcraft trickery is this?'

She nodded to the route map he'd been studying. 'Plus this is the stop for the number 400 bus, so the number was already floating about in your head.'

He glared at her. 'You tricked me.'

'No, but I proved your random choice wasn't random at all. Now, if we can just figure out why the hell he left her here, maybe we'll move closer to figuring out who *he* is.'

CHAPTER TWENTY-FOUR

59 DAYS UNTIL I DIE

The atmosphere is thick with despondency. I know that the men and women gathered in this incident room have worked day and night to try and find something to link the three victims, other than the manner in which the killer left their bodies. But it's been weeks since Steph was discovered and nobody has been able to present a tangible solution.

The DI looks exasperated. 'Come on, people! There must be one of you who can offer a potential insight. You've lived and breathed the victims' lives for days. Why did he choose them? ANYBODY?'

My hand is tentatively rising before I realise it's happening. Her eyes are wild as she looks over to me. 'Amy?'

I feel the eyes of the room fall on me, and my cheeks burn with embarrassment. As I open my mouth to speak, it's dry and the first syllables are unintelligible. 'Online dating, ma'am,' I eventually repeat.

Her eyes narrow, and I'm sensing that she is going to chastise me for making such a stupid suggestion. But when she speaks, there is a hint of excitement in her voice. 'Go on.'

I reach for the pages behind me, eager to show that the idea isn't totally insane. 'We know that Steph Graham went on a date the night she died, and we've ruled him out. But what if she was followed home by someone else from the site? Maybe someone she dated and spurned, or maybe she wasn't even aware of his interest.' The pace of my voice is increasing as I speak. 'Roxie O'Brien's housemate said she'd been on a couple of blind dates in the weeks prior to her death. She couldn't remember the name of the site Roxie used, but the lab boys have her computer and could probably confirm what's in her internet history.'

The DI's face begins to drop as she identifies a flaw in the theory. 'Willow had only just broken up with her ex; she wasn't known to be dating anyone else.'

I've already crossed this bridge in my mind, and I'm relieved that I prepared an answer. 'Not so, ma'am. In his preliminary interview, the ex-boyfriend mentioned he was aware that Willow had been seeing several other guys, but he was convinced she'd come back to him… She had a dating app on her phone.'

The DI snaps her fingers and points at me as her eyes survey the faces of the rest of the team. 'This is the kind of out-of-the-box thinking we should be doing. I want you all following up on this. Did they all use the same site? I want the names of every person who interacted with the victims on those sites. But don't stop at names. Check for common dates of birth, addresses, bank accounts, profile images. Our killer may have multiple identities to protect himself. I want a list of potential suspects as soon as possible. I don't care how large the list is initially. We will systematically find every person on that list and check their alibis and whereabouts on each of the nights. He will not kill again. We won't let him.'

I look away as a couple of the old hands snarl in my direction, but the thumbs-up the DI flashes my way is gratefully received.

It's the first time since I saw Steph Graham's body in Finsbury Park that I don't feel so scared. He is no longer the monster under my bed. Instead he is a man that I know will be found. The DI has said on countless occasions that she'll never stop until she finds him, and there isn't a single doubt in my mind that she'll do it.

'Amy,' she calls me to the DCI's office. 'I want you with me when I visit Willow's parents. The app on her phone was a good spot, but

we need to know for certain whether she'd actually been on a date, or had been thinking about it.'

I close the door to the office to shut out the rest of the team. 'Ma'am? I wasn't going to say anything, but I overheard you and the DCI the other night. It was late and I was just logging off.'

'And you want to know why I'm so convinced the same man is responsible for all three attacks?'

I shrug pathetically. 'It's not that I doubt the logic, it's just—'

But she raises her hand to cut me off. 'You want to know why I have no doubt we're looking for one killer. Instinct. I feel it in here,' she rubs her gut. 'And I know it here,' she taps a finger against her head, 'and I've never been more certain of anything. If you're to realise your potential and become a brilliant detective, you need to start listening to that voice in the back of your mind. We all have it. Some ignore the voice, but others embrace it.'

She must still see the doubt in my eyes.

'You know, you remind me a lot of myself,' she continues. 'I once questioned every decision I made, wondering if I'd ever become the cop I aspired to be. It's been a long road, and it hasn't always been a smooth ride, but if you want to succeed in this place, you need to develop a fighter's spirit. Your dad had that spirit. He put his life on the line for this job, and he's a hero in my eyes because of that. Doing this job well isn't about the ratio of cases you close or the number of arrests you make; it's about the things you'll do to keep the streets safe, no matter the cost.'

The DI pauses and grabs her coat. 'Now, shall we go and take the first step towards proving your theory?'

CHAPTER TWENTY-FIVE

'Same as before,' Kate said, as she clambered out of the car. 'Find a parking spot and meet me back here.'

As Finn pulled away, a gust of bitter wind rustled the damp leaves around Kate's feet, and it was all she could do not to lose her balance as a shiver ran the length of her body. In daylight, Hilly Fields Park in Lewisham wasn't nearly as menacing as it was in the darkness. She could imagine it in summer packed with children running around and city folk lying on the grass, topping up their tans. But in the middle of January, the grass looked old and withered and bore the marks of a torrid downpour, pockmarked with puddles.

Bisecting the expanse of green was a winding concrete path that led from the normally busy road, through the park to the all-girls school. She could hear muffled shrieks in the distance as one of the school's sports teams participated in some event nearby.

Not prepared to risk slipping on the boggy grass, Kate stuck to the pavement and turned onto the path. The cold air on her face relieved the heat she could feel at the top of her scalp. She hadn't seen Roxie O'Brien's body in situ on the ground, as she hadn't taken over the investigation until a month after she'd been found, but she'd seen pictures; naked with her skull smashed open with a hammer of some kind. She could almost picture O'Brien walking through the park when she was set upon by a man lurking in the dark. She'd read the report the scene of crime officers had produced, and they concluded there was no sign of a struggle on the grass beneath the body. They concluded that the murder probably occurred elsewhere and that the body was then placed on the grass beneath the tree.

Kate continued along the pathway, looking all around her, trying to determine why he had chosen this exact spot. In her mind, there had to be some relevance to the location, though that wasn't a theory widely shared by her investigative team at the time. In fairness, there was nothing obvious about this or any of the other locations, other than that they were open spaces where the public would be likely to discover the body. But therein lay one of the problems with the theory: he'd taken a huge risk to leave the victims in such open places. Any number of witnesses could have happened upon him mid-act, but he'd managed to kill four times without being seen.

Finn jogged up behind her. 'Is that where…?'

Kate pointed towards the tree. 'Roxie O'Brien's body was discovered just over there. Are you okay with all this? I know it's a lot to take in.'

His face adopted a look of determination. 'Absolutely.'

'The forensic specialists examined every inch of the park, looking for any clue he might have left; but they found nothing. They did find a set of prints nearby, but couldn't say for certain if they belonged to the killer. What shoe size are you?'

'A twelve.'

'The prints found were a size ten. That's one of the most common sizes for male adults in the UK, so it didn't narrow our search significantly.'

'Were footprints discovered at any of the other crime scenes?'

'Unfortunately not. Our SOCOs estimated the killer to weigh approximately 80 kg, which again failed to narrow the search. But it did make them more certain it was a man.'

Some members of her investigative team had taken to naming their mystery killer 'Mr Average'. It wasn't a view Kate subscribed to; having seen up close what he'd done to Steph's body, she knew he was anything *but* average.

She observed the landscape around her, gazing at the tree as her head turned in full panoramic view. 'Why here?'

Across the road from where Finn had dropped her were several three-storey townhouses overlooking the park. Anyone looking out of a top-floor window at the right time would have seen him carrying her into the park.

'Do you think he wanted to get caught?' Finn asked, unsure if Kate's question had been rhetorical.

She shook the theory from her mind. 'No, that's not it. If he'd wanted to get caught he wouldn't have stopped killing after Amy.'

In the distance, heavy cloud obstructed their view of the Canary Wharf skyline. The city she'd called home for so long seemed so far removed from where they stood, even though it was only a few miles away. If her ankle was healed, she could easily have walked the distance.

Coming to Lewisham today had been a bad idea. She'd hoped that seeing the scene in person once more would help shed some light, but it had only brought up more questions.

Kate took one final look at the tree, before turning and making her way slowly back along the path towards the main road. Finn went to collect the car. As she reached the pavement, she felt the first spots of icy rain on her cheeks. She tried to pick up the pace, but her crutch wouldn't allow her to move any quicker. It was a relief when Finn pulled up a few minutes later.

'Where to now?' he asked, when she was back inside.

'Finsbury Park tube station.'

'Do you mind me asking: what are you hoping to achieve by revisiting these scenes?'

She stared out of the window as the drops of rain grew heavier against the glass, but before she could answer, her phone rang.

'Ma'am, I'm sorry to disturb you on a Saturday.'

'That's fine, Laura. Go ahead.'

'I thought you'd want to know, we've reviewed all the security-camera feeds from around the train station where Helen's body was found, and we were unable to identify the exact time the BMW passed by. In total four vehicles fitting the description passed the area between eight o'clock on Tuesday night and the early hours of Thursday morning when the victim was discovered. None of the vehicles had the same registration number as Isbitt's car.'

Kate clamped her eyes shut, pinching the bridge of her nose. 'What are you telling me?'

'I think the killer changed the plates on the vehicle to cover his movements.'

'Why?'

Laura paused. 'I spoke to SSD and they've confirmed an adhesive material was discovered in two places in the centre of both the front and rear plates. That's why we weren't able to find when the vehicle arrived at the scene.'

'I'm going to compare the registrations of the four vehicles found on the footage against the PNC database to see if one stands out.'

'That's great, Laura, but listen, now's not a good time. Why don't you stop by my place tonight and we can go over it in more detail.'

'Sure.'

'Oh, and Laura, you'd better update Underhill with your findings, but when you do, please don't mention my name. You know what he's like.'

'Understood, ma'am, I'll leave your name out of it. Shall I bring food?'

'You choose,' Kate said as a fresh wave of nausea struck her. She hung up the phone.

CHAPTER TWENTY-SIX

Leaning against the wire fence, Kate took a moment to catch her breath. She'd forgotten how steep the bank up to the railway tracks was. The rain continued to fall and her grip on the bank's edge was poor.

Kate could still remember that fateful October morning in 2015 when she'd first set eyes upon the murder scene here. Steph's face had been contorted with fear; an image that still haunted Kate's dreams to this day. Her skin had taken on a milky-brown quality, owing to overnight exposure to the elements.

She had dealt with murder enquiries before, but this had been the first that had really affected her. The murders she'd previously investigated had been motivated by revenge or anger, but Steph's murder seemed senseless.

The body had been reported by a concerned passenger on a passing tube that cold morning. Hundreds of people must have whizzed past on Piccadilly Line trains that day, but only one person had picked up the phone to report it. It wouldn't have surprised Kate if nobody else had seen the body. Rush-hour commuters are focused on getting to work as efficiently as possible; they travel in bubbles, oblivious to the world outside.

The killer had squashed Steph's side up against the wire fence, leaving her naked on the bank, with the cut across her throat exposed.

Kate looked back down the soggy bank at the concrete cycle path below. The path led directly into the park, but there were no street lights, so in the dead of night, there would be no way a potential witness passing by could have seen what he was doing to Steph up here.

Security cameras at Finsbury Park tube station had her exiting the station at 22:58, and turning to the left, instead of to the right, which would have allowed her to walk the short distance to the Seven Sisters Road, where she lived. But instead of going home, she'd headed in the opposite direction towards the cycle path into the park. To this day, nobody could explain *why* she hadn't gone straight home. Had she been meeting somebody? But why would she agree to meet someone in such a dark and secluded place? The junction where the tube station sat was a busy spot with plenty of local businesses, street lights and passing buses and cabs.

The team had investigated whether Steph could have been discreetly meeting a dealer in the park, but there was no evidence that she had a habit of any kind. She was paid the minimum wage, making just enough to cover rent and food for the one-room studio flat above the takeaway.

According to her work colleagues, Steph had been excited about going on a date that evening. She'd told them she was meeting him in the West End for coffee, and she would let them know how things had gone the following morning. She'd met this man through an online dating agency, and having exchanged a dozen or so messages, they'd agreed to meet in person, though both had insisted it be in a very public place.

Kate's team accessed Steph's computer and identified the mystery man as Daniel Papic, a Polish teacher in his early forties. They brought him in for questioning and he told them that the date hadn't been a great success, with both of them too shy to properly engage in conversation. Although they'd agreed to speak again, he admitted that he hadn't intended to get in touch with her. He confirmed he'd gone straight home after the date and security footage from a camera in a tube station in Greenwich confirmed he was nowhere near Finsbury Park at the time of her death.

Papic wasn't in the frame, but the dating site did give them a further avenue to explore. It became even more relevant when Amy spotted that O'Brien had also used a couple of dating sites in the months prior to her death. Further digging confirmed that Willow had also recently registered on a dating site after breaking up with her ex-boyfriend. Was it just coincidence? Not for Kate. It was tenuous, but all her instincts told her this was a link worth pursuing.

Kate created a sub-team to analyse the information on each of the victims' profiles. There had to be something specific the killer looked for: a character trait, a turn of phrase, or a particular interest. There had to be something that had brought these three women into his spotlight.

But as hard as they'd tried to find even a tenuous link, there was nothing that made them stand out above anyone else. Yes, they were female; yes, they were single; yes, they lived in London; yes, they were employed; but their hobbies and interests varied, as did the type of man they said they were looking for. If they were to set a trap for him, how could they leave the right bait for him to track?

'I'll do it, ma'am,' Amy had said during one afternoon brief. 'Let me hook him.'

After thanking her for volunteering, Kate had dismissed the idea in the meeting. But once the rest of the team had gone home, Amy had come into the office and had refused to leave until Kate considered the proposal. Looking back on it now, Kate could see how she should have been firmer with Amy. But the young DC had been desperate for a chance to prove herself, and had begged

Kate for the opportunity. Kate had only reluctantly agreed when Amy promised to take a self-defence course.

Kate slipped as she made her way down the muddy embankment, frustrated that her wet overcoat was now also streaked with mud. She did her best to wipe off most of the stain with a tissue from her bag, before hobbling unsteadily back to where Finn was waiting at the tube station drop-off point.

'One more stop to make,' she said, a shiver running down her spine as he looked up.

There was no need to tell him where.

They'd set Amy up with temporary accommodation in a one-bed flat in Balham, from which she was to live her cover role as a receptionist in a busy doctor's surgery. But her body had been found outside her own flat in Battersea, which meant he'd seen through the cover and had still decided to kill her.

CHAPTER TWENTY-SEVEN

Finn slammed on the brakes and gesticulated angrily out of the window. 'You bloody idiot!' He leaned back in. 'Did you see that? He came out of nowhere.'

Kate hadn't seen a thing. Her mind had been wandering again. She could feel Finn watching her, his eyes demanding a response. 'Yeah, nowhere.'

'The world's gone mad,' he continued. 'It was bad enough when they were just on bikes, but skates?'

Her mind was whirring as she tried to blot out the spikes of nausea, but as the signs for Battersea loomed close, the feeling of dread grew.

'Listen,' Finn said eventually, 'if you don't mind, I'd rather stay in the car than come to her flat with you. It's just…' his voice faded as he struggled to explain.

She touched his hand. 'It's okay, Finn. I understand why you wouldn't want to come back here. Just drop me as close as you can, and then you can be on your way. I'm sure your folks will be finished with Armitage by now. I really appreciate everything you've done today.'

He thanked her and pointed out of her window at a small alleyway between two shops. 'If you dart up there, you can cut through to the flat in no time. With this traffic, it could be another twenty minutes before I can drive you there.'

Kate gathered her bag and thrust her crutch out of the door. She waited until Finn had pulled away from the kerb before tentatively heading towards the passageway. The closest tube station to Amy's flat was Vauxhall, but it was a good ten minutes away on foot. They had extensively checked the security-camera footage at the station, but at no point had Amy passed that way that night. They had tracked her movements to the theatre, where she presumably met the killer, but despite reviewing every CCTV camera in and around that area, there was no trace of her after the theatre, until her body was discovered outside her flat later that night.

Amy hadn't used the tube to get home, or if she had, she hadn't used her Oyster card or contactless debit card to do so. But the theatre was nearly a two-mile walk from her home, and if that was how she'd travelled, they surely would have caught sight of her on camera footage, but there was no sign. They'd requested footage from each of the buses running that night, and had petitioned the London Taxi Company for details of which cabs were running in and around that time. It had been a massive operation, which Kate had unfortunately had little involvement in, but there was no way to confirm how Amy had made it home. Nor why she'd gone there instead of to her cover flat in Balham.

Two young black men wearing baseball caps suddenly appeared out of the passage, one chatting loudly on a phone, and the other wearing large headphones. The second eyed her before blowing a kiss as they continued on their way. Kate took a step closer to the passage, picturing Amy making her final journey through it.

It was no more than ten metres long, and opened out into a wider courtyard housing two cafés, a dry-cleaners and an Italian restaurant. Beyond the restaurant, a second passageway led Kate through to the back alley that ran behind two roads of local businesses. She made her way along the dark and grimy street, littered with empty drinks bottles, crisp packets and cigarette stubs.

As she closed her eyes, she could remember racing along this very stretch, flashes of blue light all around. She stopped where

Amy's body had been left; eyes open, hands by her sides, with a stab wound in her abdomen.

A cough over her shoulder caused her to spin in defensive anticipation. A young man in wire spectacles stood behind her. He was average height, and extremely thin, wearing a brown shirt beneath a yellow cardigan. He offered an awkward smile, on an acne-scarred face.

'You're blocking my way,' he offered, pointing at the staircase up to the flats.

Kate instinctively shuffled to one side. 'I'm sorry. Wait, you live here?'

He nodded, as he stepped towards the black metal staircase.

Kate reached for his arm. 'I'm sorry, which flat is yours?'

He gave her a curious look. 'Number seven… just up there.'

Before she could stop herself, Kate passed him a business card. 'I'm DI Matthews. I'd like to come up.'

He rolled his eyes. 'You're here about that woman, aren't you? I thought your lot were done with poking about.' He sighed, before indicating for her to follow him up. 'I really wish the landlord had warned me about the flat's history *before* I signed the tenancy agreement. If I'd known the woman who lived here had been killed, I might have kept looking.'

Kate shrugged her shoulders apologetically, keen not to have to explain her real reason for wanting to poke around. If Armitage had any idea she was here, she'd suffer the consequences.

'Are you going to be long?' the young man enquired. 'It's just, I have other things to get on with today.'

'I just need to look around and then I'll be out of your hair,' she promised, as he unlocked the door and held it open for her.

She squeezed through the doorway, and left him in the poky kitchen, as she proceeded through to the small living room, which led to the bathroom and bedroom. Although there were signs of attempted assault and Amy's arms displayed defensive wounds, the murderer hadn't managed penetrative sex before he'd killed her. But unlike the other women, Amy had put up more of a fight, and further bruising had been discovered on her back consistent with a fall.

Was it possible that Amy had invited the killer inside her flat? The SOCOs hadn't found her blood inside, so had ruled it out, but had that been the wrong call? The place had been in such a state that it had been impossible to tell if there'd been a struggle.

Kate could feel her migraine returning; so many questions about that night remained unanswered, and she was unable to sort the truth from the supposition. Amy's actions had been out of character, but so had the killer's. *Why had he left her in the alleyway when Vauxhall Park was only a stone's throw away? What had stopped him taking her there?*

The loud ringing of her phone interrupted Kate's thoughts. 'Hi, Trish.'

'Hi, hun. Are you nearly finished? It's gone three, and I'm shopped out. Are you still at the police station?'

'Not exactly… Any chance you can pick me up outside Vauxhall tube station?'

'Sure thing. Did you manage to accomplish what you wanted?'

Kate looked around the interior of the poky flat. 'I'm afraid not. If anything I feel further from the truth than ever.'

CHAPTER TWENTY-EIGHT

49 DAYS UNTIL I DIE

The elation of ten days ago has dissipated. For a day there was a real buzz in the office, as we pored over lists of names, pulling together possible suspects. It felt like we were only hours from discovering Steph's killer.

But as the hours have turned to days, and each suspect has been slowly crossed from the list, it feels like we are back to square one. The DI is trying to put a brave face on it and rally the troops, but the general consensus is that this case will remain unsolved for years to come.

We found profiles for Steph on one site, two for O'Brien on different sites, and even one for Willow. But none on the same site. It doesn't rule out the possibility that this is how he targets them, but it asks more questions than it answers. I desperately wish I hadn't spouted the idea originally. I feel like I've wasted so much of everyone's time. Time we don't have.

The killer has struck three times in three months. We are about to enter a new month, and we're all dreading that call. The call which announces he's struck again. The press are all over the case too, which adds an unwanted dimension. There are calls for the DI to be replaced as SIO, which would be a travesty.

But she's getting desperate for a breakthrough. She even dragged in Steph's creepy neighbour again; some hermit with a condition that means he lives by night, like a vampire. But she had to release him when he presented airtight alibis for the nights in question.

I've never known pressure like this. All other work has been put to one side while we hunt for this man, and no progress has been made. Not really.

'We need fresh ideas,' the DI finally said tonight. 'First thing tomorrow we go through everything again.'

I feel like I've let her down. She gave me a chance to prove myself, and all I did was offer a half-baked idea. It wasn't good enough, and now she's suffering because of my naivety. I need to think of a way to make it up to her. I won't be the reason we fail Steph.

CHAPTER TWENTY-NINE

Two hours later, Kate's intercom sounded, and Laura appeared at the door holding a takeaway bag. 'I've got Chicken Tikka, Lamb Balti and Beef Madras.'

Kate showed her into the kitchen and got two plates out of the cupboard. 'Wine?'

'Have you got a lager?'

Kate opened the fridge. 'I think Ben may have left…' She stopped as she realised what she was saying. 'I mean, there probably is.' She handed Laura a can of lager, and watched as the realisation dawned on her face. 'Oh God,' she said before Laura could speak. '…not a word to anyone else in the team, okay?' Laura tried, and failed, to hide a smile, but drew a seal across her lips that promised discretion. Kate reached for a plate, eager to change the subject. 'How do you want to do this? Do we have one each, or do you want to split them and have a bit of each?'

'I'm up for sharing if you are?'

Limping back to the lounge, Kate dropped to the sofa. Laura followed behind, carrying their drinks, before returning with their plates. She eyed the pages stuck all over the walls. 'I see you've been keeping yourself busy.'

Kate, slightly embarrassed, didn't reply, occupying herself with the food instead. 'What progress have you made with Helen Jackson's murder?'

For Kate, it felt good to discuss something unrelated to Amy's murder. She hadn't taken any pills since London and was beginning to feel it after a long day traipsing around, so the distraction was welcome.

'I compared the registration plates against the PNC database,' Laura continued, lowering her fork to the plate, 'and the first three were listed at locations in the county. But the fourth plate wasn't recognised, meaning whoever attached that plate to the car made up the letter-number combination. It has to be Helen Jackson's killer.'

'And what time was that seen at the station approach?'

'Three thirty-one on Wednesday morning, which confirms that Helen's body was dumped almost a day before it was found.' Laura glanced at the pages stuck to the walls. 'What is all this, if you don't mind me asking, ma'am?'

'Before I answer that, you've got to stop calling me ma'am. We're not at work, we're in my home sharing a delicious curry. Please call me Kate.'

Laura's cheeks reddened. 'Understood, Kate.'

'Good.' Kate looked around her, ready to talk, ready to share some of her burden. 'What you see before you is everything I have from my last case in London.'

Laura nodded; she knew all about DC Spencer's death, everyone did, not that they'd ever dare mention it in front of Kate.

'I am certain he chose his victims from various dating sites, but what I can't figure out is why he chose these specific women. That has to be the key to identifying who he is, but no matter how hard I stare at these reports, and no matter which angle I approach it from, I just can't see the connection.'

Laura rested her plate on the floor and moved across to the wall, skim-reading some of the pages. 'Are these their dating profiles?'

'That's right.'

'Presumably you've compared them?'

'Over and over and over again.'

Laura turned to face her. 'A fresh pair of eyes couldn't hurt. Do you mind?'

Kate shook her head, and watched as Laura pulled Willow's printed profile down from the wall. 'Have you got your laptop handy? And we're going to need a pen and paper.'

CHAPTER THIRTY

An hour later, Kate was just finishing her second glass of Sauvignon Blanc, while Laura was still nursing her lager.

'I can't believe some of the stuff people are willing to list on their profiles,' Laura said as she continued to study the laptop screen.

'This is the digital age we live in.'

'I take it you're not on Facebook then, ma'am?'

Kate fired her a look. 'Kate.'

Laura blushed slightly as she nervously glanced up. 'Sorry, it just takes a bit of getting used to.'

'Where are we with that lot?'

Laura sat back, and stared at the sheets of paper she'd been scribbling notes on. 'As you said at the start, it's not easy to narrow down. I've managed to access the Pinterest accounts for Steph and Willow, but it doesn't look like Roxie used it. She did use Twitter occasionally, however, and based on what the three of them pinned and retweeted, it's safe to say they shared interests in health and fitness. Both Steph and Roxie followed businesses promoting health and vitality drinks, as well as a number of celebrities who regularly tweeted about one diet or another. Of the three, Willow was in the best shape, but we know from the original investigation that she was a member of the gym she worked at, so it's not difficult to assume she was body-conscious too.'

Kate pulled a face. 'Doesn't exactly narrow it down, though, does it? Show me a woman who isn't body-conscious. What else have you found?'

'Well, it's kind of along the same lines, but they all shared swimming as an interest.'

'Swimming?'

Laura reached for her glass of lager and took a long sip. 'Yeah. We know from Roxie and Steph's bank statements that they both paid membership fees to gymnasiums. Roxie's was for a place in Lower Sydenham, and Steph was registered at Finsbury Leisure Centre in the months before she died.'

'And Willow worked at Watford Leisure Centre Central, right?'

'Correct.'

'Do you think the killer was also a member of these leisure centres?'

It was Laura's turn to pull a face. 'It's weak, isn't it?' She snapped a piece of poppadum.

'Well, it's an angle the original investigation missed, and something we should follow up on. If we could get hold of a list of their members we could cross-check it with the names extracted from the dating sites.'

'*If* you could get your hands on those lists. Do you know anyone on the current enquiry who could pass those along?'

The image of Armitage warning her to keep away flashed before Kate's eyes. 'I'll have to work on that. What else links the three?'

'None of them owned cars as far as I can tell. They each have Transport for London charges on their bank statements for Oyster card top-ups. I can't see any direct debits for motor insurance or breakdown cover.'

'So, swimming and public transport. Maybe if we phoned the leisure centres we could ask if they still have CCTV footage from 2015, and then we might see our perp watching them leave?'

Laura groaned. 'Please don't mention security cameras. Think I might go blind if I have to sit and watch random cars driving down the road again.'

'You should have a word with Underhill and ask him for something else to do.'

'I know, but I don't want to rock the boat. I think he's feeling the pressure of you not being around.'

Kate tilted her head. 'What do you mean?'

'You must have noticed it?'

'What?'

'Ever since you solved the Watson-Jacobs-Yen triple murder last year, he's been like a bear with a sore head. While your record has gone from strength to strength, his has been on the slide. With you out of the office, he's head honcho and he's desperate to bask in some limelight of his own.'

'The priority is solving crime and protecting the public.'

'Oh, I know that, I was just making an observation.'

Kate smiled; it was good to know she wasn't the only one on the ropes. Laura's mobile erupted to life. Fishing the device from her pocket, Laura put it to her ear. 'Trotter… Oh I see, sir. On my way.'

She stood, placing what remained of her lager on the table. 'Sorry, Kate, I need to go. That was the supe. The body of another woman has been found, it's in a car beneath some offices in town this time.' Laura reached for her coat.

Kate stood, flattening her top. 'Mind if I tag along?'

CHAPTER THIRTY-ONE

'The cleaning lady found her,' Kate confirmed, as she looked out at the six detectives. 'The pathologist is in there now, but I warn those of you with weak stomachs, from what I've seen so far it's not a pretty sight.' Until Underhill rocked up, someone had to take control, and who better than Kate? She hoped the supe would be as easy to convince.

Kate looked over Laura's shoulder at the underground car park, which was now awash with bright light from the temporary halogen bulbs the SOCOs had erected.

'There don't appear to be any security cameras inside, but I've spoken to the night manager and he says access to the car park is restricted to a set list of employees who have spaces down here. He's printing me copies of that list now. I want you to split into two-person teams and tackle the names on that list. I don't care that it's after ten, I want you to physically meet with every person on that list, secure alibis and confirm where their car-park barrier IDs are.'

Laura raised her hand. 'Ma'am, if the barrier can only be raised by a small number of ID cards, can't the night manager access the barrier's records to find who the last person to enter was?'

'We believe the cleaner was the last person to enter.'

'Yeah, but he must be able to see who else passed through the barrier tonight. That would narrow our search, wouldn't it?'

'Ordinarily, yes, but the small office where the server is stored has been vandalised and the computer is currently down. The good news is the records are backed up to a secondary location, but we won't be able to access that information until the morning. So, in the meantime, I want you to track the names on the list he's going to locate.'

'Ma'am, where was the night manager while all this was going on?'

'He started his shift at eight and claims there was nothing untoward when he arrived. He went off to do his first round of checks in the offices upstairs, which takes him an hour to complete. He left the building to enjoy a cigarette and make a phone call, and he returned to his office to find the vandalised equipment around quarter past nine. That's when he heard the cleaning lady screaming. She has to access the building via the car park.'

Kate looked back at the concrete ramp descending from the road into the belly beneath the eight-storey tower. They were only a ten-minute walk away from the West Quay shopping centre in the heart of the city. At this time on a Saturday night, the bars, clubs and restaurants surrounding the complex would be packed with revellers enjoying the damp and cold January evening. With two universities in the city, a bit of poor weather wasn't enough to discourage the huge student population.

Laura raised her hand again. 'Ma'am, what about appealing for witnesses? I know this end of town is quieter, but someone, somewhere, is bound to have seen something odd.'

'All in good time, Laura. Let's focus on what we can manage at this point. Shake down that list of names. There's every chance that our killer is on that list, and it's just a matter of narrowing down who hasn't been at home.'

Kate was eager to get a proper look at the victim up close, but Laura had the bit between her teeth. 'Ma'am, do we know if our victim worked in the offices?'

'The victim has yet to be identified. Neither the cleaning lady nor the night manager said they recognised her. All of you: work that list and we'll reconvene at the station at 1.00 a.m. If your spouses and partners were expecting you home tonight, you'd better make those phone calls first.'

Laura turned to Patel. 'You want to buddy up?'

He yawned and rubbed his eyes. 'Happy to.'

'We should grab a coffee on our way. The McDonald's drive-thru should still be open.'

He turned up his nose.

'I know the coffee's not barista-prepared, but it's cheap and cheerful. You look like you need it more than me.'

He yawned again. 'I've been awake since five with our youngest. She's teething again and not sleeping well. I was supposed to be on Calpol-duty with her tonight. My wife won't be happy I'm out.' He shrugged. 'But she knows the score.'

Kate handed out copies of the list of names and watched them leave, before signing in at the cordon at the entrance to the car park, changing into white protective overalls and ducking beneath the tape. The security barrier remained raised. She followed the trail of lights until she spotted the pathologist in his overalls by one of the cars. Why did it have to be Ben? They'd not spoken since Friday night's argument, but she wasn't ready to deal with the fallout of that yet.

'What can you tell me?' she asked, moving along beside him, sheepishly.

He jumped at the sound of her voice, lost in what he was doing. He cleared his throat, buying a few seconds to compose himself, then explained in a matter-of-fact way, 'She's been dead for less than an hour, I'd estimate.'

Both back doors to the Mercedes SUV were wide open. Ben was concentrating on the passenger side while a large halogen lamp illuminated the car's interior from the driver's side. Kate stepped forward so she could look past where Ben was crouching; the woman on the back seat was lying flat out, her legs hanging off the seat closest to Ben. Long copper-coloured hair covered most of her face, held in place over her cheeks, nose and chin by congealed blood.

The victim's long-sleeved T-shirt was torn in several places, and her right breast poked through one of the tears. Her jeans were intact, but there were several large dark patches around both kneecaps and the groin area. It was then that Kate spotted the woman's wrists, bent at unnatural angles. She covered her mouth.

Ben straightened and passed her a tissue. 'Do you need a minute?'

Kate turned away for a moment to catch her breath and turned back. 'I'm fine. What can you tell me about her? Any ID?'

'No handbag or purse found inside the car. She's dressed like she might have been meeting friends for a casual drink, so I'm surprised she doesn't have any money with her. Unless the killer took it with him. She's wearing a bracelet inscribed with the name Mary, but it could be the name of a child.'

Kate jotted the name in her book. 'What else?'

His voice remained sullen. 'At best guess, I'd say she's in her early to mid-thirties, slim, red hair is natural. She's suffered a frenzied attack, with multiple blows sustained to the face and neck. Both wrists are broken. I haven't examined the knees yet, but I'm guessing they may also be broken. I found a small sledgehammer in the footwell on the driver's side, which I've bagged up for SSD. It looks like there's blood spatter on the head and handle. I believe the same instrument was used to smash the driver's window to gain access to the vehicle.'

Kate glanced up and saw shards of glass jutting out where the driver's window had once been. 'So the vehicle didn't belong to the victim or killer?'

'That's for you to determine. My best guess is the killer lured our victim here, maybe on the promise of sex, and then jumped her. I haven't examined her genitals yet, but there appears to be large blood loss from that area, so I would imagine she was struck there too.'

Kate sighed. 'I can't believe somewhere like this doesn't have security cameras.' She paused. 'Hold on, it's the weekend, what's this car even doing here?'

She stood suddenly and studied the rest of the car park. There couldn't have been more than sixty spaces marked out, with large concrete pillars minimising access to some of the spaces. She spotted a small Fiat in one corner and a second SUV further back. 'There are three vehicles in the car park, but nobody is working upstairs. That's odd.'

'Maybe their owners are in town for the night and parked here for free? There's a night manager wandering around somewhere, you could check with him.'

Kate couldn't see any sign of the night manager from where they were, but made a note to follow up on it. 'Can you tell me anything else?'

Ben stepped away, and she watched him rifling through a case on the ground behind the vehicle. He produced a transparent evidence pouch and held it up to the light. 'I found this on the mat by the victim's head.'

She took the pouch and examined it. Inside was a thick black bag, with what appeared to be a blood spatter. 'You think the killer left this?'

'Not only did our killer leave it here, but he also used it to suffocate the victim to death. Bruising around the neck is consistent with something tight being pulled and held in place. It's not my place to say, but there's a very good chance that the victim was dispatched by the same man who killed Helen Jackson on Tuesday night.'

Kate stepped back, and the blood drained from her face. Her head span.

Two murders in the space of a week.
Tied to the same killer.
On the anniversary of Amy's murder. Could it be…?

CHAPTER THIRTY-TWO

46 DAYS UNTIL I DIE

It's been a couple of months since I've visited his grave. I invent excuses like I'm too busy, or it's too far to travel, but really it's because I feel I've let him down. I know he'll be watching down on me as I stand on the grass telling him what I've been up to.

He was so proud the day I announced I'd applied to join the force. I don't think I ever saw him look so happy. Mum wasn't, but then she'd never appreciated his vocation. I think she'd rather I'd chosen anything but to follow in his footsteps. But applying for the police wasn't really a choice I made. It chose me.

Maybe she would have learned to accept my profession if he'd still been around when I finally graduated from Hendon.

I will admit, even I had doubts as to whether I should continue after what happened to him. Well, you would, wouldn't you? I still remember the day he died. I'd stayed over at Mum and Pop's house the night before, but I was at the gym when Mum received the call. I wish I'd been the one to break the news to her. They sent an inexperienced Family Liaison Officer; immature, insensitive, robotic. We just wanted to know what had happened, but all she could say was, 'Sorry for your loss,' and 'I'm not allowed to discuss details of an ongoing investigation with you.'

But we learned eventually. It was impossible to avoid when news of the armed robbery broke on every front page and the BBC news.

Three of the robbers had already surrendered when the fourth started taking potshots at anyone in Kevlar.

'You were kneeling down, helping one of the bank's customers when his bullet struck you in the neck,' I tell the weathered stone in front of me. 'Always the hero, hey, Pop. At trial he claimed he wasn't aiming at you, and you were the unfortunate victim of a stray bullet. I think we were the unfortunate ones. I'd do anything to hear your advice now.'

I check that nobody is close, but it's pointless as the cemetery is empty. 'I made a promise to a victim that I'm failing to keep. We need a breakthrough urgently, and I feel like I'm letting down the team, and the DI. I never realised just how hard being a detective would be. They make it look so easy on the television. You'd have probably solved this thing by now, wouldn't you? You'd have found the breadcrumbs linking the victims back to the killer. But I'm not you, Pop, and I don't know whether I'm wasting mine and everyone else's time by pretending to be.

'The DI talks about real detectives having gut instinct, just like you used to. In fact, she reminds me a lot of you; the things she says, the way she doesn't take crap from anyone. I reckon she'd have driven you crazy, but you'd have respected her. And you'd appreciate the way she's keeping an eye on me.

'I just wish there was something more I could do. I've read every statement and possible lead, over and over, and there's just nothing tangible to build on. Maybe I'm not cut out for this type of work. I'll know soon enough. My probation period ends in February, and there's a strong chance my time out of uniform will come to a swift end. I wish you were here now.

'I've tried talking to Mum, but she gives me that same withered look whenever I mention work, so I've stopped telling her what I've been up to. Whenever she asks, I give her the same nod and tell her all's fine. I haven't told her I'm part of the team hunting the "Metropolitan Killer". That's what they've dubbed him. The DI hates giving him a nickname, as it turns him into some kind of celebrity.'

I don't really know why I'm pouring my heart out to a gravestone. I'm not remotely religious, and I'm sure if he is watching down on me, he knows exactly what's been going on.

I pull the dried flowers from the small pot in front of the slab and discard them in a nearby dustbin. I turn back to face the stone. 'I'll bring some more the next time I come. If you've any idea who this bastard is, or what I can do to catch him, please let me know. Really need some inspiration, Pop. Love you.'

CHAPTER THIRTY-THREE

SUNDAY

The incessant whirring of the door buzzer was what caught her attention first. Kate forced her eyes open, glimpsing the morning light stealing around the edge of the curtains. Barely five hours had passed since she'd arrived home and crawled into bed. She'd left the crime scene and started preparing the incident room to brief the teams who had been speaking to people with key cards for the car-park entrance barrier, when Underhill had arrived, bleary-eyed, demanding to take over. Kate didn't argue, she had seen what she needed to see.

She wasn't ready to share the possibility that Amy's killer was back; without a shred of evidence she knew everyone would think she was crazy. Laura would keep her in the loop and Underhill could clean up the mess while she carried on with her own investigation.

The buzzer sounded again.

'All right, all right,' she grumbled to nobody in particular. 'I'm coming!'

Pushing the duvet back, she was relieved to see the skin around her ankle had turned a sickly green-yellow with hints of plum, but the swelling was almost gone. She reached the front door without her crutch and pressed the intercom button. 'Yes?'

'Finally!' Rob groaned. 'Are you going to let me in or what? It's sheeting down out here.'

Confused, Kate buzzed him in, and opened the front door, waiting for her ex-husband to reach the top of the stairs. 'Did I miss something? It's not my day to see Chloe until next weekend. Right?'

He brushed droplets of rain from the front of his zipped hoodie. 'No, sorry, I'm alone. I was hoping we could talk about this.' He raised a brown envelope into the air, and Kate knew immediately why he'd travelled an hour to visit her without warning.

'What needs discussing? I've applied for joint custody of *our* daughter.'

He didn't seem angry. 'The letter from your solicitor came a bit out of the blue. Can I come in so we can talk about it like grown-ups?' He looked down at her foot. 'Looks painful.'

'It's only sprained. I'll live.'

'You should have told me...'

Kate waved away his concern. 'It's nothing. *Really.*' She hopped backwards to allow him in. 'Why don't you wait in the kitchen while I throw on some clothes?'

She didn't wait for a response, using the wall to balance as she hobbled quickly back towards her bedroom, closing the lounge door as she went. Yesterday's clothes were in a pile at the foot of the bed. She plonked herself down on the end of the mattress and wriggled into them. Stopping only to run her fingers through her thick brown hair, she stared at her reflection in the mirror. 'Looking good,' she whispered sarcastically.

Out in the hallway, she saw that the living room door was now open and Rob was pacing beyond the door. Why couldn't he just wait in the kitchen like she'd told him?

Pushing the door open wider, she moved inside, closing it behind her.

'Before you say anything…' Kate began.

He was staring at the pages tacked to the wall. 'Jesus, Kate, talk about bringing your work home with you. What the hell is all this?'

She tried to keep her voice low and controlled. 'What I do in my home is none of your business.'

'On the contrary, when *our* daughter is here, it *is* my business. What if Chloe had wandered in here instead of me? Do you think it's appropriate to have photos of dead bodies hung on the wall where our daughter can see them? It's enough to give *me* nightmares, let alone *her*.'

'But she *isn't* here. And I did tell you to wait in the kitchen.'

'What's going on?'

'It's… nothing.' She didn't want to tell him what she'd been looking at. 'It's just a project; an old case I was asked to review.'

The penny dropped. 'This is about *her*, isn't it? Amy Spencer?'

She raised her hands to pacify him. 'Listen, Rob, it's not what you—'

He spun on his heel. 'Listen to me. You need to let it go. There's an entire team in London investigating her death. You know that, they don't need you.'

She kept her voice quiet, controlled. 'Nobody knows this case better than me. If anyone is going to find who killed Amy, it's me.'

'Have you heard yourself? It *isn't* your case anymore, Kate. I'd have thought after the way they blamed you for her death, you'd want nothing more to do with it! We might be divorced, but you still carry my surname and I still care. This needs to stop. Now.'

He pulled the closest image to him from the wall; Willow Daniels, post-mortem, floated to the floor.

Kate rushed to it, pinning it back on the wall and lifting her arms to create a barrier between him and the remaining pages. She knew how this must look, but this wall, this puzzle, was her only release from the guilt and the anguish she'd been dragging around for the last year; a year spent trapped in a maze of her own making. Punishing as it was, finding a way out was the only possible therapy. 'Don't come into my home and start pulling things down.'

'Fine! You want this shit all over your walls, so be it, but you can think again if you think I'm going to let Chloe come anywhere near this mausoleum.'

'What's that supposed to mean?' she whispered, cold dread prickling her skin. Not again, she couldn't lose Chloe again.

'What do you think it means?' He raised the envelope again. 'You've petitioned for joint custody, but you're not ready. Until you're able to make her your priority, you've no right to request additional access.'

'No, please, Rob. I'm better now, you know that. You've seen it; I've changed. I live for the time I get to spend with her, and twice a month just isn't enough. For either of us. That's why I instructed my solicitor to raise the request. I thought you'd be pleased that I want to play a more active role in Chloe's life.'

He raised his hand to cut her off. 'I accept that she needs both her parents, but not when you're like this.'

His words stung, but she did all she could to control her emotions. 'Like what?'

'*This!* Whenever you have a big case on you become *obsessive*. It's not good for you and it's certainly not good for Chloe. She needs a mother who will put everything else to one side, and give her the love and attention she deserves.'

'I will. You know I will. I'd never let anything happen to her. I know I haven't always been there for her, but you've no idea about the horrors I've seen. I used to be so terrified that she'd look at me, or touch me, and see it too. I wanted to protect her more than anything, and I thought that meant staying away. But I realised last year that I'm the best person – the only person – who can keep her truly safe. She's the reason I go the extra mile to solve the investigations I lead. It's to make a safer world for Chloe. For our daughter.' Kate trembled at her own admission. '*Please* don't challenge the petition, Chloe doesn't deserve that. She needs me, and I – I need her.'

Rob slumped into the armchair. 'I know. She misses you, too.'

Kate saw a tiny chink of hope and grasped at it, suddenly oppressed by the wall of horrors behind her. 'She grows so quickly, and I've already missed so much of her life – and I accept that that's my own fault – but I don't want to miss any more. I don't want to disrupt her life, and I know that you and Serena do a great job of taking care of her, but I'd like the opportunity to spend more time with her. If you'll let me? Maybe our one day every other weekend could become two days every other weekend? Or maybe I could come and see her in Oxford at the weekend when she's not due to come here? You have to admit the drive to Southampton every fortnight isn't great for you either.'

He shrugged.

'I don't want to cause trouble, but I think she would benefit from having us both in her life. I'm ready to do whatever it takes.'

'What about… you know… your depression?'

'I won't pretend it's easy for me to trust myself as far as Chloe is concerned, but that's only because my love for her is so strong. I would lay my life on the line for her, and you must understand what that means. I'm sure you'd do the same. Please, Rob?'

'What about that boyfriend of yours? Ben?'

'What about him?'

'Well, Chloe seems to like him. She says he tells funny jokes. Is it serious between the two of you?'

Kate didn't know how to answer the question after what had happened on Friday night, but she realised that she hoped it was salvageable. 'He's a good guy.'

Rob squinted. 'That wasn't really an answer. Do you love him?'

'Uh, we're getting off the subject.'

But Rob wasn't prepared to let it go. 'I disagree. If you're to have more contact with Chloe, I have a right to know who else will be present during the access. Who is he? You've never introduced us.'

'He's a pathologist. He's kind, and he's funny and smart. Chloe adores him and I—'

Rob fixed her with a look. '—love him?'

Kate was about to tell him it was none of his business, but was relieved to be interrupted by the sound of her mobile ringing. Seeing Laura's name on the display, she excused herself. 'I need to take this.'

CHAPTER THIRTY-FOUR

'Ma'am? I can't get hold of Underhill, and I want authority to arrest Gavin Isbitt.' Laura jabbered into the phone.

Kate closed the kitchen door, to ensure she wasn't overheard. 'What's going on, Laura? What's Isbitt done?'

'The night manager at the car park sent over the list of visitors from Friday afternoon. Isbitt visited the offices and was signed in to the car park between two and five.'

Kate narrowed her eyes. 'What did he say he did for a living again?'

Laura consulted her notes. 'Runs an IT company with his brother.'

'That's right. He was a salesman. Why the concern? He might have had a legitimate reason for being at the crime scene.'

'There's more, ma'am. When SSD were searching the back of the vehicle for DNA, they discovered fragments of a torn business card, squashed between the seat cushions. It was a corner, showing most of the company logo. I recognised it immediately, ma'am… the business card belongs to Gavin Isbitt.'

Kate's eyes widened. 'Could be circumstantial.'

'Agreed, but it's strange that we have evidence linking him to two separate crime scenes, isn't it? At the very least it warrants a conversation.'

Kate's mind was already hypothesising. 'We don't want to frighten him off, but we should speak to him right away. Can you pick me up?'

'It's all right, Patel's here and he can go with me.'

'No. I want to be there, Laura. I need to look into his eyes.'

'Are you sure? I don't want to disrupt your plans.'

'It's fine, Laura. It's nothing I can't put off until tomorrow. I'll see you soon.'

CHAPTER THIRTY-FIVE

'Why the hell should I believe your lies?' Nicola Isbitt demanded, the baby in her arms wrestling to get free.

Kate wound her window down so she could hear the ensuing argument better.

'I'm not lying to you,' Isbitt pleaded from the rear of his latest company car. His wife, leaning out of the front door of the house, was wearing little more than a dressing gown, and her hair was wrapped up in a towel. Isbitt lifted a small case from the boot of the car and rested it on the paved driveway.

'I wonder what that's about,' Laura muttered. 'I hate prying, but we should probably ask them to go indoors before one of their neighbours reports it and gets in the way of our enquiry.' She reached for her door handle.

Kate raised her hand. 'Hang fire, let's see where this goes for a bit longer. Okay? If he *is* our man, let's find out exactly what his wife thinks of him. If we go in all guns blazing now, she'll close up, and won't utter a word against him.' A noise on the street caught her attention and she turned back. Isbitt had now picked up his case and was striding towards the front door, but his wife, now minus child, was blocking the doorway. 'Is she holding a phone?'

Laura studied the scene. 'I can't quite tell. She's holding something, oh, and now she's showing him.'

'You neglected to mention that *she* would be there too,' Nicola howled. 'How convenient. The same night you're at a conference in Colchester, *she's* at the same bloody conference. Do you really think I'm *that* stupid?'

Isbitt glanced around for the first time, but missed the car parked across the street where Kate and Laura were straining to hear every word.

'Where did you get this from?' he shouted, grabbing the device.

'It isn't hard to check other people's photographs on Facebook you know,' Nicola fired back. 'I suppose at least she had the decency not to post a picture of the two of you together.'

'How many times, Nicki, I am not having an affair with Amelia.'

'Oh no? So how come the two of you *happened* to be staying in the same hotel last night?'

He dropped his case and opened his arms passively. 'I don't know what you want me to tell you. The conference was at that hotel. I had no idea she would be there. In fact, had you not showed me this photograph, I wouldn't have even known she was there.'

Nicola folded her arms. 'Try again, Gavin. At least have the decency to admit you're screwing her. It wouldn't hurt as much if you were just honest with me.'

'Read my lips, Nicki: I AM NOT SCREWING AMELIA. I haven't seen or spoken to her in more than two years. In fact, I haven't spoken to her since she left the company. I don't know where she's working now, but clearly whatever she's now doing it must still involve IT. Shocking. I don't know what else I can tell you. Call her up if you don't believe me. Ask her if she saw me last night. Ask her when we last spoke.'

'Oh, you'd like that wouldn't you? I bet the two of you would have a good laugh about that behind my back!' Nicola's eyes widened, and she swung an arm at him.

Kate and Laura were both out of the car without a second's thought. Laura reached the driveway first, holding her ID aloft. 'Sir, madam, please take this inside. Now.'

'That man is not coming into my house,' Nicola replied, standing firm.

Kate tentatively approached her. 'Why don't you and I go inside and discuss things, while my colleague asks your husband a few questions. Is that okay?'

A look of confusion descended. 'Questions? What about?'

'I'll explain when we're inside,' Kate urged. 'Please?'

Nicola watched her carefully, before stepping aside and allowing Kate to enter. She made sure to close and lock the door behind her. Kate followed her through to the dining room where she'd first spoken to Isbitt on Friday. The child she'd been holding at the door earlier couldn't have been much older than a year and was playing happily in an enclosed pen.

'He's cute,' Kate commented, nodding at the child.

'Yeah, well hopefully he won't grow up to be a cheat like his father.' She apologised when she realised what she'd said.

'Who's the woman on the phone?' Kate asked, keen to expose the gap in Nicola's emotional barrier.

Nicola slid the phone across the table. Kate was surprised at just how striking the woman in the image was. Tall, with raven-black hair and a figure to die for. 'She used to work with my husband, until I discovered they'd slept together. I only agreed to take him back if she left the company and he promised not to cheat again. I should have listened to that voice in the back of my head: once a cheat, always a cheat.'

Kate pushed the phone back. 'Did I hear correctly: they were both at a hotel last night?'

Nicola narrowed her eyes. 'He was at a conference in Colchester, staying at the Marriott. Ever since the affair, I've kept my eye on him. I know I should trust him, but it's not easy, you know?'

'I understand, Mrs Isbitt. Between you and me, I think you were brave to take him back in the first place. I know I couldn't be so forgiving.'

Her shoulders relaxed a little. 'Please, call me Nicola, or Nicki.'

Kate offered her a reassuring smile. 'Okay, Nicki. This Amelia woman, how do you know she was also in Colchester?'

'We have a mutual friend on Facebook. It isn't hard to keep up with her posts. She doesn't tend to write much, but she does post the occasional photograph. As she did last night. From the Marriott in Colchester. Some people really should update their privacy settings.'

'I see, and you think the two of them were meeting up?'

'What else can I think? It's only a two-and-a-half-hour drive from Colchester to home, yet he insisted on staying overnight. And I mean, who the hell holds a conference on a Saturday, anyway? I was suspicious from the moment he told me he *had* to go.'

'Are you certain your husband was in Colchester last night?'

'He showed me the email confirming his reservation. Unless he cancelled it at the last minute, he was there.'

'The reason I ask is…' She paused for effect. 'Another woman was murdered and left in the back of a car last night. We have reason to believe she was killed by the same person who stole your husband's car.'

The blood drained from her face. 'How do you know it's the same person?'

'The victims were killed in a similar way. Now, the reason we're speaking to your husband is that we have reason to believe that he was in the vicinity at the time of the second murder. When we spoke to you on Friday you advised us that your husband was home all night on Tuesday. In light of this new evidence and what you believe he has been up to, I'm wondering if you wish to revise your statement?'

'You think Gavin killed those women? *My* Gavin?'

'We certainly can't rule him out at this stage.'

'He's not a…' Her words trailed off.

Kate reached for her hand. 'Forgive me if I'm speaking out of turn, Nicki, but I can see some faint bruises on your neck and arm… you're safe here with me and you're free to speak openly. Has Gavin ever hit you?'

Nicola pulled her hand away and pressed it against the patch of colour on her neck.

Kate leaned closer. 'You don't have to be afraid. I have spoken to dozens of women in exactly the same situation as you. You feel trapped because you have a child to take care of. All I'm saying is, you don't need to be scared. There are people and programmes out there who will protect and help you.'

There was a coldness in Nicola's eyes as she spoke. 'I want you to leave my house.'

'Please, Nicki. My colleague will keep your husband at bay. Okay? He's not going to get in here, or retaliate. I just need you to be honest with me. Where was he on Tuesday night?'

'I've told you: he was here.'

'All night?'

'Yes.'

'And you're certain he didn't get up and leave? If you have any reason to doubt what I'm saying, the man we're looking for beat and suffocated these women, who can tell what he might do next? Please, Nicki, I don't want you to be another victim.'

'He was in bed with me when I went to sleep, and he was there when I woke up.'

'And he was there all night? Did you wake up at any point in the night and see him still there? Maybe you went to the toilet or got up to check on the baby? I need you to remember.'

Nicola looked nervously towards the front door.

Kate saw the movement. 'Don't be afraid. If he's the man we're looking for, we'll take him in now and he won't ever bother you again. Two women are dead already. Don't be the reason there's a third.'

Nicola looked back at her, tears welling in her eyes. 'I suffer with migraines sometimes. I felt one coming on, on Tuesday night, so I took one of my pills. They knock me right out. All I can tell you is he was there when I went to sleep, and there when I woke up. Whether he was there or went out in between, I – I really can't tell you.' The tears broke free and rolled down her cheeks. 'Oh God, do you really think he…?'

Kate jotted Nicola Isbitt's comments in her book, found a tissue in a box on the side and passed it to her. 'He's now our prime suspect. We'll monitor his phone and vehicle movements for both dates, as well as checking if his DNA profile is at both scenes. Thank you, Nicki. I promise I'll keep you safe.'

Kate left the room, unbolted the front door and stepped out into the cool breeze. Laura was leaning against a wall with her arms folded, while Isbitt paced around on the driveway.

'Finally!' Isbitt declared. 'Can I go into my own house now?'

Kate raised her arm to block his path. 'I'm afraid not.'

He tried to push past, but she grabbed his arm and pulled it behind his back, pressing her knee into the back of his. He dropped to the ground. 'What the bloody hell are you doing?'

'Gavin Isbitt, I am arresting you on suspicion of the murders of Helen Jackson and an as-yet-unidentified victim. You do not have to say anything. But, it may harm your defence if you do not mention when questioned something which you later rely on in court. Anything you do say may be given in evidence.' She cuffed his wrists and helped him to his feet.

'Murder? What the *hell* did she say to you? I'm not a murderer. What the hell is going on?'

Kate didn't respond, leading him to the car and securing him in the back. She took Laura to one side. 'What did he tell you?'

'He said he was at some conference in Colchester last night.'

'That's what the wife said too. But I'm not convinced.'

'You think we've got our man?'

Kate considered the question. 'We need to get SSD to check the second vehicle for traces of his DNA. If they find a match, I think we'll have a better idea. You and Patel had best interview him, but I'd like to observe.'

Laura radioed control to confirm they were bringing him in. Kate knew there'd be no way to keep her involvement from Underhill or the supe. But if she was right, and they'd caught the killer, she wouldn't need to justify her actions.

CHAPTER THIRTY-SIX

45 DAYS UNTIL I DIE

I woke in the middle of the night with a crazy idea. I got up and started writing it down immediately. My heart was pounding in my chest as I rehearsed my speech in front of the mirror. It could work, and it could give us the inside track we've been desperately craving. My hands are still trembling.

I have spent the day trying to get the DI alone so I can speak to her, but the top brass have kept her away from the incident room all day. As crazy an idea as it is, I'm sure she'll go for it. Matthews is not afraid to challenge convention.

But it gets to 7.00 p.m., and she calls the team together for an evening brief. She admits that the DSI is considering replacing her on the enquiry, to bring fresh eyes in. The DSI has never been convinced that the murders were linked, and our lack of progress gives him all the rope he needs to hang her out to dry. But I am certain she is right. I have studied the post-mortem reports, and the images of the scarring left by the killer's blade. I've even taken copies of the images home to study more.

She is about to end the brief when I tentatively raise my hand again. 'What about an undercover op, ma'am?' I say weakly.

She looks confused, so I try and explain how it could work. The speech I spent all night rehearsing has disappeared from my memory, and I struggle to get my words out. There are murmurs of derision from some of the team. They think I'm just out to make a name for myself, but it isn't that. I made a promise to Steph, and I'm determined to fulfil it.

The DI thanks me for my suggestion, but dismisses it out of hand. She releases the group, and I see her walk into her office and close the door. She sits behind the desk and buries her head in her hands.

I saw the newspaper article this morning. One of the tabloids ran a fourth-page story about her marital problems and how she isn't fit to head this investigation. It was vicious, and I can't help but pity her. I'm relieved that nobody has dug up my secrets. Imagine if your worst – most shameful – secret was laid bare for all to devour and judge. How would you feel?

I find myself knocking on the door. When I begin to speak about going undercover, she raises her hand to silence me, but she doesn't realise I won't take no for an answer. I tell her that it's our last shake of the dice. I tell her we can upload my profiles to different sites and I add that I'll do it with or without the Met's support.

She says the DSI won't sign off on the budget needed to surveil potential suspects. I tell her we don't need a big team. Just enough cover for one officer to watch the hidden camera I'll wear, and another in support.

The DI warns me that I'd be putting my life on the line, and that my dad wouldn't have approved. I remind her that he lost his life in the line of duty, and would want me to risk everything for the career he dedicated his life to for more than twenty years.

I can see she is waning.

Deep down, I've already decided that I'm going to act on this idea whether she gives it the green light or not. I'm sure it was Pop who sent me the idea. He'd want me to do it.

'There's no way to guarantee he'd bite,' she argues.

'We've nothing to lose, ma'am. With respect, it beats sitting on our arses hoping he drops into our laps.' I blush at my outburst, but she smiles.

'I admire your passion, Amy. We'd have to create an unshakeable cover story for you, and set you up in temporary accommodation.'

'I'm willing to do whatever it takes, ma'am.'

'If we were to do this, we'd need to keep it quiet. God knows there have been enough leaks from this office already. The fewer who know what we're doing, the better.'

I can feel my lips curling into a smile. 'I understand, ma'am.'

'Tell me one thing first: why do you want this so badly?'

I'm not sure how to answer her question, as I'm concerned the wrong answer will dissuade her from pursuing it. I could tell her it's because I made a promise to Steph, or I could tell her it's to honour my father's memory, or even that it's my duty as a Met police officer. But none of those answers feel right. They're all true, but what drove me to step into her office and petition her, was more than that.

'Would you hate me if I said I felt it was my destiny, ma'am? Every decision I've made to this point has led me here. I feel deep down that I need to do this if we're ever to stand a chance of catching him.'

She is silent as she watches me, and I can almost hear the cogs turning in her mind. Her face is neutral. Oh God, does that mean she hated the answer? Although a 'No,' won't stop me, I know it will work better with her support.

Matthews finally breaks the suspense with a smile of her own. 'Okay, Amy, I'll run it up the line to the DSI. I'm sure he'll reject the suggestion, but I have a trick or two up my sleeve.' She winks, before dismissing me.

I feel like a massive weight has been lifted from my shoulders as I close her door behind me.

CHAPTER THIRTY-SEVEN

'How many times do I have to tell you?' Isbitt shouted from the back of the car. 'I didn't murder anyone. I'm *not* a killer.'

Kate rolled her eyes so Laura would see. 'And how many times do we need to remind you that anything you say will be given in evidence? It's in your best interests to pipe down for now, Mr Isbitt. You'll have your chance to speak when we're inside.'

They left the roundabout, and Laura waited for the security barrier to lift, before pulling into the car park. 'We'll check him in, and then we can roll straight into interview, assuming Patel has prepped the interview suite.'

Laura parked and they exited the car, Laura dragging Isbitt from the back. But as they reached the door to the secure detention centre, it opened and Ben emerged. He held the door open for Laura and Isbitt, but did a double take when he saw Kate behind them.

He looked at her and nodded, his face expressionless.

Ben was the last person she'd expected to bump into at the station. Kate desperately wanted to apologise, to make things right. She could feel him drifting further away as the moment to make amends slipped by.

Kate took the edge of the door, allowing him to pass through in silence. 'Wait,' she called after Ben, before turning back to Laura. 'Would you mind checking Isbitt in? I need to speak to Ben about something.'

Laura nodded and pushed Isbitt towards the custody desk, explaining his arrest. Kate closed the door, checking it was properly shut, before doing her best to hurry after Ben. He was already at his car when she caught up to him. 'Ben, please wait.'

He stopped, but didn't turn to face her, his voice barely more than a whisper. 'What do you want, Kate?'

She reached out for his shoulder, but he shook her hand away. 'I wanted to check how you are?'

'I'm not sure how to answer that question.'

Her heart ached with the pain she had caused. He deserved to be treated far better. 'Did you manage to complete the post-mortem on the Jane Doe?'

What was wrong with her? Every fibre of her being wanted to apologise, for scaring him with the painkillers, for the harsh words she'd said, for hurling the tea at him. She wanted to beg him to forgive her, and to tell him that she would try harder to let him in to her mixed-up world, but her thick skin wouldn't allow that voice through.

He remained with his back to her. 'Yeah, I completed it this morning.'

'Did you establish COD?'

'I'm waiting for test results, but it's looking increasingly likely that she was suffocated like Helen Jackson.'

'Okay, thank you. We have a suspect in custody.'

'Good.'

Why couldn't she just say the words? How difficult could it be to apologise, to let herself be vulnerable? She looked away. 'What are your plans for the rest of the day?'

'I've been up all night, so a shower and bed, I guess.'

'If you're free later… we could meet for dinner…'

He spun round, his usually sunny eyes looked tired and defeated. 'What would be the point?'

What did that mean? Had he given up on them already? She wasn't ready to let him go yet. She was a fighter, and she would fight for him. She reached for his hand, and this time didn't allow him to break her grasp. 'Ben, I'm… I'm sorry. Please, we need to talk about this.'

A glimmer of hope flickered across his face. 'I think that's the first time I've *ever* heard you apologise.' His lips curled slightly up at one side.

Kate couldn't stop a thin smile forming on her own face. 'Well, you'd better not get used to it; I'm not often wrong.'

His smile grew wider. 'I guess we'll have to agree to disagree on that one.'

She playfully slapped his arm. 'I need you to know that what happened on Friday… it *was* an accident. I would never—'

'I know,' he interrupted. 'You just scared me.' He leaned in conspiratorially. 'Don't let on, but I kind of like having you around. I don't know what I'd do if—'

It was her turn to interrupt, pressing a finger to his lips. 'Nothing's going to happen to me. I'm made of strong stuff, remember?'

He nodded as she pulled her finger away.

'So, are we… okay now?'

He stepped forward, wrapping his long arms around her shoulders. 'Yeah, we're okay. I really should get home though,' he added with a yawn. 'I've been up all night.'

She broke free of his embrace, conscious that anyone could come out and see their little moment of intimacy. 'I'd better let you get on home then.'

Kate watched Ben get into his car and pull out of the car park, before heading to the secure detention centre and inputting the daily code. She felt less weighed down. There was finally light at the end of the tunnel.

CHAPTER THIRTY-EIGHT

'And you're sure you've got everything you need?' Kate asked, pacing the room.

'Certain, ma'am,' Laura replied, resting her hand on the thin paper folder in front of her. 'We know he wasn't at the Marriott in Colchester. I just need him to admit where he was.' She glanced up at Patel who was nodding beside her.

'Has he called for a brief?' Kate asked.

'He's requested the support of the duty solicitor,' Laura replied. 'She should be talking to him now.'

'And what about the forensics? Any word from SSD yet?'

'No word from them yet. They said they'd phone when they've finished testing the samples taken from the second car. We already have his DNA in the BMW.'

'It's hardly a smoking gun. Patel, are you happy supporting Laura in the interview?'

'I agree, ma'am. Isbitt's our guy.'

'Although we have the bag he used to suffocate them, his DNA wasn't on it. We don't have anything concrete to put him at the second scene, so we're going to be reliant on a confession to charge him. Are you confident you can get it?'

'I won't let you down, ma'am.'

Kate dismissed them, and made her way to the viewing booth so she could watch the interview unfold via the inbuilt cameras in the interview suite. She desperately wanted to be in the room with them, so she could directly influence the questions being asked of Isbitt, ready to pounce on any weakness or slip-up. But she was already taking a big chance even observing it. She had to trust her team and their training. Fixing herself a large mug of coffee, she switched on the screen, just as Laura and Patel entered the room.

'I need to consult with my client,' the solicitor demanded.

Kate had crossed paths with her several times before and the woman had done little to endear herself. Wearing a dress suit a size too small, Cindy Everidge had as much respect for the police as Kate had for her.

'It's okay,' Isbitt piped up. 'I've done nothing wrong. I just want to get this over and done with as soon as possible. It's already been a long day.'

Kate smiled to herself as Laura and Patel took their seats across the table from him. Laura started the recorder and introduced everyone in the room, before reminding Isbitt he was under caution. 'Should I call you Gavin, or would you prefer Mr Isbitt?'

'Mr Isbitt.'

'Good, okay, Mr Isbitt, before we begin I want to remind you that you're well within your rights not to answer any of my questions, but I would encourage you to do so. I want to hear your side of the story. I'm not here to trip you up or trick you. You understand that, don't you?'

Kate saw him briefly glance at the solicitor before nodding.

'Can you verbally confirm that for the tape, Mr Isbitt?' Laura said.

'Yes. I understand.'

'Good. Can you start by telling me where you were on Tuesday night?'

'Tuesday night? Is that what this is about? The car? I told you on Friday, it was stolen while I was asleep at home.'

Kate could see Laura working through her nerves. 'I know you've already informally discussed what happened to your BMW, but now we need to do so for the record. So, for the tape, please talk me through the events of Tuesday night. Try and be as specific as you can with timings.'

Kate watched Isbitt nervously glance at the solicitor again, before shaking his head in frustration. 'As I said before, I drove home from Cornwall, arriving at my house around eight o'clock. I went in and chatted with my wife, had a large glass of red wine, and headed up to bed around ten o'clock. I woke at six the next morning, showered and dressed, and when I went to get into my car, I saw it was missing.'

'And that's when you reported it stolen?'

'Yeah. I called you lot, and they said they would send someone round to fill in a report. I said they'd have to come later as I had a meeting with a client, and ended up calling a taxi to get to the meeting.'

Kate had written a list of questions she wanted Laura to ask, and so far, she was sticking to the running order. 'Does your wife not have a car you could have borrowed?'

'She does, but she needed it to take my son to the doctor's.'

'Your car was relatively new, wasn't it?'

'It wasn't *my* car. I leased it from an agency. It was for business.'

'But it was new, right? It had a 17 plate.'

'What's that got to do with anything?'

Laura paused. 'It would be difficult to break into and drive away.'

'Yes, but as I told you, my keys were missing too.'

'That's right. You have a theory about how the thieves got your keys, don't you?'

'One of my neighbours had his car stolen the other week. The police reckoned they'd used a wire coat hanger to hook his keys through the letterbox. It was probably the same thieves who took my car.'

'The thing is, Mr Isbitt, in those types of crime – which aren't uncommon – the thief will often require several attempts to actually hook the keys and remove them from the property. And what we often find is tiny scuff marks or scratches around the edge of the letterbox where the hanger has caught it. I had a look at your letterbox earlier today, and couldn't see any scratch marks at all. You haven't replaced your letterbox since Wednesday morning, have you? Before you answer, I'll remind you you're under caution, and that if you have replaced the letterbox, we'll need to see a receipt for the new one.'

Kate clenched her fist in satisfaction. To illicit a confession, Laura and Patel would need to shed enough doubt on his version of events, before questioning the entire statement.

Isbitt looked glumly at his solicitor. 'No, I haven't replaced it, but that doesn't mean that's not how they got the keys. Maybe the thief who took them was a bit of an expert at hooking keys? Or maybe he got lucky and hooked them on his first attempt? I dunno.'

Kate recognised the desperation in his voice, and was pleased when Laura removed a photograph of Helen Jackson from the folder and slid it across the table. 'Do you recognise the woman in this photograph?'

Isbitt took a quick look and shook his head. 'No.'

'Are you sure, Mr Isbitt? This is the woman we found beaten and suffocated in the boot of your stolen BMW. Are you sure she doesn't look familiar?'

He was biting his nails. 'I don't know her.'

'Your wife informed us she took a pill for her migraine on Tuesday night and cannot recall if you were in bed with her all night. I put it to you, Mr Isbitt, that *you* were the person driving your car, and that it was *you* who killed Helen Jackson and left her in the boot of your car.'

'That's ridiculous!' he shouted. 'I didn't even know the woman.'

Anger and denial were common when suspects felt the walls closing in around them. Kate took a short breath, waiting for the inevitable slip to unfold on the screen.

'What about last night, Mr Isbitt?' Laura continued. 'Can you confirm for the tape where you were?'

'I've told you: I was in Colchester.'

Kate saw Laura slide a second sheet towards him.

'What's this?'

'This is a satellite map showing cellular activity. The green spot represents the signal from your mobile phone, taken from 10.00 p.m. last night. The red spot is Colchester. Note the distance between the spots.' She passed him a second image. 'This is the same map, but we've zoomed in on the green spot. Tell me, Mr Isbitt, if you were in Colchester all night, why was your mobile phone just down the road in Portsmouth at 10.00 p.m.?'

CHAPTER THIRTY-NINE

'How much longer do you think they'll be?' Patel asked, popping a mint in his mouth and waving the packet in Kate's direction.

Declining the offer, she leaned back on her desk chair and stretched her hands high above her head. 'Your guess is as good as mine. I'm half-tempted to observe their private conversation in the interview suite. I would, if it didn't breach his rights.'

'Do you reckon he's spilling the beans to her?'

Kate cocked an eyebrow. 'If he is, you can bet she'll tell him to give you nothing but "No comment" to all your remaining questions. Did you see the look of panic on his face as he asked to speak with her alone? He knows you're on to him. I used to think criminals were getting smarter. With so many cop shows on the television, you'd think he'd have covered his tracks better.'

'Maybe the first one wasn't planned, he panicked and has been trying to clear up the mess. Who knows what goes through a psychopath's head.'

Kate's eyes narrowed. 'You reckon he's psychopathic then?' She wasn't sure whether to share her suspicions about Isbitt's possible connection to the London crimes.

'Well, whatever the correct term is, he's definitely not right in the head. He wanted her dead. That's why he used a bag to suffocate Helen. He'd have felt every last breath as her body tried to cling to life. And then to go and do it all again… he's not right.'

'I agree. Which is why I'm going to come in with you for the second part of the interview.'

She saw him fire a glance towards Laura who'd been sitting at her desk, quietly observing their exchange.

Kate turned to face her. 'I think you've done fantastic job, Laura, I'm proud of you, but we need to make sure we press him in the right way. We need him to confess. A new voice will unsettle him and help catch him off guard.'

'What about the supe?' Laura challenged.

'Leave him to me. When he realises we managed to catch the killer, he won't be worried about my involvement.'

It had been an hour since Cindy Everidge had demanded a quiet place to review matters with her client. Kate had spent most of that time on the phone to SSD chasing up the forensics. Now she was growing impatient. They could only hold Isbitt for twenty-four hours before they'd have to either charge or release him. She needed the DNA match or a confession; ideally both.

She had disclosed to Everidge that they'd found fragments of Isbitt's card in the second vehicle. Isbitt's face was puffy and red, and he was nursing a tissue when they entered. Everidge wore a coquettish smile, which Kate tried to ignore.

Restarting the recorder, Kate confirmed the interview was reconvening and introduced herself, reminding Isbitt he was still under caution.

'My client wishes me to read a statement on his behalf,' Everidge declared, picking up a pad of handwritten notes.

Kate nodded for her to continue.

'My client, Mr Gavin Isbitt, wishes to put it on record that he was not responsible for the unfortunate death of Helen Jackson. He has never met or seen Helen Jackson, and cannot explain how she wound up dead in the motor vehicle he was leasing for business. Mr Isbitt reported the vehicle stolen when he first became aware of it on Wednesday morning. He has followed the correct procedure for the theft and was issued with a crime reference number, which you're already aware of.'

She paused for a sip of water. 'You have disclosed that my client's DNA was discovered inside said motor vehicle, but as he freely admits to leasing and driving the vehicle for business reasons, it should come as no surprise that his DNA was present. You have not disclosed that his DNA was discovered on the victim's body, and unless you are later going to confirm this, there is nothing linking my client to her death, other than circumstantial evidence, which we all know the CPS will not uphold.'

Kate remained quiet and still until the statement was complete.

'Now, to the matter of my client's mobile phone activity yesterday. Mr Isbitt originally advised you that he was at the Marriott hotel in Colchester, attending a technology conference. My client now wishes to revise that statement. Whilst there was a conference at that hotel on Saturday night, and my client had booked a room there, he in fact decided against attending the conference. He says the hotel will be able to confirm he never checked in. My client admits to misleading you originally, but his reason for doing so was to validate the lie he had told to his wife, who was present at the scene when his whereabouts were first questioned. Mr Isbitt was in fact in Portsmouth from lunchtime yesterday, and spent the night there too. Mr Isbitt has provided me with the name of a woman who will confirm he was with her between midday on Saturday until eight this morning. Mr Isbitt has been conducting an extra-marital affair with this woman for several months, and using the guise of conferences to cover his actions. Whilst there is nothing illegal about such activity, Mr Isbitt is deeply ashamed of the lies he has been telling his wife, and would like the opportunity to come clean to her in his own time.'

Everidge passed them the piece of paper. Patel excused himself to make a copy of the page, returning two minutes later. Kate restarted the recorder. 'Who is this woman in Portsmouth?'

He was slouched in his chair. 'I've known her for years. We used to go to school together, but lost touch, and then she added me on Facebook. We met for a coffee, and it was like we'd never been apart.'

'Your wife told me she thought you were having an affair with a former employee. Why perpetuate the lie?'

'I love my wife and my son, but you don't know what it's like living with her. She gave up work when he was born, but since she took me back, she's become paranoid about my every movement. Ironically, it was her behaviour that drove me to having another affair.'

Kate couldn't control her reaction. 'It's always the wife or girlfriend's fault with men like you, isn't it?' She shook her head in disbelief. 'It's nobody's fault but your own. If you think otherwise, you're kidding yourself.'

'I should have known you'd take her side. You women stick together.' He leaned forward. 'Is it normal that she checks every email I receive? That she goes through my bank statements, and my Facebook timeline – is that normal? A marriage should be built on love and trust, but she doesn't trust me.'

'With good reason, from what you've admitted today. Did you ever plan to tell her the truth?'

'I don't know… yes… maybe… What's it to you, anyway?'

'I think she was a fool for taking you back the last time you abused her trust, but I'd be very surprised if she makes the mistake again.'

Everidge raised her hand. 'I'm sure I don't need to remind you that the details of this interview are confidential, detective. If you tell Mrs Isbitt about what my client has said, we will seek civil redress.'

'I don't need you to remind me of your client's rights,' Kate said, glaring at her before turning back to Isbitt. 'What were you doing at the Teletron offices on Friday afternoon?'

He frowned. 'Uh… oh that's right, I had a meeting with the Managing Director there. They're looking to upgrade all their systems to Windows 10 and he wanted me to quote for the business.'

'You had a guest pass to enter the building and car park, didn't you?'

'Yeah. What of it?'

'What happened to the pass, Mr Isbitt?'

'What? I handed it back in to the woman in reception when I left.'

'So you didn't keep it and use it to gain entry back into the car park late last night?'

'*No*. I've told you, I was in Portsmouth last night.'

'Your phone was in Portsmouth, but that doesn't necessarily mean you were.'

'Phone my girlfriend and she'll confirm I was there all night.'

'I'm sure she'll tell us anything you ask her to.'

He gasped in exasperation. 'It's the truth! What is it with you people? I am not a killer!'

'Can you explain why fragments of your business card happened to be found squashed into the cushion of the vehicle where our second victim was located?'

'How the hell should I know? Maybe I met the killer at some point and gave him one of my cards?'

'Do you give out many business cards?'

'All the time. I give one to every new person I meet. Even if they don't need our services, they often know someone who does.'

'Our Scientific Services team are currently comparing samples taken from the second vehicle to your DNA profile. You're going to have a lot of explaining to do if they find a hit. This is your chance to come clean and tell us what you did.' She slid the autopsy photograph of the second victim towards him. 'Who is she? How did you meet her?'

He sat back and folded his arms. 'I don't know who she is or who killed her. For God's sake, how much more of this do I have to put up with?'

'Did you meet this victim online too? Is that how you met Helen Jackson as well? Were they both former girlfriends?'

He spoke through gritted teeth. 'I don't know either of these women.'

'My colleagues are conducting a search of your home as we speak, so just come clean and spare us the effort.'

'I've had enough of this. Ask your bloody questions, but don't expect an answer from me.'

'Did you kill Helen Jackson and leave her body in the boot of your business car?'

'No comment.'

'Did you kill the woman in this photograph and leave her on the back seat of a Mercedes you'd broken into?'

'No comment.'

Kate suspended the interview and stopped the recorder, before storming out of the room.

CHAPTER FORTY

39 DAYS UNTIL I DIE

The DI wasn't kidding when she said she had a trick up her sleeve. I still can't quite believe the DSI agreed to let me go undercover. Everything has moved so quickly since we spoke in her office. I now have a flat where I'm to sleep for the next few weeks. It's smaller than my own place in Battersea, but it's adequate for what we need. There are cameras and recording equipment in the ceiling to monitor all activity inside, so I don't need to worry about making notes about who I speak to or when.

I had to undertake a three-day intensive course with one of the Met's undercover units. I got the impression they weren't happy not to have been approached about the operation, but the training delivered is thorough and professional. They've taught me how to discreetly check for and lose suspected tails. I don't mind admitting I found it all very thrilling; like being a spy. They also showed me how to use the camera in the small brooch I'm to wear on each date. It has a directional microphone and needs to be pointed at the suspect in order to pick up what he says.

Matthews wanted to act as my handler, but the DCI running the undercover unit insisted we use one of his trained handlers. She wasn't happy about it, but her face has already been plastered over the papers, and the handler needs to be someone not recognisable as a police officer. I take an instant dislike to the guy they've assigned me, after the lewd look he gave me when we first met. I need someone I can trust, not someone who wants to screw me. I told the DI this privately, and she slipped me her personal number, telling me to call day or night, whenever I needed someone to talk to.

The handler thought it best if I keep my own name, to avoid confusion, and in case anyone I know spots me while I'm out with a potential suspect. During the day I'll be working as a part-time receptionist at a local GP surgery. It isn't exciting work, but feels as far removed from my real job as possible. As far as I know, only a handful of people know about my assignment, including the DI, DCI and DSI. Everyone else thinks I've returned to uniform after completing my probation.

'We will be watching you at all times,' Matthews tells me, but doesn't inform me how or where they will be monitoring from. She thinks it is best I don't know, in case my behaviour changes and alerts him to their presence.

They have put my profile on each of the sites the victims used, as well as others. All message requests will be received in a dummy email account that the DI and her small team will monitor. Each potential date who messages will be thoroughly assessed before any agreement to meet is made. At the moment, what worries me most is that he won't want to target me. We've still yet to identify what attracted him to the other three, and I can't escape that doubt in my mind; though I do my best to ignore it.

I'm taking a self-defence class outside of work. I want to be prepared in case things go wrong. I'm sure I'm being paranoid, but there's no harm in taking added precautions. The gym work is tough, but it'll be worth it in the long run.

Mum didn't react well when I told her I was going to be too busy to come round for the next few weeks. She thinks I'm turning my back on the family, but she'd go ballistic if she knew what I was really doing. It'll be better for her and the others if they don't know what's really going on.

I shower after my latest gym session, and return to the GP surgery. But I struggle to concentrate once I receive a message from the DI saying we are on for our first date this evening. I am due to meet him for coffee in the West End at six. The DI wants to see me beforehand and will be at the cover flat when I finish work.

As I leave the surgery and make the short journey back to the flat, I can't help but wonder whether he's watching me now… waiting to strike.

CHAPTER FORTY-ONE

The flat seemed so quiet now. Ben hadn't called yet, and since getting home, Kate hadn't been able to concentrate as she read and reread her notes. The answer had to be in there, but she couldn't escape the fact that she was reviewing old material. She would give anything to see copies of what the new team had. She'd thought about reaching out to Armitage again. Ultimately, they both wanted the same outcome: to catch Amy's killer. The only difference was, she wanted justice, where he wanted a promotion ladder.

Making her way towards the kitchen, she opened the freezer, removed a frozen ready meal and threw it into the microwave.

The door buzzer sounded, startling her. He must have decided to come over rather than call. She buzzed the door open, but was surprised to see Laura on the stairs, rather than Ben.

'Sorry to come around unannounced,' she said, raising a chilled bottle of wine into the air. 'Can I come in?'

Kate moved away from the door and reached two glasses down from the kitchen cupboard. 'Are you okay? You look… well, you don't look happy. Is this about what Isbitt said in the interview?'

Laura opened the bottle and poured generously into both glasses, before following Kate through to the living room. 'His wife doesn't deserve to be treated like that. It makes me just want to phone her up and tell her what's going on, but if I did—'

Kate interrupted. 'I know it's tough, but unfortunately we can't interfere at that level. However, I do think he might have assaulted her. She didn't want to admit it, but I saw the signs.'

'Poor woman.'

Kate sipped her wine. 'Did you manage to get hold of his girlfriend? Did she confirm his alibi?'

'Of course she did.'

'But you don't believe her?'

'SSD extracted multiple DNA sources from the vehicle, but one in particular – a hair from one of the carpet mats in the front of the car – belongs to Isbitt. If he didn't kill her, how the hell did a stray hair wind up in the footwell?'

'Have you put that to him yet?'

'Not yet. Underhill is applying for an extension to his custody so SSD can continue searching the car for more samples. Underhill told me to go home and rest, and to be back in for seven tomorrow to have another go at Isbitt. I had to explain to him that you'd agreed for us to bring Isbitt in. He didn't seem happy, but he should have answered his phone the six times I called him.' Laura took a long sip of her wine as the microwave pinged from the kitchen. 'Sorry, am I interrupting your dinner?'

'It's only a lasagne. It can wait.'

Laura looked at the walls. 'Have you made any more progress with this lot?'

'Not really… I wish there was a way to get an inside track on what the new team are looking at. I feel like we'll never solve this if we don't see the whole picture.'

'I could log into HOLMES2 and see what I can find, if you want?'

'No, it's a high-profile case. If anyone not connected with the op starts searching for information, Armitage will know. If he then sees that you work with me, he'll be on to the supe.'

Laura growled. 'I'm still angry about Isbitt. Not content with a wife and child, he's off shagging another woman. And some of us can't even find one man who'll take them out.'

Kate was surprised by the sudden outburst. 'Are you all right?'

Realising that this wasn't the time or place to be discussing her personal life, Laura apologised.

'What about that barista at the café?' Kate asked. 'You could ask him out. I'd always assumed you had a boyfriend out there you didn't talk about.'

'We should change the subject. I'm fine on my own,' Laura snorted. 'Maybe online dating really is the way forward.'

Kate choked her wine back. 'Trust me, it's not a good idea.' She said, reaching for her laptop and beginning to type. 'Don't tell anyone about this, but…' She indicated for Laura to come and join her on the sofa.

'Oh my God,' Laura said when she saw what was on the screen. 'This is *your* dating profile?'

Kate could barely look at it. 'Embarrassing, right? My neighbour Trish put it on there for me, it's how I got hacked by that stalker. Do you remember?'

'I bet you get loads of hits from potential dates though.'

'I just delete the emails. I keep meaning to have the profile removed, but I've never got round to it. My reason for showing it to you now, is to show you that you have *nothing* to worry about. You're still young. You're – what, twenty-four?'

Laura nodded.

'There you go then. You're not old enough to be worrying about settling down yet. I'm sure the right guy is out there somewhere. If you stop looking, he'll probably come looking for you.'

'And, in the meantime?'

'Ask that barista out.' Laura was about to return to her own seat, when Kate suddenly grabbed her hand. 'It's her. Look, on the advert. It's the woman we found in the car park last night.'

CHAPTER FORTY-TWO

'If her profile was on this site, then we must be able to find out who she is,' Kate exclaimed as she feverishly tried to narrow the search criteria. She thought back to Ben's initial summary in the car park. 'She was in her early to mid-thirties, so that's as good a place to start as any. She was found in Southampton, so let's assume for now that she lived locally…' She hit the filter button. 'Jeez, there's hundreds… Okay, what else do we know? Her name might be Mary.'

Kate moved from profile to profile, her pulse quickening with every swipe. 'Come on, come on, she must be one of their clients. If they've used her face in their advertising banner, they must have got the image from somewhere…' She paused. 'Unless she's a model they hired…?' She shook her head. 'No, I'm sure they'd use real people.' She continued to click the arrow button.

Her mind was racing with questions, while the wine in her stomach swirled. She hadn't eaten since breakfast, and now a bubble of nausea was slowly rising. She clenched her teeth to quell the growing anxiety. It couldn't be a coincidence that Isbitt was selecting his victims online, just like the killer she'd hunted before. She was beginning to believe her crazy idea was anything but.

The breath caught in Kate's throat as the car-park victim's smiling face appeared in the right-hand corner of the screen. Her fingers hovered above the keyboard as she took in every freckle, every wrinkle and stray strand of the copper-coloured hair. 'Holy shit! It's her… I'm sure of it. Laura, look, this is Isbitt's second victim.'

Laura leaned over. 'It says her name is Mary Eden. God, you're right, it's her.'

Kate nodded, her anxiety boiling over. He'd kept himself out of the headlines for a year following Amy's death, but the press coverage of the anniversary must have sparked something in him again. And this time she knew who he was. But why?

Laura stood. 'I need to call this in. Can I use your phone? My battery's nearly dead.'

'Sure, but before you do that… you don't think… what was the first victim's name?'

'Helen Jackson. Why?'

'Well, if Mary Eden is on this site, is it possible that Helen is too?'

Laura's eyes widened, as she realised what Kate was suggesting. 'You think—'

Kate interrupted her. 'We have no evidence… yet.'

Laura leaned over her and adjusted the filter settings. 'There are only 104 profiles this time…' she said, as she began clicking through them. Kate pulled herself up and began examining something on the far wall.

'I'm not sure that Helen was looking for love, to be fair,' Laura said, as she neared the end of the list of profiles. 'She hadn't long split up from her boyfriend. I mean, it would be a huge coincidence if she happened to…' Her words trailed off as she blinked at the screen in front of her.

Kate, who hadn't really been listening, turned to Laura as she picked up on the sudden silence. 'What is it?'

'I don't believe it.' She turned the laptop for Kate to see the screen. 'There she is. Helen Jackson, the girl from Isbitt's boot. Do you realise what this means?'

Kate couldn't begin to comprehend what the evidence was suggesting. The hairs on the back of her neck stood as a tingle of fear and excitement raced down her spine. Laura was still speaking, but she couldn't hear a word as competing thoughts jostled for position. It had to be just a coincidence, right? It was ludicrous to think that he'd lain dormant for a year and had suddenly struck again. And why here? Southampton: to toy with *her*? A wave of nausea swept through her, but she choked it back feeling a cool sweat descending from the top of her head all the way down.

During the investigation she'd spent every waking minute thinking about the day she would finally put cuffs on him. And every day since he'd killed Amy, she'd lived with the regret that she might never discover who he was. And just as things seemed so bleak, he'd returned, as if taunting her for her failure. Was this a reprieve? Was this fate's way of giving her a second chance to stop him once and for all? With Isbitt in custody, the clock was ticking to find the evidence to prove they had their man. She bent low and sucked breath deep into her lungs.

'Ma'am? We've got to call this in.'

Laura was right, of course she was. As personal as this case was, she had to handle it appropriately. There was too much at stake to risk screwing up because she had failed to follow protocol again.

Kate raised her hand. 'Wait, before we jump to conclusions, we need to establish whether Isbitt could have found them through that site. Can you run a search to see if you can find him on there too? Presumably SSD have taken his computer for analysis? They could check his internet search history and see if he has visited the site too.'

'I didn't think she'd be on there. I—'

'Laura, we can't get ahead of ourselves.' But even as she spoke the words, Kate knew she'd already lost that battle with herself.

'How do we prove it's him?'

Kate's brain was firing out questions and accusations faster than she could process. Grabbing her glass, she necked what remained of the wine to steady her trembling fingers.

CHAPTER FORTY-THREE

39 DAYS UNTIL I DIE

I can't stop fidgeting as I sit at the tall table, waiting for him to arrive. I shouldn't feel this nervous. It's not like he's going to attack me in such a public place. And given the DI is listening to everything at a table in the seating area upstairs, I have nothing to fear.

Yet still my head jerks up every time I hear the door open. I've emptied and refilled the small dish of sugar sachets too many times to count. But it is already five minutes after six, and he is yet to show. Is he just running late? Or did he realise who I was and decide to go on his way? Or worse still, is he not our suspect, saw me through the window and decided he didn't fancy me?

My head is spinning.

'Calm down,' the DI's voice says through the earpiece.

I've been told not to react to anything she tells me, but it's hard not to. I'm about to speak when a voice catches my attention over my shoulder.

'Amy?'

I look up, confusion descending. 'Finn? What are you doing here?'

'I was about to ask you the same question. This isn't your usual neck of the woods. Do you mind if I sit down for a minute?'

Oh God, what do I do now? The team at the undercover unit warned me that this might happen, but in a million years I'd never expected my brother to show up while I was on assignment. He sits before I can answer, so I shrug.

What's the suspect going to think if he sees me sitting here with someone else?

'Get rid of him,' the DI says in my ear.

'I'm waiting for a friend,' Finn continues, oblivious to the panic rising in my throat. 'We're seeing the new Star Wars *film.'*

I nod, keeping one eye on the door.

'Yeah, he said to meet him in here, but I've been all over and haven't spotted him yet. You don't know my mate Sam, do you?'

I shake my head, willing him to leave.

'No, I didn't think so.'

'Maybe you should call him,' I muster.

'I'm sure he won't be long. We've got ages until the film starts. Hey, you're more than welcome to join us if you don't have other plans.'

He's sweet to offer, but even if I wasn't in the middle of work, I wouldn't choose to watch sci-fi.

'I'm kind of on a blind date,' I tell him, rolling my eyes.

He stands quickly. 'Oh, I see. I'm sorry. You don't think I frightened him off, do you?'

'He's probably just running late too, or he's stood me up.'

He frowns. 'I can't imagine why you'd think that. I'm sure he's just late too. Hey, wouldn't it be funny if your guy rocked up at the same time as Sam? Hey? Maybe they're travelling on the same train and don't even realise they're heading towards the same place.'

'Maybe.'

He steps away from the table. 'I won't cramp your style anymore. But if he doesn't show up, give me a call, and you can join me and Sam.'

I nod as he disappears off towards the back of the café, and am relieved when the bell on the door goes again, and I see my date arrive. He thrusts his hand out for me to shake, but I'm already leaning forward to kiss his cheek, and his hand brushes my chest. We both blush, and settle for shaking hands.

'I'm so sorry I was late. The tube got stuck in a tunnel. Have you been waiting long?'

I wave away his apology. 'I was early, anyway.'

He sits, noticing I already have a latte in front of me. 'Do you want another drink?'

I've only had one sip, but nod eagerly, thanking him. My head feels like it is on fire. When did it get so hot? He heads off to the counter to order.

'Just relax, Amy,' the DI says. 'We've got a good view of him on the brooch-cam and the audio was good when he spoke. You're doing fine.'

It's kind of her to be so positive, but I can't help but feel that he can see straight through me. As he returns with the drinks, he points at my ear. 'What's that?'

I frown as I don't know what he's talking about.

He leans forward and pulls something hard from my ear. My eyes widen in horror as I see the earpiece between his fingers. It must have slipped out and been hanging there without me noticing.

He looks around, as if expecting a television camera to be suddenly thrust into his face. 'Is there something you want to tell me?'

I open my mouth to speak, but no words will come out. My mind is blank. How do I explain why I was covertly wearing an earpiece without giving the game away?

'I'm partly deaf,' I offer. 'It's to help me hear better in this ear.'

But he isn't fooled as he studies the small device. 'I know what this is, but the question is: why are you wearing it? Who's on the other end? What is this, some kind of police sting operation?' He lifts the earpiece closer to his mouth and speaks directly to it. 'Come out, come out, wherever you are.'

I snatch it off him, but he doesn't stick around to hear my feeble explanation, darting for the door and disappearing into the busy street.

I close my eyes and let out a long sigh. 'Fuck!'

The DI is at the table a moment later. 'Listen, it happened and there's nothing we can do about it.'

But I can hear the frustration in her tone, even if she doesn't intend it.

'I'm sorry, ma'am. I fucked up.'

'We know where he lives and we'll send a unit by to question him tomorrow. It probably wasn't him, so don't blame yourself for what happened. It was one of those things.'

I know she is trying to shield me from the pressure she's under, and she must be questioning whether I'm up to the task. 'Please, ma'am, don't bump me from the op. We've put in too much groundwork to give up after this. Maybe it would be better not to wear the earpiece anyway. I found it distracting not answering you.'

She fixes me with a stare, as if weighing up my value. 'I need to get back to the office and update Armitage and the DSI.'

I instinctively reach for her hand. 'Don't give up on me, ma'am. If we can move past this, I know we'll find him. Just give me a second chance.'

But she leaves the café without another word, and I'm left wondering whether my inexperience has just cost us the chance of catching Steph's killer.

CHAPTER FORTY-FOUR

MONDAY

'I really appreciate you coming with me,' Kate said, making eye contact with Finn.

'I'm just glad you called me. If you're right about this guy, then Armitage will have to act.'

She didn't like it, but he was right about the *if*; she had no evidence to suggest that Isbitt was the man she'd been hunting for so long. She was certain in her mind that he'd returned, but convincing Armitage and making it stick was a different game altogether.

Kate checked her watch anxiously. 'What time will he be here?'

'Any minute now,' Finn confirmed, opening a sachet of sugar and tipping it into the espresso on the table.

They were in the same café as their meeting on Saturday. Trish had reluctantly agreed to Kate borrowing her car to make the journey, but only after Kate had assured her that her foot was healed enough to drive. Not that she needed her left foot in Trish's automatic.

She lifted her own mug and took a large gulp. She was taking a huge risk in reaching out to Armitage at this stage, but with his contacts and the size of his task force, having him onside would be vital in putting Isbitt at the scene of each of the crimes. She'd phoned Nicola Isbitt and asked her to confirm where her husband was on certain dates in 2015, under the pretence that it was in connection with other matters. Nicola had said she would check and let Kate know. If they could establish that Isbitt was away on the date of each murder, they'd be a step closer to confirming Kate's worst fears. She had little doubt they'd find what they needed this time.

At least he was in custody for now, but if Underhill's extension request was unsuccessful, it would only be a matter of time before he was out and free to strike again.

'He's here,' Finn muttered under his breath to catch her attention.

Armitage's tan looked even darker as he sat down at the table, not noticing Kate hunched over her own drink, her back to him. 'Matthews! I should have guessed that you'd be behind this in some way.'

'This isn't Finn's fault. I asked him to invite you here. Please, just hear what I have to say.'

Armitage looked around the small Italian café. 'You know I'm going to phone your DSI about this, don't you? You'll be finished, Matthews.'

She shuffled her chair over to their table. 'For once I'm trying to do the right thing. I've uncovered a suspect in Southampton who I believe may also have a connection to the London victims.'

Armitage crossed his arms and sighed, making it very clear to Kate how tedious he was already finding the interruption to his day. 'You have five minutes.' He called a waiter over and ordered a latte to take away.

Kate took a deep breath. 'Two young women have been found beaten and suffocated in Southampton in the last week. We believe that both were attacked by the same man, and that he used some kind of polythene bag to kill them. Our prime suspect is a computer engineer and sales rep for a company he owns with his brother. The first of this week's victims was discovered in his allegedly stolen BMW, and our SOCOs found one of his hairs and fragments of one of his business cards inside the second vehicle. We have him in custody, but his solicitor has instructed him to deny the allegations.'

Kate paused to make sure Armitage was still listening. 'Last night we found both victim's profiles on a dating website.' She paused again, allowing her words to sink in. 'I am pursuing the likelihood of his work taking him to London in late 2015, and will confirm as soon as I have that information.'

His face remained neutral. 'Is that it?'

'I know it isn't concrete, but I felt I should share the information in case his name has come up in connection with any of your other leads.'

He sighed and pushed his chair back from the table.

'Wait,' Kate said eagerly. 'There's more. Finn has confirmed that the week before Amy's death, she hired an engineer to come and reformat her computer because it had contracted a virus of some sort. Isbitt is a computer engineer.'

Armitage remained seated. 'And was he the engineer who visited her flat?'

Kate looked at Finn. 'Describe the engineer you saw at Amy's flat.'

Finn looked off into the distance, and his hand involuntarily ran through the thick stubble on his chin. 'Mmm… I'd know him if I saw him. He was probably average height, average build… he was wearing a baseball cap and glasses… I remember thinking he looked a bit older than I'd expected. But the guy was well presented in company overalls and seemed to know what he was doing.'

Armitage looked from Finn to Kate. 'You should know better than this, Matthews. It's bad enough you wasting my time, but to unnecessarily raise the hopes of the victim's family is not fair, nor professional. And invoking Mr Delaney to get involved in your twisted games too? You should be ashamed.' He stood and moved to the counter to await his drink.

Kate was about to follow him over, but Finn beat her to the punch.

He pulled on Armitage's shoulder, spinning him round. 'You need to listen to what DI Matthews has to say.'

Armitage sized him up, before offering his winning smile. 'With all due respect, Mr Delaney, I know how to do my job, and I will do everything within my power to find the man who murdered your sister. I know that DI Matthews appears to offer hope with all her wild-eyed theories, but she was out of her depth twelve months ago, and she's even more out of her depth now. Why do you think she was forced to leave the Met? Because she wasn't worthy enough to wear the badge. I understand the pain you're going through and I apologise on behalf of the Met for Matthews' reckless actions, but I implore you to let us do our job, and to stay clear of this woman.'

The barista placed a cardboard cup in front of Armitage, who grabbed it. 'She's paying,' he added, pointing in Kate's direction. 'It's the least she can do for wasting my time.' He left the café, and a frustrated Finn returned to the table.

'I'm sorry he wouldn't listen,' Finn offered.

Kate's cheeks felt warm after the character assassination. 'I understand if you want nothing else to do with me.'

'Are you kidding, if anything, I think you're even more right. Do you have a photograph of this Isbitt character I can look at? I'm sure I'd recognise him if I saw him again.'

'What are you doing for the rest of the day? I think you should return to Southampton with me now and I'll see if we can get him in an ID parade.'

'Can't you just show me a photograph of him?'

'I don't have one on me, but if we hurry, we might still catch him at the police station.'

CHAPTER FORTY-FIVE

'Wait for me in here,' Kate said, as Finn sat in the soft interview room. 'I'll check that the suspect is still here and then I'll set up a chance for you to identify him. Do you want tea or coffee?'

Finn didn't look comfortable in the confines of the windowless room, and Kate had to question whether she was doing the right thing in putting him through such an ordeal. If he was right, and Isbitt was the engineer who'd fixed Amy's computer, she would be putting him face-to-face with his sister's killer, and that wouldn't be easy.

He shook his head. 'Don't be long.'

She tried to smile reassuringly. 'I'll be as quick as I can.'

Closing the door behind her and marking it as engaged, she made her way back along the corridor, and up to the third floor to look for Laura when she heard a familiar boom.

'MATTHEWS! Get in here. NOW!'

Kate shut her eyes and took a moment to compose herself before turning and heading through the supe's open door. She remained silent as he paced furiously by the large window overlooking the sea. He finally slowed, stooping to rest both hands on his desk, clearly exasperated.

'Well? What's the explanation this time?'

She hesitated, uncertain which specific actions he was referring to.

'Have you nothing to say for yourself?'

She remained silent, her head dipped.

'Okay, well I'll start, then. Tell me on whose authority did you approach DCI Armitage and discuss a case that you've been warned to go nowhere near?'

So Armitage had followed through with his threat, she couldn't say she was surprised. 'Sir, I have reason to believe that the suspect you currently have in custody is the man responsible for not only the two women killed last week, but also the four women murdered in London a year ago, including DC Amy Spencer.'

The supe looked like he might erupt, but she carried on before he had a chance.

'Hear me out. We believe that the same person killed Helen Jackson and the woman discovered in the car park on Saturday night, whose name we now believe to be Mary Eden, from a dating website that both her profile and Helen's were found on.'

'Who's *we*?'

'DC Trotter and myself.'

He threw his hands into the air in mock surprise.

'So, not only are *you* breaching procedures, you're dragging the ever-eager Trotter down with you.'

'Sir, if you—'

He held up his hand to silence her. 'No, enough is enough, Matthews. I've given you the benefit of the doubt since that Vaughn mess last year, but you've taken advantage of that, and it has to stop. You've crossed the line this time.'

'But, sir, please, we suspect Isbitt was at Amy's flat—'

'I warned you about this on Thursday. This was precisely what I was trying to avoid.' He turned his back to her and stared out at the sea. 'I understand the frustrations of not solving a case that you're personally invested in. With your own involvement in what happened a year ago, I can see why you would want to find links between what happened then and now. If you could link the crimes, you'd have the closure your mind demands. But as your superior and friend, I need you to listen very carefully to what I am about to tell you: *let it go*.'

'But, sir, if you'll just—'

He spun round. 'There is no connection! We released Isbitt half an hour ago. He has an alibi for Saturday night. He didn't murder the second victim.'

'But, sir—'

The hand flew up again. 'I made it abundantly clear to you that you were to go nowhere near Underhill's investigation. Even when you disobeyed and tried to take control of the second murder, I *reminded* you of my expectations. And despite all those chances, you continue to defy me!'

'Sir, I'm not—'

'I don't want to hear anything else from you, Matthews. You're done here. I have already spoken to Professional Standards and they support my decision to suspend you from duty with immediate effect. You've left me no other choice. You are hereby suspended as per regulation 10 of the Police (Conduct) Regulations 2012. Your suspension will be on full pay and will last until such time as a hearing can be arranged. I will confirm the terms of your suspension in writing in the next day or so.'

Kate remained where she was, until he pointed to the door. With her head low, she left his office, slamming the door behind her. She'd come too far to stop now. Amy's killer was free, and it was her duty to nail him once and for all. Even if it cost her the only job she'd ever loved.

CHAPTER FORTY-SIX

'Grab your coat,' Kate demanded, as she burst through the door of the soft interview room, 'we need to get out of here.'

Finn stood unsteadily. 'What's going on? What about the identity parade?'

'Isbitt's not here. They've released him.'

He crossed his arms. 'What do you mean they've released him? What about Amy? What about the other women he killed?'

Kate's cheeks were still flushed from her encounter with the supe. 'I'll explain everything when we're out of here. But we need to go, now.'

He remained still, waiting for more of an explanation.

'I've been suspended,' she finally confessed.

His eyes widened with shock.

She stared straight ahead. 'It doesn't change anything. We know who we're after, and now it's only a matter of time before we find what we need. Come on.'

Finn draped his jacket over his arm, and followed her out of the room, back along the corridor and out through the front door. Kate kept her head down; news of her suspension would spread through the station like wildfire, and she didn't want to still be around when it did.

'Where now?' he asked as they stepped out into a cool breeze. The grey clouds overhead threatened rain, but were holding. For now.

Kate was about to reply, when she heard her name being called.

Turning, she saw Laura bursting out through the same door, and rushing down the stairs to where they were standing. 'Ma'am, tell me it isn't true.'

'Who told you?'

'Underhill just briefed those of us in MIR-1. Should I speak to the supe? After all, I was the one who got you involved in Helen Jackson's case.'

Kate smiled, grateful for her support. 'It wouldn't do any good. This isn't your fault, and you'd be best served steering clear of me. I don't want to be the reason you throw your career away too.'

But Laura stood firm. 'If I had any doubt that Isbitt killed Helen and Mary, I'd be back inside at my desk. What can I do to help?'

Kate, Laura and Finn bundled into the back of Trish's car as the rain began to fall, and relocated to Laura's favourite café. They huddled around their drinks in a vacant corner where their hushed conversation wouldn't be overheard.

'Under the regulations, you have the right to appeal, ma'am.'

Kate stirred her coffee. 'In writing, I know, but it won't do any good. The supe has valid grounds for suspending me and referring my actions to Professional Standards. The day will come for me to justify my behaviour and clear this whole thing up, but nothing will justify it more than if we solve this thing. We don't have long. He's killed twice in a week, and it's only a matter of time before he does it again.'

Finn had been sitting quietly, obviously trying to wrap his head around what was going on and to pick a side. Eventually, he leaned in. 'What can we do? If what Amy told me about you is true, then you must have a plan.'

Kate looked away. 'Not exactly, but if we go at this thing from opposite ends, then maybe there's a chance we can meet somewhere in the middle. Laura, I don't want you doing anything that will see you suspended or booted out of the trainee detective programme. You've worked hard this last year and I'm not going to be responsible for holding you back.'

'I'll be careful, ma'am. I won't do anything to draw attention to what I'm doing, but I wouldn't be any kind of detective if I sat idly by and allowed Isbitt to go free.'

Kate forced a thin smile. 'Okay, then do your job. Do everything Underhill asks you to, but keep digging on Isbitt. Speak to his wife. When I saw her yesterday, I got the impression that there was more she wanted to tell us, but that she was afraid to speak. I promised we would keep Gavin away from her, but now he's back at home so you're going to have to rebuild her trust, and let her know we'll keep her safe. She'll have access to his email and diary and you need to convince her to share that information with us. She told me she took a sleeping pill on Tuesday night, so push to find out what she takes and whether it's possible he slipped her an extra dose to ensure she didn't wake and wonder where he was. Also, try and track the allegedly stolen car's movements back from its arrival at the train station. He must have grabbed and attacked Helen somewhere. Find that footage and we tie him to the crime.'

Laura busily scribbled notes in her pad.

'Also,' Kate continued, 'you need to visit Isbitt's girlfriend in Portsmouth. Find out if he's threatened or paid her off in some way to give him an alibi for Saturday night. It's possible he left his phone with her in Portsmouth so he could travel back to Southampton and strike undetected. Remember, he's remained off the radar for more than a year; he's smart. We need to be smarter.

'Finn, you and I need to tackle it from the London end. I can't go anywhere near Armitage's investigation, and after your involvement earlier today, he's unlikely to trust you with updates. However, he will keep Erin and your dad informed. Stay close to them and ask them to keep you posted with any updates, however small. When are you due to go back to Devon?'

'I can't go back to Devon until we catch him. We – I *need* this closure.'

She watched him carefully. 'Are you sure you can afford to be away this long?'

He nodded, but Kate could see from his eyes he was lying. She decided not to press him now with Laura around.

'Speaking of which,' he said, holding up his phone to show he had an incoming call. He moved away from the table to answer it.

'What are you going to do?' Laura asked.

'I need to go back over every witness interview we took during the original investigation. If I'm going to place Isbitt in London, I need to identify exactly how and where he went. If he found the four initial victims via dating sites, how did he find out where they lived? And where did he stay while he was in the capital? We're creatures of habit, so there will be patterns, we just need to know where to look. That's where your work with Nicola Isbitt will help.'

'It's going to be hard to keep this all under wraps,' Laura admitted, the first traces of doubt creeping into her voice.

'But it's essential that we do. I'm going to return to London with Finn later, so I can speak to the family and friends of the victims again. If Isbitt was watching those girls and waiting to strike, someone must have seen him. It may be that he used his computer business to get into the homes of the other girls, like he may have done with Amy. Can you get me a photograph of him?'

'Leave that to me, ma'am.'

'It's Kate, remember? Besides, if we fail, I won't be your superior for much longer.'

Laura nodded her understanding, but Kate could see the look of pity in her eyes. She didn't need pity, she needed support.

'I'd better head back before Underhill wonders where I am,' Laura said, checking the time.

'Understood. Keep me posted. Call any time, day or night.'

Laura put on her coat and ducked out into the rain, hurrying along the pavement and over the footbridge above the railway tracks.

At the other side of the café Finn's voice was rising, but she couldn't hear what he was saying. She tried not to listen, and stared out of the window until he returned to the table.

'Sorry about that,' he offered. 'What happened to your friend?'

'She had to go back to the office. Finish your drink, we have a long journey ahead of us.'

CHAPTER FORTY-SEVEN

The rain eased as they passed Fleet Services, and the sun poked through the few remaining clouds, reflecting off the wet road ahead and making it almost impossible to see. Finn had been silent for most of the journey.

'Everything okay?' Kate asked when she could no longer take the silence.

He turned to face her, confused. 'Sorry?'

She offered him a look of concern. 'Are you thinking about Amy?'

'Is it that obvious?'

'We'll catch him, Finn. Okay? I promise you.'

'What if you lose your job?'

She didn't want to even consider the possibility. 'This is bigger than that.' She smiled affectionately.

He didn't return the smile, facing the window again. 'I haven't been able to stop thinking about that night, about that sick monster who killed my sister. That he might have been in her flat the week before, and...'

'None of this is your fault, Finn. You have to stop blaming yourself for what happened. I know it isn't easy.'

'I want to make him feel the pain that he's caused all of us. Does that make me a bad person?'

'Bad, no; human, yes.'

'I... I want him to suffer, you know? Amy was such a fire-cracker; the life and soul of family gatherings. Nothing's been the same since… if only… I probably shouldn't be telling you this. You'll have me arrested.'

'I'm hardly in a position to do that at the moment,' she half-joked. 'I understand how you feel, but when it comes down to it you'll do the right thing, that control is what differentiates us from them.'

'You think too much of me.'

It was an odd response, and something was niggling at her mind. 'What is it you're not telling me?'

His attention remained fixed on the road out of his window. 'I don't know what you're talking about.'

'The call you took back at the café, was it your wife?'

He glanced back at her and nodded. 'How did you know?'

'It didn't look good, that's all. You don't have to tell me.'

He sighed. 'I agreed to move to Devon to try and fix things, to get away from it all, but things haven't been right with me since… I feel so guilty that I wasn't able to protect Amy. It eats away at me. I try to hide it, but my wife, she can tell. The thing is – I've never told anyone before – but she called me that night.'

Kate almost swerved into the hard shoulder. 'What? They checked her phone records and I was the only person she called.'

He nodded gravely, staring down at his hands. 'It was from a payphone, I think. I missed her call, because I was driving home from work. She left a message asking me to call her back. We were due to see each other for lunch at my dad's place on the Sunday, and I figured she would just speak to me there about whatever she wanted to discuss. Instead of calling her back to see what was wrong, I went to bed. I had a stinking virus, and the doctor had me on these really strong antibiotics. And then the next morning, my dad phoned and broke the news. I was physically sick there and then; I barely made it to the kitchen sink. The guilt has been eating away at me ever since; in her hour of need, she reached out to me, and I didn't take her call.' He pressed his hand to his eyes in an effort to stop the tears escaping.

Kate had already been suspended when the full details of Amy's last night had been uncovered. Most of her understanding of what had happened, she'd drawn from the tabloid coverage of the crime. Coverage that ultimately held her accountable for what had happened, and led to her being chased out of the Met.

'So, she called you too. Did the investigating team speak to you about the call?'

He shook his head. 'They never asked, and I didn't mention it, in case they suspected I might have had something to do with it. It was only a ten-second message.'

'Why do you think she phoned you?'

'I tell myself every day that her call had absolutely nothing to do with what happened that night, but I can't escape the more probable truth: that she reached out to me because she thought her life was in danger.' He covered his face with his hands, and gently sobbed.

Kate reached over and rubbed his shoulder. 'She called me too, Finn, but my battery was dead. I was the one who should have had her back. This isn't your fault. It was mine. It was my job to protect her. You shouldn't feel guilty.'

His tears continued to flow freely. 'The image of her in the street haunts my dreams. She didn't deserve to die like that. She should have been older and at home with family who loved her; not left out naked in the gutter like… like trash.'

'Can I offer you some advice?'

He nodded, as he wiped his nose with the back of his hand.

'Call your wife and tell her everything you just told me. If there's one thing I *do* know, it's how to wreck a marriage. If what you have is worth saving, then you need to let her in.' She fixed him with a stare. 'I promise you, I *will* catch whoever killed your sister. Okay? I won't stop until I do, and I know I'm getting closer. We just need the last piece of the jigsaw and we'll have him.'

He acknowledged her statement with a faint smile. 'I meant what I said, too; I am at your disposal. I promise I won't do anything stupid if you find the evidence you need. You can trust me, Kate.'

'Good. Well, the first thing you can do is open the file by your feet. Steph Graham's address should be in there. I want us to go back to where this all started for me.'

CHAPTER FORTY-EIGHT

34 DAYS UNTIL I DIE

Mum is waiting for me in the kitchen. 'What's this Finn tells us about you going on a date? Who is he? What's his name? Where did you meet him?'

I should have known Finn would let slip about seeing me at the café the other night. I'm relieved I didn't tell him the real reason I was there.

I carry the dirty plates to the counter next to the sink, and gently lower them. 'It didn't work out,' I tell her.

She begins to rinse gravy from the top plate. 'Was he married?'

'Mum! I don't chase after married men.'

She raises an eyebrow. 'Oh really? The last two you were seeing had wives at home, didn't they?'

I blush, more concerned about how she knew who I'd been seeing, let alone my shame at being their bit on the side. 'It wasn't like that.'

'So who was he then?'

'Just some guy I met online.'

She drops the plate back into the sink with a thud. 'You ought to be having your head examined, young lady! Do you know what kind of eejits lurk on the internet?'

'It's not like that anymore,' I lie, to put her mind at ease. 'He wasn't some weirdo I met in a chat room. He was someone from a dating website.'

'Hark at her who's suddenly got time to be meeting men on dating sites, but doesn't have enough time to pick up the phone and call her mother.'

I pick up a tea towel and begin to wipe the cutlery dry. 'Please don't have another go at me. I came around today, didn't I?'

'Aye, you did that,' she sighed, 'but you've hardly taken your eyes off that phone of yours. You expecting a call?'

The truth is I'm waiting for the DI to call and tell me whether to continue my cover role, or whether I should return to the station. I can't be certain which way her decision will go. Not that I can tell Mum any of this.

'I bet it's that job of yours,' she concludes when I don't answer. 'I mean it's a Sunday, for pity's sake. Do they not understand you're entitled to a day off as well?'

I don't answer.

'It was the same when your father was alive. Even when he'd booked time off for important occasions, there was never any guarantee he wouldn't be called in for one thing or another. The only peace we ever got was when he'd had to fire his gun and was waiting for clearance to return to work.'

'It's the life we chose, Mum.'

'Some life!'

But for once I'm in no mood for her usual lecture. 'No, Mum, you're wrong. I'm sorry but I love my job, and there isn't anything else I'd rather do with my life.'

She hushes me with a wave of her Marigolds. 'Okay, okay, I don't want a row with you. I was just trying to get you to share some juicy details about your love life, that's all. I'm not getting any younger, and it would be nice to meet my grandchildren while I'm young enough to be able to play with them.'

I sigh loudly so she knows just how angry I am that she's managed to steer the conversation back to my lack of procreation. 'There's plenty of time for all that.'

'Mark my words, my girl, the end will creep up on you before you know it. One day you're young with the rest of your life ahead of you, and then suddenly death sneaks up, and you'll look back wondering what you could have done differently.'

This is how every visit to my mother ends. It would probably help if Finn and his wife would produce a child, just so my mother can show it off to her friends. She believes it's quite the scandal that she's the only one without a grandchild to parade at the knitting circle.

I'm relieved to excuse myself when my phone starts ringing, and I step outside to answer.

'Okay, we're still on,' the DI says, and relief floods through my body. 'Get yourself back to the cover flat tonight. We need to up our game, so I hope you didn't have any plans for this week, as we've lined up dates for every night.'

CHAPTER FORTY-NINE

Thumping her hand against the door, Kate called out, 'Mr Brookes? It's Detective Inspector Kate Matthews. Do you remember me?'

She pressed her ear closer to the door, straining to hear any movement inside. She looked back at Finn who was leaning against the staircase wall. She banged her hand again. 'Mr Brookes?'

'Seems like he's not home.' Finn shrugged.

The smell of fried onions drifted up the narrow staircase from the fried chicken takeaway below Brookes's flat. It made Kate's stomach grumble. At the top of the stairs, the small corridor to the left led to what had been Steph Graham's one-bed studio flat, with the opposite corridor leading to her neighbour, Wallace Brookes. Kate made one more effort to reach Brookes, before signalling for Finn to head back downstairs. They exited and returned to the car.

'Who is this Brookes guy?' Finn asked when they were seated.

Kate opened the file she'd brought down. She thumbed through it until she found the image she was seeking, and showed Finn.

His eyes widened. 'Jesus! Freaky-looking, isn't he?'

Kate closed the folder and nodded. 'We interviewed him the week following the discovery of Steph Graham's body. He suffered with vitiligo, which meant his cells didn't produce enough melanin to colour his skin. His face was as white as chalk, and there wasn't a single hair follicle on the top of his head. His skin was hypersensitive to UV rays, and he had to cover himself if he ever left the property during the day. I remember we brought him in to take a witness statement a couple of days after we'd found her body. He wore this pale-yellow mac, with the collar turned up and a scarf around most of his face. It was only when we were safely inside a windowless interview room, with the lights dimmed, that he removed his scarf and spoke to us.'

Finn studied the image. 'Why was he brought in?'

'Under the premise he'd confirm Steph's comings and goings from the flat; because of his condition he rarely went out during the day and was up for most of the night. You should have seen his place; windows covered with thick, dark card and blackout blinds, dimmed lights, no fresh air. The place reeked.'

'You said the witness statement was a premise. Why did you really bring him in?'

'Steph had made a complaint to her landlord about him a couple of months before her death.'

'About?'

'Something innocuous, from memory. Uh… she'd seen him lurking around, shadows of footsteps under the crack of her door or something. She thought he'd been listening at her door. He denied it, stating that he would have been asleep at that time of the day.'

'You suspected him?'

'I definitely felt there was something not quite right about him, but he had an alibi for the night of her murder.'

'Which was?'

'He runs an internet radio station from his flat, and he was talking on air from 10.00 p.m. until 3.00 a.m.'

'That's a long stint. Could he not have pre-recorded the show?'

'We thought that, but a couple of people called in with requests and he was there to pick up.'

'What about CCTV?'

'The only street camera between here and the park where Steph was found wasn't working. I had an officer review the footage we managed to pull from private cameras, but there was no sign of him. He had alibis on the nights of Willow and Roxie's murders, too.'

'Did you check to see if he was known to either of the first two victims?'

'Yeah, we showed his picture to Willow's parents, but neither of them recognised him. He has a face you would remember, so you wouldn't have missed him if he'd been hanging around. We ran some background checks, just to be sure.'

'So why the urgency to speak to him now?'

Kate pulled her phone from her pocket, unlocked it and slid it across the table.

Finn looked at the image on the screen. 'Who's this?'

Kate narrowed her eyes. 'That's Gavin Isbitt. Don't you recognise him?'

Finn picked up the phone and studied the face again, the blood draining from his face. 'Yes, that's him: that's the man who was in Amy's flat.'

Kate returned the phone to her pocket. 'Well, I'm hoping Wallace Brookes recognises him, too. I'll leave a note under Brookes's door and we'll move on to Willow Daniels' parents. I want to show them Isbitt's face too.'

CHAPTER FIFTY

As Kate clocked the condolence cards still propped up on every surface, it was clear that Mrs Daniels hadn't moved on from that night in 2015 either.

Kate had suggested that Finn wait in the car while she spoke with Willow's parents. Although she had no jurisdiction or right to speak with them about their daughter's murder, he had even less right, and it didn't feel fair to lie to the family about who he was and why he was there.

Mrs Daniels carried the cup and saucer of tea through from the kitchen, and rested it on a coaster on the dining table near where Kate was sitting. 'Do you take sugar?'

'Thanks, no,' Kate said.

'Do you mind if I smoke?' Mrs Daniels asked, placing a cigarette between her lips and lighting up with a trembling hand before Kate had a chance to answer.

'It's your house,' Kate replied, leaning back to try and avoid as much of the smoke as possible.

Mrs Daniels inhaled deeply, exhaling smoke towards the small open window over her shoulder.

'How have you been keeping?' Kate asked. She'd first met Willow's parents two months after the murder, when she was linking Steph and Roxie's murders with Willow's. She'd tried to keep them updated, but following Amy's murder, Kate had been banned from making contact with anyone related to the cases.

Mrs Daniels puffed on the cigarette. 'I have good days and bad days. Most mornings I wake up still expecting to hear her voice. She was terrible at getting up for work in the morning, and it would take me several attempts most days. It used to drive me nuts, but I'd give anything to go back to those mornings now.' She dabbed the cigarette against the ashtray. 'It's funny, innit, the silly things we miss when they're snatched away from us?'

'Mr Daniels isn't home today?'

'Nah, he was back at work within a month of it happening. We've had many a row about him burying his feelings. At first I thought he was avoiding grieving properly, but then I learned that was how he needed to cope, to survive.'

'Does he still work for the council?'

'He's still in social care, if that's what you mean? I don't know how he does it sometimes. Some of the stories he tells me about what some parents do to their kids… it makes what happened to our Willow even crueller. We was good parents, and she was a good girl. Nobody had a bad word to say against her. Yet there are other people out there who treat their kids like shit, and they can continue with their lives.'

'Did you see the *Crimewatch* re-enactment on Thursday night?'

She flicked more ash into the glass dish. 'I couldn't bring myself to watch it. Pete did, but it would just bring it all up again. Did they mention Willow much?'

In truth, the murders of Willow, Roxie and Steph had been slightly glossed over, but she didn't need to hear that.

Kate nodded. 'They're hoping by focusing on the most recent crime that someone will come forward with information that will tie the killer back to the other murders. Are you still attending the victim-support group you were going to?'

'Nah, gave that up last year. It was too difficult to get to the community centre every week, what with Pete going back to work. I wasn't getting much out of it anyway.'

Kate took a sip of her tea, trying to work out how to phrase her next question. 'I want you to know, Mrs Daniels, that I haven't given up hope of finding your daughter's killer. If it takes me the rest of my life, I will catch the person responsible.'

Mrs Daniels squashed her cigarette into the ashtray and placed her cold hand over Kate's. 'I don't doubt it, love. I was shocked when I heard they'd kicked you off the investigation. I said to my Pete they were making a mistake, but nobody cared what we thought. You was the only one who seemed to care about our Willow. After that young detective got killed, she became their main focus. We've heard hide nor hair this past year.'

'I'm surprised to hear that. Did anyone come and speak to you before the *Crimewatch* programme?'

'Some lad in uniform, who looked like he should be in school, came here and interviewed us, not that it did any good. We wasn't able to tell him anything we hadn't said a hundred times before.'

Kate unlocked her phone and slid the image of Gavin Isbitt across the table. 'Do you recognise the man in this photograph, Mrs Daniels?'

She glanced at the phone. 'Hang on a tick, I'll need my glasses.' She left the room.

Kate was taking a huge chance in showing her the photograph Laura had sent through, but if Mrs Daniels could identify him as someone in Willow's life, it would put Kate a step closer to nailing him.

Mrs Daniels returned, wearing a pair of bifocals with a colourful cord around her neck. She lifted the phone into the light and squinted as she scrutinised it. 'No, love, sorry, I don't recognise him,' she said, as she offered the phone back.

'Please, Mrs Daniels, look again. I have reason to believe this man *may* – and I use the word cautiously – be the man who attacked Willow that night.'

Mrs Daniels studied the image again. 'Who is he?'

'I'm not at liberty to divulge his name at this time. I just need to know whether you can remember seeing him around the time that Willow was killed, or whether Willow mentioned or described someone like him.'

She passed the phone back, the face now committed to memory. She retook her seat and removed the glasses, allowing them to hang from their cord. 'How sure are you that he did it?'

'I'm sorry, Mrs Daniels, I'm not at liberty—'

Mrs Daniels waved her hand as if she'd heard the excuse a hundred times before. Reaching for her cigarette packet, she lit up a second. 'Let me put it this way, if I was to say that I'd seen him hanging about the place, would that give you what you need to arrest him?'

Kate didn't like the way the question had been phrased. 'Are you saying you *did* see him?'

'I think so… *if* I say yes, does that help you?'

As much as Kate wanted him caught, she had to be sure and she had to do it by the book.

'I can't answer your question, Mrs Daniels. I'm sorry, but either you *do* or you *don't* recognise him. I can't influence that.'

Mrs Daniels took several puffs of the cigarette, her eyes studying Kate, looking for any kind of sign. Kate kept her expression as neutral as she could, determined not to offer even a flicker, even though she desperately hoped for affirmation.

Mrs Daniels tapped the ash into the dish. 'Yeah, I recognise him.'

Kate's eyes widened. 'You're sure?'

She nodded.

Kate wasn't convinced. 'Mrs Daniels, I don't want you to say what you think I want to hear. You have to be certain. If this ever went to trial, you would be required to swear an oath and confirm what you've told me in front of a jury. Where did you see him?'

'Oh, I don't know, it was more than a year ago.'

'I'm sorry, Mrs Daniels, but that isn't good enough. *If* you recognise him, you must remember from where.'

'Must have seen him hanging around the gym where Willow worked.'

Kate pulled out her notepad and scribbled the questions and responses down, even though she suspected Mrs Daniels would have confirmed anyone's identity to see someone convicted. 'And when would this have been?'

'Now you're asking too much! I'm lucky if I can remember what I had for lunch yesterday. It would have been in the fortnight prior to her death.'

Kate made a note to call the gym and ask to see their security-camera footage from the period, if indeed they still had copies. She was sure Armitage's task force probably had copies from her original investigation, but there was no chance she'd get her hands on that.

Mrs Daniels finished and extinguished the cigarette. 'Well? Are you going to tell me who the bloke is then?'

'I need to chase a couple of other things down first. But I promise you'll be the first to know when I have something concrete.'

Kate stood, eager to be on her way, and headed to the front door. Mrs Daniels looked at her with a glimmer of renewed hope, before gently closing the door behind her. As she wandered back to the car, Kate reflected on Willow's mother's desperation to identify Isbitt. In a way, she could understand exactly why Mrs Daniels had so urgently wanted to pin her daughter's murder on someone. It seemed everyone was after the same thing: closure.

CHAPTER FIFTY-ONE

24 DAYS UNTIL I DIE

The moment he sits down, I feel something isn't quite right. When he messaged me online, he'd come across as confident, arrogant even, but the man before me is quiet and withdrawn. His eyes dart towards the diner door every time it opens.

He looks nothing like the handsome forty-something man in the profile picture either. My heart is racing, and it's all I can do to stop my hands from shaking.

I keep reminding myself that the DI is parked in a van outside, so if he tries to abduct me or force me into a vehicle, they'll be ready to intervene. They also have an image of his face from the brooch-cam pinned to my lapel.

It's then I remember I've removed my jacket. Despite the cold rain outside, inside the diner it's like an oven. The place is packed, and there is a queue for tables at the door. It was his idea to meet here. Should I have scoped out the place first? This is the fifth date I've been on this week, and until now I haven't felt concerned. But this guy's vibe isn't right.

I try to glance down at the brooch, to judge whether they can see him, but I'm sure my left arm is in line of sight. After the horror of the first date, we have agreed I won't wear an earpiece, so I now have no verbal relay from the van. They can hear everything we say, but not vice versa.

The diner door opens again and two loud youths enter; my date practically falls off his seat.

My voice tremors as I try to calmly ask him if he's okay. He forces a thin smile and brushes off my concern, passing me a menu and asking me if I'd like to share some wine with him.

'I don't drink,' I tell him, smiling back. 'Too many bad experiences as a youngster.'

It's a line the DI and I agreed upon. In the event that I need to arrest one of the dates, it's better if there is no question mark over my sobriety. I could murder a drop of white right now, just to settle my nerves.

'You don't look much like your profile picture,' I comment for the team's benefit, more than my own. 'I was expecting someone with light brown hair, but in person it looks much greyer.'

He blushes slightly. 'It's an old photo. I should update it. Are you disappointed I'm older than I said?'

He's testing me, so I dismiss the suggestion with a wave of my hand. 'Age is just a number.'

The team vet each of the dates before they arrive, but they struggled to get any information on this guy. He's the first of the six to set alarm bells ringing. The DI told me I didn't have to go through with it, but I told her I'd be fine. I wish I hadn't been so stubborn. I desperately want this date to end: the sooner the better.

The waitress takes our orders, and we settle into small talk. He tells me he is a delivery driver by day. I picture him in a large van. A van large enough to transport a body, hidden from view. And how many of us would question a delivery van pulled up on the side of the road? It's the perfect cover.

When the food arrives, I ask if he works for a major delivery company, but he shakes his head and says he freelances. 'Keeps the taxman off my back,' he adds with a snigger.

Which means his van probably isn't registered with a delivery company, making it more difficult to track. His head snaps around at the door again.

I want to arrest him now. Even if it turns out he isn't the killer we're hunting, it would give me an excuse to get out of here. But if I panic, the DI might think twice about continuing this assignment, and I can't do that to Steph.

I tell him I do secretarial work in a doctor's surgery.

'You don't look like an admin assistant,' he says, as a creepy smile stretches his cheeks wider.

'What do I look like then?' I ask, terrified my cover is blown.

'You could be a model.'

It's a cheesy line, but I pretend to be grateful for the compliment. He reaches out and takes my hand in his. His is warm and clammy, and my skin crawls. I want to pull it away, but I need to find out more about him. Why did I ever volunteer for this assignment?

'I really like you,' he says. 'You're so beautiful, and I know you're out of my league, but what would you say if we get out of here and go somewhere a bit more intimate?'

My instinct tells me to grab his neck and slam his face into the table, before yanking his wrist behind his back and cuffing him, but I hold my nerve. 'Where were you thinking?'

'I have my van around the corner… we could go for a drive…'

Is this what he said to the others? Did he give lifts to Willow, Roxie and Steph? Or did they refuse rides and that's why he attacked them?

I leave my hand where it is, and act coy. 'I hardly know you. Why don't we eat first, and then when we're done, I'll give you my answer.'

He raises my hand and I can feel the dried and cracked skin of his lips as he kisses it.

A camera suddenly flashes to our right and a woman approaches us. She places a business card on the table, and as I read it upside down, I'm amazed to see she's a private investigator. My date looks crestfallen.

'Your wife wants a divorce,' she tells him with a grin, snarling in my direction. 'We have all the evidence we need. If you don't want

her to take you to the cleaners, you call that number in the morning, and we'll talk.'

And with that she disappears out of the door. He is propping his head up with his hands, his eyes darting as he tries to process what's just happened. I can't quite believe what I've just witnessed either, but before I can speak, he grabs his coat from the back of his chair and tails it out of the diner, just as the waitress brings our food over.

He's left me to pay the bill. Asshole.

CHAPTER FIFTY-TWO

Standing in the queue at the reception desk, Kate was surprised at how many people were waiting to gain access to the pool or gym this late on a Monday afternoon. As she checked her watch for the umpteenth time, she wondered how much longer she'd have to wait until a second staff member manned the reception desk. Finn was waiting in the car again, and he'd be concerned that she was taking so long.

She would have pushed through the queue, had she still had her identification, but she would have to wait like everyone else. She willed the line to move quicker.

Kate finally made it to the front, and was pleased when she recognised the young man behind the desk. He couldn't have been much older than twenty-five, with a toned physique, and a smile so white he must have had veneers.

She pushed her business card across the desk. 'Could we have a word in private?' she asked.

A look of guilt descended on his features as he nodded and called for a colleague to take his place at the desk, before leading her through to the small office behind the desk.

Kate made sure the door was closed before she began. 'I'm DI Kate Matthews. It's Ethan, isn't it?'

'That's right,' he said, his shoulders tensing. 'Have I done something wrong?'

Kate kept a straight face. 'Not that I'm aware of. If you have, that's not why I'm here. You don't recognise me, do you?'

He frowned as he studied her face. 'Are you a member here?'

'No. I came in here and spoke to you, must be… just over a year ago. I was investigating the murder of your colleague Willow Daniels.'

He clicked his fingers, and the broad smile returned. 'You were after security-camera footage, weren't you?'

She smiled to acknowledge that he'd made the connection. 'That's right.'

'I remember you now. How've you been?'

'I'm well, thank you, Ethan.'

'Do you want to join the gym? We offer a special discount to the emergency services. The package includes—'

She cut him off. 'I'm not here in a personal capacity. The case has been reopened.'

His eyes widened with trepidation. 'What do you need?'

She was relieved he was so willing; clearly he wasn't going to ask too many questions.

'Well, Ethan, I need you to run me off another copy of those recordings, if you don't mind.'

'Sure.' He nodded, reaching for a pen and scrap of paper. 'Remind me which dates you needed again?'

'Well, Willow was killed Thursday, 20 August 2015, so that day and each day in the four weeks prior.'

He jotted the dates down. 'I'll have to go and grab them. Do you mind waiting here while I go to the security office? I'll try not to be too long.'

Kate did her best not to look too relieved. He would have been within his rights to refuse her request without a warrant, or confirmation from the SIO on the case, but he had accepted her at face value. Not that she expected to see Isbitt's face on the footage. She still wasn't convinced that Mrs Daniels had ever seen him, let alone down here, but she had to be certain.

'I'm happy to wait,' Kate confirmed.

'Would you like a tea or coffee while you're waiting?'

'No, just the footage, please.'

Kate sent Finn a message, explaining that she wouldn't be too much longer. She'd missed a call from Laura while she'd been talking to Ethan, but she didn't want to call her back from here. Wallace Brookes hadn't made contact, but if he was away, he wouldn't have seen her note yet. She would return tomorrow and if he still didn't answer, she'd reach out to his landlord and find out if he knew where Brookes was.

It was tempting to find a hotel for the night, as she planned to show Isbitt's image to some of Willow's friends, as well as to Steph's colleagues and Roxie's friends. But Trish would already be wondering where her car was.

Twenty minutes had passed when Ethan returned to the small office. He handed eight DVD cases to her. 'There you go.'

'Oh, couldn't you have put it on a memory stick or something?'

He puffed out his cheeks. 'Sorry, that's how they come.'

Kate's laptop didn't have a DVD drive, which meant she'd have to be at home in front of her TV to watch them. She forced a smile. 'Forget about it. I'm sure these will be fine. And this is everything from the four weeks prior to Willow's death?'

Ethan nodded solemnly. 'Everything up to and including 20 August. Are you any closer to catching the guy who did it?'

'Getting closer every day.'

She slipped the cases into her bag, and allowed him to open the door for her.

'If you need anything else, you know where to find me,' he said, looking pleased he'd done his bit. 'And if you change your mind about that membership, tell them I recommended it.' He leaned closer. 'We get commission for signing up new members.'

'I'll bear it in mind,' she lied. The queue of people waiting to enter now snaked back to the sliding doors.

'Did Amy use a gym?' Kate asked, as she returned to the car.

Finn nodded. 'Yeah, there was one up the road from her flat, I think. Not that she needed to. There wasn't an ounce of fat on her.'

Kate knew it was common for police officers to use gyms to keep in shape, and to work out the stresses of the job, but it wasn't a link she'd made before. So all four of the London victims had spent time at a gym. Was that the connection they'd been missing? Were Helen and Mary gym members too?

'Did you get what you were after?' he asked.

'I got the footage if that's what you mean. But it'll take days to review everything he's given me. And I won't be able to review it on my computer, as I don't have a DVD drive.'

'Can I help? I've got no plans for this evening. I could watch them and let you know what I find.'

She wrinkled her nose. 'I'm not sure—'

'Please?' he interrupted. 'Let me do this. You said yourself we're against the clock. And Amy would want me to help.'

Against her better judgement, Kate relented. 'Okay, but I'll be back first thing to see how you're getting on. Now, it's probably best if I drop you around the corner from Erin's place. The last thing I need is her reporting my presence to Armitage.'

CHAPTER FIFTY-THREE

Kate's head was beginning to pound as she joined the M3, and came to an immediate halt as a stream of red lights filled the road ahead as far as she could see. Keen to think about something else, she called Laura back, plugging into the car's hands-free system. 'Sorry I missed your call. Is now a good time to speak? How's everything at your end?'

There was silence, followed by a shuffling noise, before Laura finally came on the line. 'Yes, just had to step out of the office.'

'No worries. You're busy then?'

'You could say that… Are you still in London?'

'On the way back, but traffic is terrible. Thanks for the photograph. Finn confirmed Isbitt is the engineer who fixed Amy's computer the week before she died.'

'That's great! I'll get him to sign a statement to that effect.'

'I'm sure that won't be a problem. Willow's mum also said she recognised Isbitt's face, but I'm not totally convinced she wasn't just saying it because she thought that's what I wanted to hear. I presume you managed to speak with Nicki?'

The enthusiasm left Laura's voice. 'Yeah, but it isn't good news. I drove to their place at lunchtime, but Isbitt was home; she didn't want to let me in at first and it was difficult to speak privately. She looked terrified, but I did my best to reassure her that we haven't given up on trying to secure the evidence against him. I asked her if she'd gone through his hotel receipts and invoices, but she said she wasn't prepared to help us prove his guilt. She doesn't believe he murdered Helen or Mary.'

'Poor woman,' Kate admitted, as the cars in front began to edge forwards.

'I was with her for half an hour. Apparently she confronted him about the affair with the woman in Portsmouth, and he came clean. Admitted the affair, but says she means nothing to him, and he wants another chance.'

'She's not going to give it to him, surely?'

'She hasn't decided. I saw a duvet and pillows on the sofa in their lounge, so I guess he's sleeping there for now.'

'How did she seem when you got her talking? Do you think she could be persuaded to help us?'

Laura considered the question. 'I'm not sure. I think if we push too hard, she'll refuse to let us in the house. We need to tread carefully. Ultimately, she can't testify against him in court, but we need to get our hands on his timeline for late 2015. I was thinking we could request a warrant for the company's records. If he was servicing computers in London at that time, it might help establish he was there.'

Kate beeped the horn as the driver in front slammed on his brakes. 'Only if we want to tip him off that we're onto his earlier crimes. Don't forget, at the moment he only thinks we suspect him for the deaths of Helen and Mary. He has no idea we know about his earlier record. Besides, you can't request a warrant and leave Underhill and the supe out of the loop. They'll shut us down before we get anywhere near a magistrate. Maybe I should try and speak to Nicki? I felt we had a good connection the other day.'

'There was one thing, Kate. While I was there, she went off to deal with her screaming child and I heard a beep, like a phone going off. I looked around and found Isbitt's mobile on the work surface in the kitchen, charging. He'd received a message from someone called Rick, asking to meet him tonight. The thing is, this *Rick* signed the message with a kiss. My guess is *Rick* is in fact some woman he's been after, but he covers his tracks by giving her a male name. He said in interview that Nicki checks his phone and emails.'

Kate narrowed her eyes. 'I don't suppose you…?'

'Took a note of the number and ran a search? That would be a breach of protocol, ma'am,' she paused for effect. 'The number is registered to one Rachel Chatsworth from Winchester.'

Kate couldn't keep the proud smile from her face. 'So he's probably meeting this Rachel tonight, behind his wife's back?'

'I was planning to go along to the pub and watch him. If she's the next on his list, then we have an opportunity to catch him in the act.'

'Now might be a prudent time to reach out to Underhill.'

'May I speak freely?'

'Of course. Always.'

'Underhill won't listen to anything I have to say. The reason I'm back at the office now is because he wants us to pull in Helen's ex-boyfriend Rhys Leonard for questioning. I'm about to head to his place to make the arrest now.'

'Leonard is a no-good junkie, but I don't peg him as a serial killer.'

'Agreed, but this leaves us in a spot. I don't think I'll be finished here in time to get to the pub.'

'Don't worry about it. I'll go. Send me the time and address, and I'll watch.'

'Are you sure? I can meet you as soon as I'm done here.'

'It's fine, Laura. You've done too much already. I'll observe from the car park, and I'll call for backup if I sense he's going to make his move. This is the chance I've been waiting for.'

CHAPTER FIFTY-FOUR

22 DAYS UNTIL I DIE

'It's Christmas Eve,' the DI says, adding a yawn. 'I told you to take a couple of days away from the office.'

I close the door to her office, and pull out a chair. The rest of the team have already packed up for the day, and the night sky outside the incident room is as black as I have ever seen.

'I'd only be sat at home thinking about the case,' I offer with a smile. 'Do you not have plans? You have a daughter, don't you?'

She smiles. 'That's right: Chloe. But she lives with her dad. I'll try and see her at the weekend.'

'How old is she? Does she still believe in Father Christmas?'

'She's nearly five, and I guess so. It's amazing the lies we tell our children to try and keep them safe.'

It's the most honest statement I've ever heard her make, and the most personal conversation we've had, but it feels good that she trusts me enough to speak frankly. She apologises for sullying the tone.

'Do you have any plans for the festive period, Amy?'

It still feels weird when she uses my first name. She calls the rest of the team by their surnames, but she always calls me Amy. Nobody else seems to have paid it much attention. At least, not that I'm aware of.

'I'll probably go to my mum and stepdad's when I've finished here,' I say, pretending I'm not that keen to be there.

The truth is, I can't wait for a couple of days away from the office. I intend to get very drunk from Christmas Day through to Boxing Day and forget all about this investigation, and my failure to lure the killer into our honeytrap.

'That'll be nice,' she says, looking misty-eyed. 'Are you shooting straight off?'

'I've got a couple of bits and pieces to finish up first.'

She slides open her drawer, and removes a bottle of vodka and two glasses. 'Have a drink with me?'

I got stupidly drunk on vodka when I was seventeen, and can't stand the stuff, but I don't want her to misinterpret a 'no thanks', so I nod eagerly. She pours two generous helpings, and hands me a glass. She raises a toast to our three victims. Just hearing their names still sends a chill down my spine. We clink glasses and I hold my breath as I take the first sip, trying to lessen the sting and flavour.

I wonder if the killer is planning a turkey dinner with all the trimmings. Whoever he is, does he have a family, and someone who will buy him a Christmas present? I hope not. I hope he is in a deep dark hole somewhere, and part of me hopes he never resurfaces. It would mean we'd never catch him, but at least he wouldn't be able to kill again.

She finishes her drink and pours a second, offering me a top-up. I pass, and rest my glass on the edge of the desk. 'Ma'am, do you still think we'll catch him?'

I don't know why I've asked her the question. I mean, it's been playing on my mind for days, but to verbalise it makes it more of a real doubt.

'I don't know, Amy.'

It's not the answer I was expecting or hoping for. The DI has been the shining beacon for us all to follow since that cold morning in late October, and now even she has doubts.

'If we don't make a breakthrough soon, the DSI will have no choice but to replace me as SIO.'

'I'm sorry, ma'am.'

'It's not your fault, Amy. It's mine. I thought my experience would be enough to see us over the line. I've let those women down, not you.'

I've heard enough. I stand and straighten my trousers. 'We will catch him, ma'am. Don't give up.'

I exit the office, knowing in my heart that I will do whatever it takes to find him. Even if it means risking everything I know and love. We will *find him.*

CHAPTER FIFTY-FIVE

The traffic was flowing better as Kate passed the exit for Andover. She'd have given anything for the blues and twos fitted to her Audi. Pushing the accelerator past eighty, she moved into the outside lane and ate up the road. The satnav said the pub was near Cadnam on the western side of the city, and Laura's message had confirmed they would be meeting at half past seven. It was already after seven, and if she didn't hurry, they could have been and gone before she arrived.

Identifying Steph Graham's murderer had been a battle from the very beginning. When she'd first suggested that the same person was responsible for Roxie and Willow's murders, she'd met with adversity. But she'd battled through it and set up her team to prove the theory. And then when Amy died, she had battled against the forces who wanted her out of the Met. In Southampton, she'd fought back again, proving how formidable her detective's mind was. After fifteen months, she was now so close to catching the killer that she found it tough keeping her mind on the road.

She wasn't even thinking about how great it would feel to have all her theories and efforts vindicated. It wasn't about proving others wrong. It was about seeing a murderer locked up and making the world ever-so-slightly safer. A world in which her daughter would grow up, hopefully never realising just how scary a place it could be.

Kate pushed the accelerator up to ninety, racing to her destiny.

*

The venue was a traditional English pub. It was a long, white building with a thatched roof, and tiny windows, through which Kate could see little from her car parked at the edge of the road. Outside, heavy rain fell on the dark, unilluminated road, causing condensation to fog the windows and windscreen. In fact, the only light she could see was coming from within the pub. Kate wasn't certain what car Isbitt would show up in, but there were no BMW SUVs in the vicinity.

The clock on the dashboard read 19:31. Had she missed them? Or were they already inside? She needed confirmation, but if he saw her, he would cancel his plans, and she'd be no closer to catching him.

There was no other choice: she would have to go inside.

Pushing the car door open, she hurried across the car park, holding a hand over her head, which did little to shelter her against the heavy downpour. The five picnic tables outside the pub were sodden, and rain dripped into puddles on the concrete beneath. Kate tried to peer through the small window in the door, but she could only just make out the bar through the angled glass.

Pushing the door open slowly, she peered through, eyes darting left and right for any sign of them. She wanted to take her time, to fully assess the location, but in the back of her mind, she couldn't escape the possibility that Isbitt and Rachel were both running late, and could arrive at any moment, catching her there.

Inside it was pretty empty, with only two older men standing at the bar, chatting loudly with the white-haired barman. The pub opened out to the left where tables and chairs were neatly laid out, but she could only see two couples dining. No sign of Isbitt.

Moving further in, she nodded towards the barman.

'What can I get for you?' he asked, his accent from somewhere in the West Country.

'I'm meeting someone, mind if I have a look around?' she said quietly, wiping rain from her fringe and straining to see round the bend to where Isbitt could still be seated. But the tables there were vacant too.

Kate breathed a sigh of relief and returned to the bar, ordering a lemonade and requesting a menu. She carried her drink over to a table by one of the small windows towards the back of the restaurant, so Isbitt would be unlikely to spot her with a casual glance. Even so, she kept her head tucked behind the menu, glancing up every few seconds to see if he'd arrived.

Heavy rain continued to batter the window, but as the minutes ticked slowly past, nobody else entered the pub. A waitress approached the table, asking for her order, but she batted her away, not wanting to draw attention to herself. Every time headlights flashed past, Kate fixated on the vehicle, looking for Isbitt's SUV, but she couldn't clearly identify makes and models. Five minutes later, the door to the pub opened, and straining to see that end of the building, she saw a large man in a hat and coat approach the two men who were still chatting loudly at the bar.

Deciding her trip out had been a bust, she phoned Laura, whose phone went to voicemail. She left a message advising her that Isbitt hadn't shown, and that they should regroup first thing, before Kate returned to London.

She settled her bill at the bar, and opened the door, stepping out into the heavy rain. The road was empty in both directions, so she raced towards where she'd parked Trish's car, unlocking it with the remote as she jumped to avoid puddles. Opening the driver's door, the sound of rain on the roof of the car covered the sound of someone approaching from behind. Kate felt a sudden pain against the back of her head, and then she was tumbling towards the wet and muddy ground.

CHAPTER FIFTY-SIX

Her neck lolling from side-to-side combined with the vehicle's stop-start motion, and occasional rise and fall, sat unkindly with Kate's semi-conscious mind. As she lay on her back staring into the abyss, she was reminded of a roller-coaster ride she'd been on as a child. She'd begged and pleaded with her dad to take her on it, even though he'd warned her she wouldn't enjoy it. But still they'd waited in line for twenty-five minutes, the nervous tension building and building as they'd drawn closer to the front.

The ride attendant at the head of the line had held the measuring stick up to her, and she'd looked pleadingly into his eyes. After a glance at her father, he'd allowed them through. It was the first time she'd been on a ride for older children, and as the safety bar had clicked into place around her middle, she remembered thinking how envious her friends would be back at school.

Within ten seconds of the ride starting, Kate had known she'd made a terrible mistake. It had shunted her left and right, and when she'd thought it would stop, it had only picked up speed. After thrashing them up and down, and then slowing again, it tipped over the edge of the horizon and hurtled them vertically down at rapid speed. She'd screamed and wailed the whole way around, her eyes clamped tightly shut for as long as possible, but with occasional dared glimpses when she'd prayed it was over. It had been the first and last roller-coaster she'd ever ridden.

The back of Kate's head throbbed from where she'd been struck and, as she focused on the pain, a flashback to the feeling of something striking her filled her mind. But she couldn't remember anything afterwards.

Kate tried to open her eyes, but the strain felt too much. Nausea continued to sweep through her, and all she could hear was the hum of the road below. Her body continued to rock as they sped onwards. She forced her eyes open. She couldn't remember receiving a beating, but now her upper body ached as the vehicle jolted along.

The car's interior glowed orange from street lights flashing past overhead. Kate was lying flat on the back seat, and as she tried to overcome the pain and shuffle her body, she became aware of something tight over her torso keeping her in place. A harness of some kind – maybe for a large animal? Whatever it was, it was pinning her in place on the rear cushion. Her wrists were bound with a cable tie, but she had limited movement in her arms. Keeping her upper body still, she tried to shift her legs without drawing the driver's attention, but a further cable tie had been applied around her ankles, and was secured in place with the seatbelt on that side. She was trapped.

The pain in her head was replaced by rising panic. She tilted her head and looked between the front seats, trying to catch a glimpse of her attacker in the driving seat. He wore a thick quilted puffer jacket, and the fur-lined hood was pulled up over his head. The coat was as black as night, and perfectly shrouded its occupant.

She wanted to sit up, hoping a glance out of the window would confirm exactly where they were. If she recognised her surroundings, she could assess where the nearest help would be. But as she tried to shift her arms into a better position, she felt the plastic cable tie digging into the skin around her wrists.

Kate closed her eyes again, not wanting him to catch her conscious just yet. She was sure he'd be checking on her, but did he realise who she was? If it *was* Isbitt, had he mistaken her for Rachel, or had he known all along that she would take the bait?

The car slowed, she heard the indicator clicking, and it suddenly swung into a poorly lit area. Darkness fell across the car, and the speed didn't increase again. They had reached their destination. The car's brakes squeaked to a halt, and she heard the click as the driver lifted the handbrake.

Kate kept her eyes clamped shut and her body limp. She heard the swish of his puffer jacket as he turned and stared directly at her. Clearly satisfied she was still out cold, he exited the car. His footsteps crushed the gravel beneath his feet, and a cool blast of air blew through the back of the vehicle as the boot beeped open. The scraping of heavy objects against the boot liner was followed by the beep of the boot lid closing, and more footsteps on gravel.

Her only chance was the element of surprise. She held her breath as the door closest to her head opened and he leaned in. Opening her eyes, the breath caught in her throat as she came face to face with the killer.

CHAPTER FIFTY-SEVEN

It was difficult to tell who was more surprised: Kate as she stared up at the face buried deep beneath the fur-lined hood, or the woman wearing it, who didn't seem to have anticipated Kate being awake.

Kate was the first to react as she took in Nicola Isbitt's soft, feminine features and the long-handled tyre iron being held menacingly above her head. Struggling against the harness that kept her pinned to the car seat and unable to turn, the weapon came crashing down towards her. She screamed as she frantically tried to cover her face and the tyre iron smashed onto her hands.

'Don't struggle, bitch,' Nicola sneered.

Kate forced eye contact. 'Please, you don't have to do this. You're making a huge mistake.'

Nicola hoisted the tyre iron back into the air, this time bringing it down into Kate's abdomen. Kate winced in pain, the wind knocked from her, unable to raise her legs to protect herself.

'You're the one who made a mistake by contacting my husband.'

'Nicki, it's me, DI Matthews. Remember? We spoke yesterday.'

The mention of her name only seemed to anger Nicola further, and her fingers made to gouge at Kate's eyes. 'You knew he was married, and you still went after him. What is it with women like you? He's *mine*.'

'*Please*, you have to listen to me. I wasn't after your husband.'

'You must think I'm stupid. I saw the message you sent him.'

'Message? What message? I didn't send…' but her words trailed off as she realised Nicola must have mistaken her for the woman Isbitt was supposed to meet.

'I bet you had a real good laugh at me, didn't you? When did you decide to try and lure him away? Was it while you were talking to me, or when you got him back to the station? You thought you could see him behind my back?'

'Don't do something you'll regret, Nicki. It isn't too late.'

She howled with laughter. 'There's nothing you can say to save yourself now.'

The pounding stopped as quickly as it had started, but the crunching of gravel told Kate that the attack was far from over. Kate's head snapped up as the other rear door flew open; a bitter chill whooshed through the car, making the hairs on her arms stand up.

Nicola must have seen the strapping on her ankle as she brought the tyre iron crashing onto it. Kate lashed out wildly as it erupted in scorching pain. But it was hopeless.

'You killed Helen Jackson and Mary Eden,' Kate desperately screeched.

The mention of their names was the distraction she'd needed. Nicola pulled the hood back slightly so her mouth could be seen through the fur edging. 'He thought I didn't know what he was doing. He thought I wouldn't discover that he had a second email account. Every time he left the house I knew where he was going.'

'Neither of them were having an affair with your husband—'

'Bullshit! I saw the exchanges between them. They wanted him, and he wanted them. And all behind my back.'

Kate couldn't see Nicola's eyes clearly, but she could hear the emotion in her voice. Insane as she was, Kate could recognise the betrayal, the hurt, the anger.

'I understand what you're going through; my husband cheated on me too.'

'Liar!'

Kate raised her head as much as the restraint would allow. 'Look into my eyes. Tell me if I'm lying. My husband cheated on me while I was caring for our baby daughter. I know what it is to be betrayed. But *this* is not the answer.'

'You're trying to stall.' Nicola raised the tyre iron high again, Kate bracing herself for another strike, but then it clattered against the gravel and Nicola was gone.

Kate blinked against the darkness, listening for the sound of footsteps crunching, but there was only deathly silence and the all-enveloping black beyond the car's door. Gripping the belt strap between her teeth, she tugged at it, but it was fastened beneath her, and with her wrists still tied, she had no way of releasing the catch.

Instinct told her that Nicola hadn't abandoned her plans, but Kate had no way of knowing what she intended next. Her panicked mind raced through terrifying possibilities.

Opening her mouth, Kate was about to call out Nicola's name, when a distinct scraping sound shattered the silence. Something solid and sturdy was being dragged against a plastic surface. The scraping temporarily stopped and was followed by a wheeze and a solid thud as something heavy hit the ground, instantly cracking the stones it came into contact with. After a second wheeze, the object was scraped through the gravel, scattering the shingle. Whatever Nicola had pulled from the boot, it was getting closer to the door by Kate's feet.

Nicola's hooded profile appeared at the edge of the doorway again, but her eyes and mouth were no longer visible, lost behind a thick plastic visor. Then Kate saw the shiny end of the blowtorch and the rubber pipe leading down to the large methylacetylene canister.

Kate's eyes widened in sheer terror as Nicola's plan became all too clear. 'Please, you can't do this. I am a police inspector, and I demand you lower that equipment and release me.'

The mask tilted to the side, before gently shaking left and right.

'Please, I'm begging you, I have a daughter… it isn't too late for you. Let me live, and I swear I'll help you. Murder is not the answer now, no matter what you did to those women. You have to listen to me.'

Nicola looked at the canister by her feet, and reached down, slowly turning the valve. The hiss of the gas escaping through the end of the torch sent a shiver from Kate's head to her feet. Nicola reached into her coat pocket and pulled out a small, shiny cigarette lighter. When she spoke her voice echoed off the visor. 'I bought this lighter for him on our first wedding anniversary. I had it inscribed. Do you know what it says? "*To the man who brightens my every day, love always, Nicki.*" I found it last week in a drawer in our kitchen. It was still full of gas. He's never used it. It means nothing to him. Well, now I've found the right use for it. You're going to suffer for trying to steal him from me, and then I'll watch you gasping for air in your final seconds.'

Opening the end of the lighter, she sparked it and held the small orange flame to the end of the blowtorch. The hiss transformed into a roar as the methylacetylene ignited with a blue-orange flame.

'Jesus Christ! Nicki, please, you don't have to do this,' Kate shouted.

'Oh, but I do. How else will you learn not to chase married men?'

'But what about Amy Spencer? She never knew your husband. Why did you kill her?'

The blowtorch dropped slightly as a moment of doubt flickered in Nicola's mind. 'Stop it. Stop all this talking.'

'What about Willow Daniels? Or Roxie O'Brien? What about Steph Graham? Did they all deserve to die as well?'

'I don't know those names.' Nicki reached down to adjust the gas valve once more. The blowtorch dropped ever closer to Kate's prone legs.

Kate's tied hands clutched at air as she tried to raise her body and grab the torch handle, but she couldn't get close enough. If only she could open the harness. Shifting her body away from the seat as best she could, her hands scrabbled with the fastener, until her finger managed to depress the button, and suddenly her shoulders were free. Lunging forward with all her might, she grabbed at the torch handle, desperate to keep the hissing flame from her tired body. But Nicola was stronger than her slight frame suggested, and cackled at the challenge, forcing Kate's shoulders back towards the seat.

Kate wasn't ready to give up. With all her might, she pushed back, gritting her teeth, ready for one last push, but as Nicola lost her footing, the blue-orange flame caught the fibres of her fur hood. The smell of burning plastic filled Kate's nostrils, and suddenly Nicola's entire hood was ablaze. The torch clattered to the stony ground as Nicola lost her grip on the handle, stumbling backwards, fighting to pull the hood from her burning head. But as she batted at it, the flames quickly spread down the coat, engulfing her in a giant ball of flame.

Kate groaned as she did whatever she could to pull her legs further up into the car and away from the fire. Nicola spun around in panic, like a Catherine wheel. Kate buried her face behind her bound hands as the fiery spinning top continued to flail in the darkness outside.

Kate couldn't hide her relief that the orange glow was getting further away from the car, but she couldn't ignore her duty – she grasped the belt in her teeth again, but it still wouldn't budge.

'Roll – *roll*, for God's sake!' she bellowed out through the door.

But either Nicola couldn't hear Kate's instructions or didn't believe her, and she continued battling to unfasten the melting zip.

Kate pushed her blistered palms together and growled as she prised her fingertips apart, trying to snap the cable tie with the strength of her metacarpal bones. 'Hang on,' she yelled towards the orange mass, which continued to burn brightly, even though Nicola had now fallen to her knees.

Keeping her palms together, Kate brought her fingers together as if in prayer, and separated her elbows as far as she could. Then, bending her knees, so they rested in the gap between her wrists and her chest, she counted to three, and with all her might pulled her arms quickly towards her chest.

She screamed, as much in agony as satisfaction, as the plastic tie snapped. Seconds later, she had removed the seat belt and was diving out of the car door, barely able to crawl along the sharp stones towards the dying orange flames. The warmth contrasted sharply with the cold night air, which fanned the shrinking flames, but it was clear already that the mass beneath the orange glow was no longer moving.

CHAPTER FIFTY-EIGHT

The stench of burned flesh hung in the air above Kate. Forcing herself up on one arm, she removed her own coat, and squashed it over the smoking mass before her, suffocating the last of the embers. 'Nicki? Nicki? Talk to me.'

There was no reply.

'Nicki? Stay with me. I'll get help.' Kate stared out into the pitch-black night, and realised she had no idea where they were, let alone where she might find help. Dragging her coat from the body, she tried to locate Nicki's face, to clear an airway and check for a pulse, but the visor was too hot to touch. What remained of the puffer jacket was shrivelled and hardening, forming a cocoon around its victim.

A sudden flash of blue illuminated the car behind them, and another car came screeching across the gravel. Kate waved her arms frantically. 'Help us. Help us.'

The car crunched to a halt, and Laura was at Kate's side a moment later. 'Thank God I found you.'

'Call an ambulance. Quickly.'

Laura relayed the message into her radio. 'Who is this?' she asked, lowering the radio.

'Nicki Isbitt. She killed Helen and Mary. It wasn't Gavin.'

Laura gulped as the news sunk in.

'We need to get her out of this coat,' Kate continued, wincing every time her skin came into contact with the smouldering material.

Laura pulled her back, keeping her arms tight around Kate's shoulders. 'She's gone, ma'am.'

Kate fought against her embrace. 'No. We have to help her.'

Laura's grip remained firm. 'Paramedics are on their way, but I fear it's too late. Come on, you're shivering. Let's get you back to my car.'

Kate continued to struggle as Laura dragged her to her feet, pulling her away from the still mass on the floor.

'How did you find me?' Kate asked as the medical team fussed out of sight.

'I tried calling you after we finished interviewing Leonard, and I thought it was strange that you hadn't answered. I drove to the pub, and when I saw you weren't there I had a trace run on your phone. It led me here.'

'I don't know where my phone is,' Kate admitted. 'She must have taken it from me when she bundled me into the car.'

'You're lucky to—'

'Please don't.'

Laura's forehead was creased with worry lines. 'I'm sorry. I never should have let you go to the pub alone. You could have been killed.'

It wasn't relief flooding through Kate's body as she considered the woman who'd just attacked her. 'We were wrong about Gavin Isbitt. He didn't kill Helen and Mary. Nicki did.'

Misjudging Nicola's situation wasn't even the gravest mistake they'd made. The effects of tonight's horror would live with Kate for the rest of her days, but what haunted her now was the knowledge that she'd been wrong to link the new spate of killings with the London ones. The supe had been right, she was too close to see the truth. She let her guilt get in the way of her instincts and it had nearly got her killed. What else had this tunnel vision stopped her from seeing?

If the murders weren't related, then Amy's real killer was still out there. They were no closer to learning the truth of what had happened to Amy, Steph, Willow and Roxie. And that hurt more than any physical beating she could ever endure.

'Do you want me to call Ben?' Laura eventually asked.

'I just want to go home.'

CHAPTER FIFTY-NINE

15 DAYS UNTIL I DIE

I've not had a date since before Christmas, and there's been no progress in our investigation. We lost another detective from the team today, moved on to a higher priority case. What can be more important than a triple homicide?

Our killer hasn't struck since Steph, not that we're aware of, anyway. The DI has had her ear to the ground but no suspicious deaths involving women discovered in public have been identified. My relief at this news is tempered by the frustration that we have no fresh evidence to work with. The DI says each time he kills, he reveals a clue to his identity, but that's only helpful while he's at work.

What's troubling me most right now is the very realistic possibility that we've already seen him and not realised he was our suspect. I rack my brains, reliving every date I've been on since the assignment started. Was one of them responsible? After each date, the DI sent a unit to check each man's alibi for the three nights, but I know alibis can be faked. God knows how many times I've lied about my real whereabouts. If my mum knew about half the times I wasn't at a friend's house when she thought I was, she'd disown me.

As frightened as I was when my cover role started, I didn't for one moment think we wouldn't identify him. It seems so silly now. In a city of more than four million men, how on earth were we going to track the one we were looking for? That's probably why the

DI agreed to use me as the bait, rather than wasting a fully trained undercover resource.

The DI has told me to take tonight and tomorrow off. What does she think I'm going to do stuck at home on New Year's Eve? I told her we should all be out there, hitting every bar and club in the capital, watching over his potential victims. Any woman on the party scene is a potential victim. Now is not the time to take our foot off the accelerator. If anything we should be pressing harder.

Well, I don't care what she says, I'm not going to stay home and wait for him to catch us off-guard. Even if I have to drag myself all over the city, I will speak to every woman I see and warn them to be on their guard.

CHAPTER SIXTY

TUESDAY

The incessant buzzing at the door forced Kate to drag herself from bed. The stench of smoke clung to her skin like an unwanted rash. Back on both crutches, she swung her way over to the door to buzz Finn up.

He was panting as he reached the top step.

'What do you want, Finn?'

'Did you forget we were meeting today?'

Kate shook her head and stood aside to allow Finn in, before dragging her sore and tired body through to the living room. The empty bottle of wine remained where she'd left it last night on the coffee table. She hadn't wanted to go to bed when Laura had dropped her home. She'd forced herself to watch the *Crimewatch* recording again. She knew she was missing something.

Finn saw the tired and frustrated look on her face. 'What's going on?'

She relayed the events of the previous night to him, albeit a redacted version.

The look of shock on his face was tempered with concern. 'So it was his wife? Jesus.'

Kate nodded solemnly. Last night, when not even the wine helped her to sleep, she'd gone over all the mistakes she'd made, furious that she hadn't spotted Nicola's guilt sooner. She should never have assumed the bruises on her neck were from Isbitt.

'She attacked me last night believing I was somehow trying to steal her husband away from her.'

'And are you okay? That ankle looks worse than I remember, and I'm sure those bruises weren't on your face yesterday.'

She ignored his question. The truth was, the pain felt good this time; it was a penance for missing what had been right in front of her all along. She fixed Finn with a stare. 'Why did you lie about Isbitt being at Amy's flat?'

Finn wrinkled his nose, and raised his hands in defence. 'I'm sorry. I didn't get a great look at the engineer who was there, but I wasn't lying when I said he resembled the guy in the image you showed me. All I can really recall is the red uniform, the cap and glasses. I'm sorry. You seemed so certain it was him that it felt easier to go along with it. I wasn't lying to you. For all I know, he was the engineer there. I certainly can't say for sure he wasn't.' Realising there was no way to justify misleading Kate, he apologised again. 'I'm sorry.'

But she wasn't willing to let him off that easily. 'Do you realise that your actions indirectly resulted in what happened last night? If you'd been honest and said you hadn't recognised him, there's a chance we wouldn't have been so incorrectly eager to connect him to the murders in London? Another woman lost her life last night, because we all blindly waded in without the facts.'

He frowned at her. 'I said I'm sorry. I don't know what else to say.'

'I was wrong to involve you in this. I'm the one who should be sorry.'

He removed a memory stick from his pocket and threw it towards her. 'You'll be glad you involved me when you take a look at what's on that.'

She lifted the small drive out of her lap. 'The gym CCTV?'

'I watched it in fast-forward as I made the conversion and his face was unmissable. Open the drive. I took a screenshot of what you need.'

Kate did as she was instructed and saw a folder labelled 'FOOTAGE', and then a picture file. She opened the image, and turned back to Finn with a look of utmost horror. 'What the hell is *he* doing there?'

Finn looked at her seriously, a glint of excitement in his eye. 'Get dressed, I'm taking you to London.'

CHAPTER SIXTY-ONE

Finn overtook a lorry stationed in the middle lane of the motorway. 'Do you think this is the breakthrough we've been hoping for? It feels like the beginning of the end.'

Kate didn't want to answer, fearful of once again raising his hopes of justice for Amy, only to have them dashed later. But even she couldn't explain the coincidence of Wallace Brookes's face appearing on the footage from the gym. He lived miles away, so there was no reason for him to go out of his way to attend the gym, unless he had an ulterior motive for being there.

'Should we tell Armitage?' Finn pressed, glancing from her back to the road.

'We have nothing yet,' she cautioned. 'We need to know for sure before we act.'

'But what if we're too slow and he does a bunk? Surely it's better to arrest him and then find what we need?'

'Suspects can only be held in custody for twenty-four hours before being charged, and that includes time for interviews, food, solicitor consultation and sleep. If we move without the evidence, we risk allowing him to slip through our fingers. I promise you, as soon as we have something concrete, you can call Armitage. In the meantime, let's see if there is any proof. For all we know, there is a perfectly reasonable explanation for Brookes having been there.'

Even Kate was struggling to be convinced by her own argument. Yet she'd interviewed Brookes before, and she hadn't felt he was responsible. Either she'd made a mistake then, or she was making a bigger mistake now.

The phone in her hand erupted to life. 'Laura? Thanks for calling me back.'

'Where are you, Kate? I stopped by your place to see how you're feeling after last night, but there was no answer.'

'I'm with Finn – it's a long story – but we might be on to something. I need you to work something from your end today.'

'I'm not supposed to be in today.'

'Please, Laura. I need someone I can trust to dig up information on Wallace Brookes.'

'Who's he?'

'Steph Graham's neighbour in Finsbury Park. We interviewed him as part of the original investigation, but we dismissed him.'

'And what's changed?'

She looked to Finn, hoping to God they were on the right track this time. 'We have reason to believe he had contact with Willow Daniels, which ties him to one of the earlier crimes. I need you to pull up everything you can on him. We're talking bank accounts, credit cards, criminal record, known family, anything and everything. Understand?'

Laura finished scribbling her notes. 'Anything else?'

If she was to connect him with all three murders, she needed to establish a link to Roxie O'Brien. 'See if you can find out his shoe size. There was a male size-ten print left at the second crime scene. It's not conclusive, but if that's his size, it would help.'

'Understood. Okay, let me see what I can find, and I'll call you with an update in a bit.'

'Thank you, Laura. And keep your head down. If we're wrong about Brookes, no one can find out we were looking into him.' She hung up the phone, the anticipation sending her insides into a swirl.

*

The leisure-centre car park was much quieter than it had been the previous afternoon. Finn dropped Kate at the door, so she wouldn't have as far to hobble on her crutches. The pain was far greater than the sprain she'd been diagnosed with last week. Deep down, she knew her injury was more serious this time, but to have it reviewed in hospital would waste valuable time she simply didn't have. She promised herself she would visit hospital once Amy's killer was behind bars. In the meantime, she swallowed the final two painkillers the doctor had prescribed.

There was no queue at the counter, but there was no sign of Ethan either. Kate smiled warmly at the young woman behind the desk, who couldn't have been much older than Willow had been. 'Is Ethan around, please?'

The girl didn't return the smile. 'Day off.'

Kate slid her business card across the counter. 'I wonder if you could help me instead?'

'What with?'

'I'd like you to check if a man called Wallace Brookes is a member here.'

The girl blew a bubble with her gum, nonchalance plastered across her face. 'That badge looks fake.'

It was a mistake to have come in in person. Kate had to tread carefully. She'd been suspended from duty and if Armitage or the supe caught wind of what she was doing they'd probably have her arrested for impersonating a police officer.

'Is your manager here?' Kate asked, making her threat clear.

'Day off,' the girl replied.

'What about your security team? I understand there's someone who monitors the security cameras?'

The girl continued to watch her in silence, waiting to see if Kate would give up, before finally putting a radio to her mouth. 'Vern, someone at the front desk for you.' She lowered the radio to the desk, picked up her mobile and started tapping away.

A large man in a navy jumper bursting at the seams waddled up to the counter a few moments later. He sounded out of breath as he introduced himself with a baritone voice. 'I'm Vern. Can I help you with something?'

'I'm Detective Inspector Matthews. I'd like to look at your list of members and ask you some questions about your security footage.'

He considered her, a wayward look in his eyes. 'You know I was going to join the police once.' He shuffled off, indicating for Kate to follow, and led her to a small, dark room the size of a broom cupboard. He unlocked the door and entered, holding it open for her to follow. Inside the narrow room, there was a desk against the far wall, on top of which stood half a dozen black-and-white monitors and a stack of what looked like DVD players. The chair in front of the desk was tattered, its yellow stuffing pushing through the threads. A computer monitor and desktop PC completed the furnishings.

'What can I do for you?' he asked when the door was closed. The room was windowless, and the only light came from a single energy-efficient bulb over their heads.

'Does that computer link up to the front desk? I want you to see if a particular man is a member.'

He nodded and punched some keys on the keyboard. The monitor flickered to life and a search window with various fields opened. 'What's his name?'

She spelt out Brookes's name as Vern typed it into the search window. A small egg timer span on the screen as it searched, before a new window flashed up stating 'no results found'.

Kate cursed under her breath. Of course it wasn't going to be that easy. She sighed. 'Okay. All of your members have photographs on their member cards, right? Is it possible to look at each male photograph? Maybe I can identify him from that.'

'It could take some time, love. Our database is shared with a couple of other sites. There will be hundreds.'

Kate checked the watch on her wrist. 'Can you filter it by age? The man I'm looking for must be in his forties or fifties by now.'

Vern nodded, rolling the mouse around on its mat until a folder of images opened. 'Okay, here are all our male members over the age of forty. Do you see him?'

'I don't get it,' Kate huffed. 'More than a hundred images and he wasn't in any of them.'

Vern was leaning against the wall near the door, the mug in his hand cooling rapidly. 'Maybe this man is not a member. Why are you so sure he is?'

'He appeared on your security-camera footage in the weeks leading up to Willow Daniels's murder.'

A wide smile grew on Vern's face. 'You're the one who asked for the videos yesterday, right? Ethan's friend.'

She tried to smile back, but felt exhausted. 'That's right.'

'And you saw this man on the videos?'

Kate yawned. 'Yeah.'

He launched forwards, placing his mug on the desk near her. 'Show me on the video what he looks like. Maybe I'll recognise him?'

Kate checked her notebook and gave him the date and time of the shot of Brookes. Vern located the relevant DVD case in the cabinet hanging above the desk and loaded the disc into one of the DVD players. He fast-forwarded to the time reference and Brookes's face filled one of the smaller screens.

'That's him,' Kate gesticulated.

Vern leaned closer to the screen, his navy jumper pressing into her shoulder as he did. 'Oh, I remember him. But he isn't a member. He was an engineer sent in to service the water boilers. Yeah, I remember him, well, with a face like that, he's hard to forget.'

Kate's breathing quickened. 'Did you catch his name? Or the name of the company he worked for?'

Vern frowned. 'It was a long time ago. But there might be a way to check.' He stretched up to the cabinet over the desk. Removing a new case, he loaded the disc into the next machine. An image of the car park appeared on a second monitor. He spun though until he found what he was looking for. 'There you go. There's his van.'

A grey short-base van was parked on the right-hand side of the screen. As Kate continued to watch, she saw a man in overalls, wearing a thick woollen hat, open the rear doors of the van. If Vern was right, Brookes and his van were at the leisure centre the day before Willow Daniels died. She jotted the van's registration number on her pad, and asked him to make her a copy of the footage, then Kate turned and hobbled out of the room, reaching for her phone as she stepped back into the light.

CHAPTER SIXTY-TWO

7 DAYS UNTIL I DIE

'Come on, Amy, it's been ages since we went out for a proper girlie night.'

Kelly doesn't appreciate that I've been out every night since New Year's Eve, and can barely think straight I'm so tired.

'Just come for one drink,' Kelly pleads.

She's my best friend so I relent, promising myself I will only stay for one drink, before getting some much needed rest.

It may have nothing to do with my one-woman crusade around the clubs and bars of London, but our killer still hasn't struck. Maybe my message is finally getting through. I'll never know how many lives I may have saved by reminding women just to be more wary of who they're with and their surroundings.

We've been in the bar for half an hour, and I've nearly finished my rum and Coke. The group are talking about moving on to a nightclub, but I can barely keep my eyes open. The DI had us in first thing to confirm that the investigating team will be disbanded and we will each be reassigned to new investigations. The DSI has ruled that there is insufficient evidence to link the three murders, and Willow and Roxie's cases will be passed back to their relevant divisions to follow up on. At least Steph was in our jurisdiction, which means we can keep plugging away at her investigation.

I stand and make my way to the toilets to freshen up. I've already thought of the excuse I'll offer when I return: if I don't get home to bed, I'll pass out with exhaustion. But as I'm making my way back to the table, I feel a hand grab my forearm.

'It's Amy, isn't it?'

I look up at the face of the man talking and recognise him immediately as the second or third date I went on before Christmas. But for the life of me I can't remember what his name was.

I force a smile. 'That's right.'

He pulls me closer to him so I'll hear him over the background noise. 'You never messaged me back after our date. Did I do something wrong?'

I can see my friends looking for me over his shoulder. 'Uh, it wasn't you, it was me,' I lie. 'Sorry, that's just the way it goes sometimes.' I try to move away, but he holds my arm firm.

He leans closer. 'You should give me a second chance. We could have a lot of fun together.'

I pull my arm free and fix him with a glare; cover-Amy is gone. 'Listen, pal, I'm not interested. Okay?'

But his fingers are around my forearm again before I can move it back to my side. 'No, maybe it's not okay. I want to know the real reason you wasn't interested.'

My friends are still looking for me, and I don't want to do anything to draw his attention to them. An image of the DI pops into my mind: what would she do in this situation?

I grab his pint glass from the corner of the bar and deposit the drink over his head. He releases his grip in shock, and I turn on my heel, but I've barely moved a step, before he's grabbing my shoulders and calling me a bitch.

Boy, did he pick the wrong night to fuck with me.

I reach up to his hand and bend his fingers back until I hear a satisfying crack. But before he has time to process the pain, I twist his wrist, causing him to spin around and face the bar, and then I kick the legs from under him. He crashes to the floor, spilling more drinks as he falls.

I lean in while he's on his arse, and point my finger into his face. 'No means no, you fucking creep. And if I ever lay eyes on you again, I'll fuck up that pretty little face of yours. Now, clean up this mess, you're making a scene.'

With that I return to my group of friends, who are gawping, open-mouthed.

'Don't worry about him,' I tell them. 'He asked me to blow him in the toilets.'

I stride off, nodding at the bouncer as he passes, having been called in because of a disturbance. He must recognise me from one of the previous nights because he grins and salutes as he passes.

Suddenly I don't feel so tired anymore, and the thought of letting loose with my friends seems like a great idea. I can't help thinking that we were closer to catching Steph's killer than we realised, I just wish I could put my finger on his identity.

CHAPTER SIXTY-THREE

Kate pressed the phone to her ear as it connected. 'Laura, what did you manage to find on Brookes?'

'Honestly, not much that I think will necessarily help you. I spoke to his landlord who reluctantly confirmed the account number he receives monthly rent from. It's with a national bank, and after some arm-twisting I managed to get hold of copies of his bank statements for the last eighteen months. Money has continued to enter his account on a regular basis, and two direct debits have left the account each month like clockwork, but there have been no cash withdrawals in the last year.'

'What were the direct debits for?'

'The first is to the landlord for £700 on the first of every month. Apparently the eighteen-month lease on his flat is about to expire, but the landlord hasn't received word of whether Brookes wishes to extend.'

'And the second?'

'That's where the plot thickens. It's to a charitable organisation called the Sisters of St Jerome. I looked them up and they're a convent who specialise in homing orphans, runaways and former residents of Young Offender Institutions. They offer shelter while they're trying to place children in new homes. They're based in the Lake District, but their website looks pretty dated and home-made.'

'So does Brookes have form? If so, what did he do?'

'There's no record of a Wallace Brookes matching our suspect's age range in the Young Offender register.'

'Did you manage to speak to the charity to see if Brookes ever stayed with them? Maybe they saved him and he feels he owes them?'

'I managed to get an administrator on the phone, but she wasn't willing to cooperate without sight of a warrant. She told me their visitors are entitled to data protection as much as the next person.'

'How big a donation does he make?'

'That's the interesting part: it's more than £500 per month on, or around, the tenth of each month. I tried asking the administrator if she could tell me anything about one of their significant benefactors, but again, she played the warrant card. I'm not sure how easy that'll be to get without alerting Armitage to it.'

'So, a dead end then?'

'It looks like it for now.'

'Is he still receiving a regular work income? If he's working, he shouldn't be too hard to find.'

'I was going to ask you what he'd listed as his profession when your team spoke to him in 2015?'

Kate checked her notes. 'Uh… listed as unemployed. Is he on benefits?'

'If he is, it isn't paid into this account. But he does receive a regular income from a company called HLE Records. Their offices are in Fareham, so I called by and got chatting to one of the secretaries there. I showed her the bank statement and explained that we were treating Brookes as a missing person. She didn't ask for any kind of warrant, and was more than happy to tell me that Brookes is one of their artists.'

Kate couldn't hide the surprise from her voice. 'Wait, you're telling me he was a singer? No, wait, is this something to do with his DJ-ing?'

Laura choked back a laugh. 'No, this is nothing to do with the radio, and he's not a singer either, but apparently a composer of some sort. Turns out he used to write jingles for them. You know that one for the nappy company? They still play it on the radio today. You must know the one I mean.'

Kate had no idea. 'Can't say I do.'

'Anyway, he wrote the music and receives royalties every time it gets played. He wrote several other pieces of music used in television commercials too, so, every month HLE Records send him royalty payments ranging from two to three grand over the last eighteen months.'

Kate whistled through her teeth. 'Ever thought you're in the wrong profession?'

'Tell me about it.'

'So, he receives his royalty, pays his rent on time and makes a regular charitable donation. He sounds like a model citizen. What aren't you telling me?'

'As I said, he's made no withdrawals for the last year. In fact the last withdrawal was on the day DC Spencer died.'

'You're kidding me!'

'Nope. In fact he withdrew £300 every day in the week leading up to her death. I don't know what he was planning to use two grand to buy, but he's never withdrawn a single penny since.'

'Two grand's not a lot to live on in London, especially for a year.'

'I also ran a search for his name on HOLMES2 for activity here in the south but his name hasn't come up in any investigations at all. I even spoke to a contact at the hospital and there is no record of him down here at all.'

'Can you run a check with the credit agencies to see if he has other accounts we're not aware of?'

'I can, but if I do, it'll flag up with both Armitage and DSI Williams. I thought I should play it safe for now.'

'Yes, you're right. Damn!'

'Where are you now?'

'Still at the leisure centre where Willow Daniels worked. Their security guard has confirmed Brookes was here the day before Willow died. Apparently, he was servicing the centre's water boilers. He arrived and left in a van. I'll text you the plate, can you run it and see what name it comes back in? Also, see if you can call in a favour and speak to the Met's team who monitor traffic cameras in the capital. They should be able to trace the plate and provide a picture of where it's been and where it currently is.'

'Okay, will do. Where are you headed next?'

'I still need to tie him to Roxie O'Brien's murder. I'm going to go and visit her flatmate and see if she remembers seeing Brookes hanging around. It's a long shot, but I've got to try.'

CHAPTER SIXTY-FOUR

Kate watched the hands tick by on the large clock on the wall at the back of the salon. Finn continued to flick through an out-of-date magazine, but Kate could tell he wasn't reading.

They'd been waiting for nearly twenty minutes to speak to Jen Laithwaite, but the salon had been full when they'd arrived, and without an appointment they would have to wait for her to become available. The walls of the small back room were bright pink, which was starting to make Kate feel claustrophobic. She was about to step out for some fresh air when the curtain to the room swished open and Jen stepped through.

'Sorry about that,' she beamed with a full set of white teeth. She had to be a similar age to Kate, though the make-up plastered on her face could have been covering more wrinkles than it showed. Her skin glowed bronze, which Kate guessed was probably the result of the tanning machines the salon advertised in its front window. 'You caught us in a rush. You're here about Roxie?'

'That's right,' Kate replied, as Finn closed the magazine he'd been leafing through. 'We just wanted to ask you a couple of follow-up questions.'

She tutted. 'Not caught the bastard yet then?'

'I assure you we're working on it.' Kate pulled out her phone and loaded up the image of Brookes. 'Do you recognise this individual? He suffers from a rare skin condition that makes his skin as white as chalk. He's tall, but with a slight build.'

Jen squinted at the image, before shaking her head. 'Christ! Now there's a man in need of a bit of colour. But no, sorry I don't recognise him. But then I suppose he probably wouldn't visit this kind of place, would he?'

Kate held the phone in place. 'You don't remember seeing him hanging around nearby, or near the flat you rented with Roxie?'

'I think I'd remember a face like that! Sorry.'

Kate tried to keep the frustration from her voice. 'Can you remember anyone else hanging around that you thought twice about?'

'I wish I did. It's hard to remember that time now. I've moved on. Don't get me wrong, I miss Roxie every day, but I've kind of accepted that she's gone. It doesn't matter whether you catch the bastard, she ain't coming back. Sorry, I wish I could be more help.'

Kate was returning the phone to her pocket when it began to vibrate in her hand. She answered Laura's call without a second's thought. 'Go ahead.'

'I ran the plates through the DVLA. They were and *are still* registered to one Dominic Coleridge, who almost shares a birthday with Wallace Brookes.'

'What does that mean?'

'It means that Brookes was born on 04-01-1969, and Coleridge was born 01-04-1969. Only, Coleridge does have a criminal history. Want to know more?'

The cogs were already turning in Kate's mind, as she stepped outside the salon. 'Tell me.'

'Coleridge was sentenced to three years in a Young Offenders Institute – well, I suppose it would have been a borstal back then – in 1983, aged just fourteen. He was out eighteen months later, but only free for two months before he was back inside, released the day before his eighteenth birthday.'

'What was he inside for?'

'First time, he was caught beating up a younger lad and the lad needed hospital care after the attack. It wasn't his first offence, but he kept his nose clean inside. But shortly after his release he beat up his probation carer and the judge had no hesitation in sending him back. I've just emailed you a copy of the report, but I think you'll find the picture of the younger Coleridge of interest.'

Kate lowered her phone and opened the app for her emails, before downloading the report. The young man with ghost-like skin and no hair on his head was unmistakeable. She put the phone on speaker so Finn could listen in. 'Coleridge is Brookes. So, what, Brookes is an alias?'

'That's my guess,' Laura agreed.

'So that's why we couldn't find anything on him when we brought him in in 2015, because he was a figment of Coleridge's imagination.'

'It's a shame you didn't arrest him prior to interview as his fingerprints probably would have brought out his background.'

'What else can you tell me about Coleridge?'

'Not a lot. He had a sister, but she's dead. As are both his parents. His mother died while giving birth to the sister, and his father passed away from alcohol poisoning shortly after Coleridge went inside the second time.'

'What happened to the sister?'

'Can't find much on her. Presumably she went into care when the father died, as she was only eleven. I'll see what else I can dig up on her.'

'What's the last known address for Coleridge?'

'Would you be surprised if I told you it was St Jerome's? The place he's been donating money to for more than the last two years.'

Kate couldn't piece together any of the new information, but her gut was screaming at her that she'd misjudged Brookes before. 'Okay, Laura, thank you. Keep digging. See if you can find anything to directly link Coleridge to Willow Daniels,

Roxie O'Brien and Steph Graham. We need to establish why he chose them. Was it random, or was there a more sinister reason? We also need to know where he is now. Finn and I called at his flat yesterday, but there was no answer. It could be that he was hiding, or he could have abandoned his home, and if that's the case, we'll need to try and find him. Presumably Coleridge has a bank account. See when it was last accessed and from where, as that might give us a clue where he is.'

Laura hung up the phone. Kate stepped back into the salon and nodded at Finn. 'I think it's almost time to go and speak to Armitage.'

'Hold on a sec,' said Jen, whose face was a mask of confusion. She disappeared behind the curtain, returning a moment later. She thrust an envelope towards Kate. 'This arrived at the flat a fortnight after Roxie's death. It was addressed to her mother, but Mrs O'Brien had passed away six weeks before Roxie, and her dad was already in a home. It was hand delivered, so I opened it. It made no sense to me, and I didn't want to burden Mr O'Brien with it.'

Kate turned the envelope over in her hands. The name 'Amanda O'Brien' was scrawled on the envelope. Kate removed the glossy card from inside and opened it, seeing a message scrawled in the same handwriting: *Now you know how I felt. DC.*

'As I said,' continued Jen, 'I didn't really know why it had been posted to us, or what it meant. Bit sinister, if you ask me. And I didn't want to add to Mr O'Brien's burden. Poor bastard. Alzheimer's.'

Kate pocketed the card and envelope as the beginnings of a crazy idea started to jump around her mind. 'Thank you for your time, Miss Laithwaite. Finn, we need to go.'

He stood and followed her through the curtain, and back out to the car. 'You look like you've realised something, Kate. Is it time to see Armitage?'

She shook her head. 'Nearly. I just need to check out one more thing first. I want you to drive me back to Watford.'

CHAPTER SIXTY-FIVE

'Are you sure you're going to be okay?' Finn asked as he pulled up at the kerb, nodding at her foot.

'It reminds me of what's at stake if I make another bad call,' Kate replied.

He shook his head dismissively, sensing it was better not to argue. 'What are we doing back here anyway?' he said, changing the subject.

Kate sat back, and allowed her eyes to fall on the semi-detached home of Willow Daniels' parents. 'I think I have an idea why he chose Willow. And if I'm right, the answer is inside that house.'

'Are you going to tell me what?'

'Not yet. Soon, I promise. I just want to be sure first.'

The front door was opened by a man with thick bags beneath his eyes, and a thinning hairline. He recognised Kate before she'd even introduced herself. 'You'd better come in,' he said glumly, holding the door open for them.

Finn led the way, with Kate hopping behind him on her crutches. She was relieved to sit back at the table where she'd spoken with Mrs Daniels the day before. 'Is your wife around, Mr Daniels?'

He collapsed into one of the vacant seats, his shoulders slumped. This wasn't the image of the man Mrs Daniels had described as hiding his grief by burying himself in work. He looked awful. 'She's out.' He said, simply.

Kate's eyes wandered over the condolence cards, looking for a specific image, but not seeing it. 'Can you tell me when she'll be back? There's something I need to discuss—'

'When are you just going to leave us alone to grieve for our daughter?' he pleaded, venom in his eyes.

'Mr Daniels, I'm trying to bring you justice—'

'Oh, don't give me that crap! This is just about getting your name in the papers. You're as bad as the rest of them! My wife was in such a state after you came here yesterday. We was up most of the night consoling each other. Every time it looks like we're on the mend, one of your lot comes over and rips the scab off.'

Kate's cheeks flushed. She was about to apologise when Finn piped up.

'You haven't got a clue, mate! This woman here hasn't stopped looking for the bastard who destroyed your family since the day your daughter was killed. Whoever it was, he murdered my sister too, and I know that *this* woman is the *only* one who's going to nail him.'

Mr Daniels looked as shocked as Kate at the outburst. Finn spun on his heel and moved away from the table.

Kate reached for his hand. 'I actually have some questions about you, Mr Daniels. I need to ask you about one of your previous cases as a social worker. Do you recognise the name Coleridge? Did you ever deal with a young girl by that name?'

He looked shocked. 'I have dealt with hundreds of children from all walks of life. Why do you want to know about one specific case?'

Kate took a deep breath. 'Because I believe that the man who murdered Willow did so to seek revenge against you.'

'Me? No, you're wrong.'

'There's one way to know for sure. Did you handle the Coleridge case?'

He shook his head. 'I don't recognise the name.'

She couldn't read his body language, but pushed forward. 'Following the murder, did you receive a strange condolence card from someone you didn't recognise? The card would have been signed with the initials DC.'

He shook his head vehemently. 'No. I really have no idea what you're talking about.'

Kate continued to watch him, her mind working backwards. Had she missed something else? Her mobile ringing broke her trail of thought.

Kate stepped away from the table and out into the hallway, leaving Daniels' shoulders gently rocking. 'Laura? Tell me you have good news.'

'I'll let you be the judge. I reached out to a contact in social services. Elaine Coleridge was the subject of four separate investigations, well, her father was. The files my contact has sent over are heavily redacted, so it's impossible to see the specifics of the investigation, but what I can see is the dates on which the recommendations were made, and the names of those who were involved in the decision-making process.'

It was all Kate could do to keep her mouth shut and listen.

'We might never know for sure what triggered the investigations, but my contact was surprised that four separate enquiries had been conducted by four different authorities. One in the Midlands, two in different parts of London, and one in Essex. He said that he would have expected Elaine to be taken away from her abusive father by a third investigation. But he also added that this was in the '80s, so everything was paper-based and many children slipped through the cracks. If Coleridge Senior regularly moved his daughter to new locations, then maybe that's how he got away with keeping her with him for so long.'

Kate closed her eyes. 'Who signed the reports?'

'A Mr P. Daniels, a Mrs D. O'Brien, a Dr S. Olufabe and a Mr J. Mickelson.'

Kate turned back to the living room, but Daniels was nowhere in sight. 'Daniels and O'Brien – we have a connection, but I don't recognise the other two names.'

'I know, right? I was asking myself the same thing: what about Steph Graham? And then I remembered you saying she was adopted, right? You said her parents were from Nigeria originally? It wouldn't be too difficult to check with adoption services whether Steph Graham was originally born to Dr Olufabe.'

Kate lowered the phone as a tearful Mr Daniels emerged from the kitchen. He held out an envelope for her to take. She removed the card from within, and held her breath as she opened it and read the message inside: *Now you know how I felt. DC.*

CHAPTER SIXTY-SIX

14 HOURS UNTIL I DIE

My whole head is pounding as I finally open my eyes, staring at the familiar brown stains on the ceiling overhead. How the hell have I ended up back here?

It's been five months since I was weak enough to sleep with him, but without looking I can already hear his gentle snoring, and last night's memories return in bright flashes.

I can feel Pop staring down at me with shame in his eyes. I have let him down: tarnished his memory. This isn't about coming full circle, I've taken an enormous leap backwards. Trevor turns restlessly, and I'm relieved I won't have to look at his face. Oh God, I wish I was anywhere but here.

We're in the same room as before, and I can't help but dread how many more times I might wake in the same room, having made the same mistake again. I thought I'd grown up, and moved on from being that selfish little girl screwing her superior, but clearly I was fooling myself. What would Mum say if she knew where I was? Ironically, it's partly her fault that I am here.

We had a blazing row on the phone last night, and both said things that I certainly regret. I hope she feels the same remorse this morning. Why won't she just allow me to focus on my job without the snide comments and constant nitpicking? Does she really think I'll just jack it all in and find an alternative career? She thinks the sun shines out of Finn's arse because he's a teacher. He's got it all: the obedient wife, stable career, nice house, and they're trying for children.

By comparison, my life is hurtling out of control.

We're all supposed to be congregating at their house this weekend, but I can't think of anything worse. I seem to remember telling her I wouldn't come.

Of course I didn't mean it, but I was lashing out. I'm not sure I'll be welcome now.

After I hung up on Mum, I headed out of work and into the nearest pub. I don't know how many drinks I was up to when Trevor approached. He took me to one side and told me I should go home and sober up before I made a fool of myself. How dare he judge me!

But I wanted to do something to spite Mum, and that's why I asked him to drive me home, before jumping him when we were in his car.

'I thought you wanted to call it a day,' he said, with just a hint of hope in his voice.

I could see he still wanted me, and I just wanted to be wanted, so I told him to drive us here, and then I let him do whatever he wanted.

I feel a tear at the corner of my eye, but I won't let it go. This is my fault, nobody else's. I seduced him. I told him to screw me here.

Despite the sharp pain behind my eyes, I push the sheet back and move unsteadily to the bathroom, collecting my clothes from the floor as I creep silently forward. I dress quickly, unable to look at my reflection in the mirror, and then I sneak out of the door while he continues to gently snore.

I don't want him to see the terrified and shameful look in my eyes. It takes me two different tubes to get back to my flat, but I need to shower and find a fresh change of clothes before I head into the station. There are no dates lined up for this evening, and for today only I get to be a proper detective again. I've missed the everyday banter of the office.

But as I open the door to my flat, I can't shake the feeling that someone is watching me. I check the courtyard beneath the staircase leading up to the flat, but there is nobody in sight. I sigh as I close the door. All this undercover work is obviously taking its toll: I'm being paranoid.

CHAPTER SIXTY-SEVEN

Leaning back in the car seat, Kate wondered if she was doing the right thing getting Armitage involved, but it was the only way. Her name had been dragged through the mud too many times to be taken seriously without his support.

She continued to watch his reflection in the rear-view mirror as he pored over the handwritten notes she'd passed him when she'd finally convinced him to get into the back of Finn's car. She could almost feel Amy's spirit nearby urging her towards the finish line. Finn would be back with the drinks any moment.

Armitage finally looked up from the papers. 'And Mr Daniels is prepared to go on record and confirm what he told you about Elaine Coleridge?'

She nodded. 'In his eyes he didn't do anything wrong. From what he told us, he first came across Elaine when one of her schoolteachers reported suspicious bruising on her back. He said he met with Coleridge Senior and questioned him extensively about the injuries, but it was concluded that Elaine was just clumsy. Daniels told me Coleridge didn't smell of booze, was well presented and spoke passionately about his love for his daughter. There was no way for Daniels to know that Coleridge Senior was a high-functioning alcoholic.

'It would seem that Coleridge and Elaine left the area shortly after, and three months later Mrs O'Brien met with the child. Again, it was a teacher who reported the suspicious markings. This time Elaine was also questioned but denied the accusations against her father. Despite her misgivings – as her dementia-suffering, widowed husband recalled – Mrs O'Brien allowed Elaine to return home, but recommended further investigation. Of course, Coleridge Senior moved her on again, this time to the Midlands where Dr Olufabe became involved.'

'So what's the motive? Revenge because they allowed the father to continue to drunkenly abuse Elaine? Why go after them? Why not go to the source of the pain?'

'Because Coleridge Senior died a month before Brookes's release. It's possible that Brookes wasn't aware of the full extent of the abuse as he was inside for years during this period. The messages in the cards – *Now you know how I felt* – tells us exactly why he did it. For whatever reason, Brookes held these four individuals responsible for his sister's death, and went after their daughters.'

'So who is Mickelson?'

Kate couldn't answer for certain. 'Maybe there's a fourth victim we haven't tied to the investigation. It will require more digging.'

'What you're suggesting is based on a lot of circumstantial evidence.'

'I know. But I think it's enough for you to take it further and focus on Brookes, sorry, I mean Dominic Coleridge. If you bring him in, I'm sure you'll get what you need. Please, Trevor. I know we haven't always seen eye to eye, but I'm not wrong this time.'

Armitage finally cracked a smile. 'I don't doubt it, Kate. And I'm not surprised that you were the one to finally piece the case together. I knew if I pushed you away enough you'd keep searching. It's who you are. Don't get me wrong, I wouldn't have you in my team, because you're far too high maintenance, but this is good work.'

Kate gave him an uneasy look, she was sure there was a compliment in there somewhere. 'So, what next?'

'We'll raid his flat and arrest him.'

'I want to interview him.'

'No chance, Matthews.'

She turned to face him. 'Please, Trevor, at least let me be there. I need to look into his eyes when he tells us why he killed Amy, too. She had nothing to do with what happened to his sister, nor did her parents, but he must have realised somehow that she was on to him.'

'I'm sorry, Kate, but you know I can't have you anywhere near the station when we bring him in. I don't need to remind you that you're still suspended from active duty. You've done really well with this and I'm glad you had the sense to bring it to me, but you need to let me carry the baton to the end now. I promise I'll keep you in the loop with what he tells us, but it's time for you to return to Southampton. And looking at the state of your foot, I'd recommend you see a doctor ASAP.'

He opened the rear door and climbed out, before leaning through her window. 'This time I mean it when I say to stay out of it, Kate. I'll make a deal with you. If you promise to stay out of our way, I will confirm the moment he's in custody. Wait for me at the station, and I'll phone ahead so they know to expect you.'

Kate watched Armitage walking away, disappointed with his reaction, but knowing he was right. For once she would do as instructed. For now, anyway.

CHAPTER SIXTY-EIGHT

Kate slammed the phone into its cradle. 'He wasn't there.'

Finn wore a veil of disappointment. 'So, what happens next?'

'Armitage and his team are going to search the property for evidence of Coleridge's involvement and any clues as to where he has gone. Apparently there was a huge pile of unopened post on the doormat, suggesting he's not been there for some time.'

'Do you want me to drive you home?'

Kate flicked on the computer on the desk. 'No way. Not while he's still out there.'

'But what can you do from here? Where do you even begin?'

'Well, we know his sister died, and was possibly the catalyst for his crimes, so maybe she had friends or family that he could be hiding with.'

Loading up a search engine she typed in Elaine Coleridge's name and skimmed the results. The first page was dominated by social media and recruitment profiles of women with the same name. She ignored these and loaded up the next page. But on the fourth page of results, an article caught her eye. Clicking the link, she was surprised to find an archived article from a local Hampshire newspaper. It recorded the suicide of a local girl, aged twenty-one. She was found in a bathtub with her wrists slit. According to the article, her unnamed brother returned from work to find her, but his attempts to resuscitate her were useless. There was an image of the young woman in happier times. Kate leaned closer to the screen. In the distance an older man was waving at her. Kate squinted at the image, gesticulating so Finn could see.

'It's him.'

'Does it say where she lived?'

Kate shook her head. There's no address, but I can contact the newspaper and see whether they have a record of it on file.'

Finn stifled a yawn.

Kate looked up apologetically. 'I'm sorry, I've had you out all day. Do you need to get back?'

He shook his head. 'There's no hurry.'

'Let's head off now. I can phone the newspaper on the way, and try to wangle that address from them.'

'You think that's where he is now?'

'It's as good a guess as any. We know he's not in London, and if he's hiding he'd want to be in familiar surroundings.'

It was nearly three by the time her phone call was finally answered. Kate didn't appreciate being on hold for almost twenty minutes, but she tried to sound calm as she spoke. 'Is that Zoe?'

The woman on the other end sounded tired, secretly longing for the end of her shift so she could get home and unwind. 'Speaking.'

'Zoe, it's DI Kate Matthews, you interviewed me when I first moved to Southampton. And again last summer when I solved Eleanor Jacobs' murder.'

'Sure, I remember, what can I do for you?'

'I need a favour. I don't like to ask, but I'd owe you one.' Reporters were always looking for currency within the force, leverage for when they wanted in on a big story.

'What do you need?' The terms of the verbal contract were clear to them both.

'You did a story years ago about a girl called Elaine Coleridge. A suicide, she was found in the bath by her brother.'

There was a pause on the line. 'Did I? It sounds vaguely familiar. What about it?'

Kate took a deep breath. 'I'm hoping you can look through your notes and tell me the address where she was found.'

'What's this about?' asked Zoe, her voice thick with suspicion.

'We're looking for the brother. He's a missing person, and we're shaking down possible leads of where he might be.'

Zoe grunted. 'If I'm going to do you a favour, you'll have to be straight with me. Someone as high profile as you doesn't run missing-persons' cases. Rumour is you're under investigation for that car chase last Wednesday. Care to comment?'

'You know I can't comment on rumours or active cases.'

'Listen, Kate, I'm only too happy to work collaboratively with you, but I need honesty. You don't have to tell me exactly why you're after this guy, but it's juicier than just a missing-person's case, right?'

Kate sighed. 'Yes.'

'And you'll give me background to go to print when you've found him?'

She closed her eyes. 'Fine.'

'I'll see what I can dig up and I'll call you back.'

The line disconnected.

'Everything okay?' Finn asked, glancing over.

Kate's eyes remained closed, hoping she wouldn't regret the trade-off.

CHAPTER SIXTY-NINE

Finn pulled into the estate and parked the car.

'Shouldn't we have phoned Armitage?' he asked, as he killed the engine. 'I mean, if Brookes or Coleridge, or whatever he's called, is in there, then he needs detaining.'

Kate answered with conviction. 'I need to be certain first. I've messaged Laura who's on her way. If he needs arresting, she can do it.'

She jumped as someone tapped on her window. Looking up, she was disappointed to see Zoe, grasping a notepad and pen. She signalled for Kate to lower the window. Kate thumbed for her to get in the back seat. The last thing they needed was for Brookes to see them hovering about outside.

Zoe closed the rear door eagerly. 'I knew you'd come straight here. So, who is he and why are you so keen to find him?'

'Our agreement was we'd speak afterwards.'

Zoe thrust her hand towards Finn. 'And you are?'

Finn reluctantly shook her hand and introduced himself.

'I know you, don't I?' she persisted.

Kate quickly shook her head so only he could see. If Zoe connected the dots, and reported that Kate was reinvestigating Amy's murder, she'd be in big trouble.

'I don't think so,' Finn replied, thankfully picking up on Kate's signal.

'So are you a detective as well?'

'Just a friend.'

'DI Matthews using a civilian to help her locate a missing man? Now I *know* there's more to this than you're letting on. Is he dangerous? Should I get a photographer down here as well? I could do you a front-page headline, with an image of you dragging the suspect from the building. That would do your career the power of good.'

'No,' Kate replied firmly. 'You shouldn't be here, Zoe. I would have called you when we were done.'

Zoe snorted. 'Yeah, right. You need to understand, Kate, that you and I could build a professional and mutually beneficial working relationship. I can share the benefit of my sources, and you can slip me the occasional exclusive. There aren't enough positive stories about the police in this city, and we could do a series about the woman cleaning up Southampton. Just think about it.'

Kate desperately wanted to throw Zoe out of the car, painfully aware that she was probably the last person who should be a poster girl for the police force, but she wasn't willing to do anything to alert Brookes to their presence before she was ready.

'Which house is it?' Kate asked eventually.

Zoe leaned forward between the seats, extending her arm to point at a mid-terrace property with orange brickwork and bright-white window frames. 'That one, with the camper van parked on the driveway.' She paused as a synapse flickered in her brain. She nudged Finn's shoulder. 'I know who you are! You were on *Crimewatch* the other night talking about your sister. What was her name…? Spencer! Amy Spencer, right? Wasn't that the case that led to your transfer down here, Kate? Oh my God! That's why you're here, isn't it? This guy you're after, is he the one…? Oh my God, my editor is going to *freak* when I break this—'

Kate's head snapped around. 'Not a word. Is that clear? You need to keep it buttoned.'

But Zoe's eyes were dancing with excitement. 'I'm right, aren't I? Goodness!'

'Stay here,' Kate warned them both as she pushed the door open and slid out, hobbling forwards towards the end of the estate as casually as she could, before doubling back and approaching the property under the cover of the neighbouring houses. She felt her phone vibrating in her pocket, but decided not to answer when she saw it was Armitage. He could wait for now.

The camper van had rust visible on the metallic bumper, with further patches on the side panels. It looked like it hadn't been moved in months, if not years.

Her mouth was dry, and she knew it was time to call Laura, but she had to know for sure. Edging out from behind the camper van, she hobbled over the small lawn leading to the front door. Taking a deep breath, she rang the bell.

CHAPTER SEVENTY

5 HOURS UNTIL I DIE

A day of normality, at last. And the best news? The DSI has given the green light for us to continue investigating Steph's murder. The DI's team is now made up of just five of us – I think she's finally called in her last favour with the DSI – but five is better than nothing.

When we were alone, Matthews told me that she still intends to prove that Willow and Roxie were murdered by the same killer as Steph. She told me not to let on to anyone else; what we do from now will be shared on a need-to-know basis. I can understand why she'd want to keep it under wraps, but I'm thrilled that she still wants me involved.

I haven't stopped smiling all day. She's told the team to have the weekend off, so we can come back fresh on Monday. I think she's planning to spend the time with her daughter, and I've decided to go along to the family gathering. I know it's what Pop would have wanted, and if I'm ever going to convince Mum that I can still lead a normal life in the police force, then I need to make more of an effort with her.

The DI has lined up a date for Monday evening, so I'll have to be in cover from Sunday night. She still believes that the dating site link is the strongest we have to tie the three victims together. Next week our team will visit each of the locations where the victims had their dates, and we will monitor security footage for common faces.

The DI now believes that the killer didn't necessarily date any of the victims, but may have been watching them during the date.

For the first time in months it feels like the investigation is once again moving forward, and I'm more than happy to be swept along with it. Last night's indiscretion is still fresh in my mind, but maybe it's the impetus I needed to get my own path moving in the right direction. I never want to wake up in that grotty hotel again, least of all with Trevor Armitage. Part of me is tempted to go and tell his wife about his extra-marital liaisons. She deserves better than that cheating scumbag. But wouldn't that make me a hypocrite? After all, I knew he was married when I got into bed with him.

My phone beeps as I exit the tube. A new message has been received on one of the dating apps. Opening it, I see it was sent by Craig, a guy I'm supposed to be meeting on Monday night. It explains that he's managed to land tickets for some show at the National Theatre on the Southbank tonight, and he wants to know if we can move our date forward.

I immediately call the office, hoping Matthews is still there and can guide me on how to reply. But her line goes unanswered. If nobody is in the office, then nobody is monitoring the email account where a copy of the message will also have been received.

When we first started the DI was adamant that I should never go on a date without backup, but I don't want to fob him off, if it's possible he is the one we've been after.

I try the office again, but the line rings out, so I try Matthews' mobile number, but it goes straight to voicemail. I leave her a message swiftly explaining what's happened and asking for her advice on what to do.

She hasn't phoned me back by the time I reach my own flat, and it's too late to head to the cover flat. Craig has messaged me again with his phone number, asking me to give him a call. He wants me to meet him at the theatre at seven. I change into something cover-Amy might wear, while I try the DI again. Still no answer.

I don't want to be the reason why he slipped through the net. I try to think of what Matthews would do in my shoes: I'm certain she would already have told him she was on her way.

I leave another message telling her I'm going to meet him and will keep her posted with my progress. I try the office phone once again, but there is still no answer there either.

I message Craig to tell him I'll be there.

CHAPTER SEVENTY-ONE

The front door opened and Kate was surprised to be looking into the heavily wrinkled eyes of a woman, her tightly curled hair almost pure white. 'Can I help you, dear?'

Kate handed over a business card. 'I'm with the Southampton police force. May I come in?'

The old lady scrutinised the card, before opening the door wider and allowing Kate in.

'Do you live here alone?' Kate asked as they entered the small living room, where the television blared loudly.

'Yes, dear. Since my husband passed last year, it's just me rattling around. Would you like a cup of tea?'

Kate smiled warmly. 'That's kind of you, but I'm fine. Have you lived in this house for long?'

'Ooh, must be at least twenty years, dear. We bought it when my Harry retired from the Royal Navy. What's this all about?'

Kate pulled out the picture of Brookes from Steph's file. 'Do you recognise this man?'

The woman reached for her glasses, snatching the photograph from Kate. 'I don't think so, dear. Does he live around here?'

'That's what I'm trying to establish. I believe he lived in this very house many years ago. With his sister.'

She passed the image back. 'I'm sorry, dear, I don't recognise him.'

Kate glanced around the room. She was sure the woman was speaking honestly, but it didn't hurt to snoop. 'Can you remember who you bought the property from?'

'My husband handled that side of things, I'm afraid.'

'And the camper van outside, is that yours?'

The woman looked off into the distance. 'That was my Harry's. He loved camping, but I don't drive, so it just sits there. I like to go and sit in it sometimes; it still has his smell in there. I should probably sell it, but I'd feel like I'm letting go of him if I did. Sorry, I sound like a silly old fool.'

Kate instinctively touched her shoulder. 'You really don't.' She took one more glance around the room, and with a heavy heart, hobbled back towards the front door. 'I'm sorry to have wasted your time, and I appreciate you speaking with me.'

'You don't have to rush off, dear. I don't get many visitors these days. Are you sure you don't want to stay for a cup of tea?' The woman's eyes were pleading.

Kate rubbed her arm. 'I wish I could, but I need to find this man before he hurts someone else.'

Stepping outside, she shook her head so Finn and Zoe would know Brookes wasn't inside. Armitage was calling again. Raising the phone to her ear, she made her way back towards the car.

'Where are you? I came back to the station and you're not here.'

'I came home. What is it?'

'I thought I should update you. Brookes is dead.'

Kate froze, the breath catching in her throat. 'What do you mean *he's dead*? What happened? How?'

'The details are still sketchy, but the DNA samples we took from his flat have been linked back to the profile of a John Doe killed in a hit and run last January.'

Kate wobbled as her legs turned to jelly. 'No, there must be some mistake.'

'No mistake. The piled-up mail on his doormat dates back to that period. All his clothes were hanging in the wardrobe, we found an envelope stuffed with three grand and his passport. It looks like he might have been planning to go away, but he never made it.'

Kate's mind raced for an alternative explanation. 'How do you know that the samples in his flat belong to him? You can't know for certain. If he was trying to get away, he might have left traces of another of his victims there, to fool us.'

'Kate, you're clutching at straws.'

'No, you're wrong. I'm telling you. You need to keep looking. I won't believe it until I see clear evidence he is dead.'

She hung up the phone, steadying herself against the car.

Finn stepped out. 'What is it? What's going on? Who was in that house?'

Kate didn't answer, she just climbed silently into the car. There was no other choice. She had to prove Armitage wrong once and for all, and the only way to do that was to return to the beginning.

'Take me home.'

CHAPTER SEVENTY-TWO

Once they were alone, Kate had done her best to relay Armitage's message to Finn. Zoe hadn't been happy to be booted out of the car, and she'd warned that she would still publish a story about their activity, but with no confirmed source, Kate felt confident the editor wouldn't allow her.

Finn didn't share her cynicism. He draped his coat and scarf over the arm of her sofa, and took a seat. 'I don't understand why you're so upset. We know who killed Amy. Okay, he's dead, rather than behind bars, but that's good enough for me. To be honest, I'm almost relieved that my dad and stepmother won't have to go through the ordeal of a trial. Now we can all move on with our lives. You should be happy.'

But Kate was adamant something didn't add up. She thought back to the first time she'd watched the *Crimewatch* reconstruction. Her subconscious mind had seen something odd, but she'd yet to identify exactly what it was.

He eyed her cautiously. 'You're not going to let this go, are you?'

'How can I? Desperate people go to desperate lengths under pressure. I've come up against a killer who faked his own death before. Why couldn't it happen again? If he's still out there… I can't leave it to chance. Amy deserves more. All of his victims do.'

He stood suddenly. 'I'm going to put the kettle on. Do you want a coffee?'

She wanted a glass of wine, but it was vital to keep her mind clear. She nodded, and watched him leave the room, before reaching for the remote control and playing the reconstruction from the beginning. On the screen, the actress playing Amy exited Waterloo station and headed towards the Southbank.

Where did she go after the theatre? How did she get home? How could these simple questions still remain unanswered twelve months on?

Kate paused the screen as her phone rang yet again. She sighed and answered Armitage's call.

'You were right. It's not him.'

Her pulse quickened. 'See! I knew it. I told you he couldn't be dead.'

'No, Kate, wait, that's not what I meant. Coleridge is definitely dead. I'm looking at the photograph of his face taken during the post-mortem. His skin's white as snow, it's definitely him.'

Thick lines furrowed in her brow. 'So, what are you saying?'

'Brookes didn't kill Amy.'

'What? Don't be ridiculous! We know she was his fourth victim.'

'Impossible.'

'No. Listen, he knew we were on to him, and that's why he killed her.'

'Kate, listen to me carefully, Brookes couldn't have killed Amy. The hit and run was on 14 January: the day before. Brookes couldn't have killed Amy, because he was already on a mortuary slab when she died.'

'There… there must be some mistake.'

'There's no mistake. I've checked and double-checked it. I've just had a conversation with the pathologist who performed the post-mortem. Brookes, or Coleridge… he was dead. You were right; Amy's killer is still out there.'

CHAPTER SEVENTY-THREE

3 HOURS UNTIL I DIE

As I pass through the barrier at Waterloo, I can't escape the sense of foreboding building in the pit of my stomach. When I accepted the date tonight, I did so believing I would eventually get backup. I've left DI Matthews a message explaining where I'm going, but no one has replied and I'm suddenly conscious of how isolated and vulnerable I am.

I'm probably just being paranoid, but it's that same feeling as I had with that married guy at the diner in December. I should have just said no, but Steph's voice is calling out to me. I vowed I'd catch him, and if this turns out to be the one, then I'll have lived up to my promise.

But it doesn't shake my growing sense of dread.

As I move closer to the theatre, I'm tempted to turn around and go home. But if I stand him up, he might not contact me again, and if he is the one we've been looking for, I'll have blown the weeks of hard work leading to this point.

As I'm about to turn, I spot him standing at the edge of the building waving in my direction. It's too late to turn and run. I'm now on an unstoppable course.

CHAPTER SEVENTY-FOUR

Closing her eyes, Kate tried to run through what she knew of Amy's final movements that night. She'd spent so long trying to link Amy's murder to the previous three, but she'd been looking at it from the wrong perspective; she should have been looking for differences, rather than similarities.

All the other victims had been found in the open, but Amy's body was left near her home, unlike the others. And it was possible that there'd been some kind of struggle inside the flat, which wasn't the case with the others. Based on the fact she'd thought the killer suspected Amy was police, she'd been prepared to overlook it. But had that been her biggest error of judgement?

Keeping her eyes closed, she tried to picture Amy. She'd used her Oyster card at Waterloo station, and they'd tracked her walking from the station to the National Theatre where she was meeting her date that night. Amy had phoned Kate during the interval to say she was fine and that the date wasn't who they were looking for. And that was the last time anyone had heard from her. Finn said he had also missed a call from her, but she hadn't left a message. *Why hadn't she called him from her mobile?*

So where had Amy gone after the theatre? Not on the tube, not on the bus, and not in a taxi. Nor had she walked home, so the only possibility that remained was that she had got a lift home from someone. Her date, maybe? Or someone else she'd met at the theatre? Kate continued to think through the timeline. Amy arrived home and either the attacker had been waiting for her there, or she'd invited him in. They'd struggled and he'd clobbered her, before dragging her down the metal staircase outside the flat. He'd then placed her in the gutter, stripped her and used a knife of some kind to slash her as Brookes had done to his victims. *So was he a copycat? If so, why had he stopped at just one victim?*

She restarted the reconstruction as the scene cut to the paramedics failing to find a pulse. It still angered Kate that they hadn't found an actress more like Amy. Her hair colour was wrong, and her cheeks looked chubbier than Amy's had.

Kate's eyes widened, and she paused the screen once more.

It couldn't be.

Was that what she'd seen?

She dived off the sofa to the pile of papers stacked in the corner, and began to tear through them, hunting for the original crime-scene photo. Even though she could still see the scene in her mind, she had to be certain. The photograph would confirm what she was now almost certain of.

CHAPTER SEVENTY-FIVE

2 HOURS UNTIL I DIE

As the curtain drops for the interval, I'm amazed I haven't fallen asleep yet. If Craig is the killer we've been looking for then his MO would be to bore his victims to death. He's nice enough, but he seems to think that his job is as exciting as that of a secret agent; he's an estate agent, for Christ's sake!

Oh, and did I mention that he has four cats? The way he speaks of them is like they're his children. He got his phone out as we took our seats and started showing me pictures of them. I think he fancies himself as a bit of an amateur photographer too.

He's not unattractive, and I suppose if I was looking for someone who thinks a night at the theatre is on a par with a trip to the movies, then maybe cover-Amy would seek a second date with him. The only positive is that I won't have to see him on Monday night now.

Craig asks me if I'd like an ice cream from the vendor and I nod enthusiastically, hoping the sugar boost will get me through the second act. He asks what flavour I'd like and I tell him to surprise me.

I leave the row and head out to the foyer. Matthews still hasn't called me back, and I'm starting to think she's turned her phone off for the night. Either that, or the battery is dead.

'Ma'am, it's Amy checking in,' I tell the messaging service. 'Just confirming that everything is okay. My date is definitely not our guy. Anyway, hope you're having fun with your daughter. I'll see you on Monday.'

I freshen up in the toilets, and as I return to my seat, Craig is just arriving back too. 'I got you vanilla,' he beams.

From where we're sitting I can see they had chocolate, blueberry and strawberry flavours as well as vanilla. He thinks vanilla would surprise me? I try not to laugh at my own fear about coming here alone.

As I'm tucking into my dessert, Craig suddenly turns to me, a panicked look on his face. He is clutching his phone and looks like he wants to cry.

'What is it?' I ask.

'It's Georgie, she's ill. I need to go.'

Remembering that Georgie is the name of one of his cats, I stand to let him out of the row.

'I'm so sorry,' he says, deep in thought. 'I'll call you.' And with that he is gone.

What is it with men running out on me? So now, here I am, alone in the theatre at a play that I'm bored with. I wait two minutes and then decide to bail out too. What a waste of a Friday night!

It's raining as I reach the exits, but I didn't bring an umbrella with me. I'll be soaked by the time I make it back to Waterloo, and I'm looking for a taxi on the streets when I spot a vehicle I immediately recognise parked across the road.

It makes no sense. What's he doing here? How could he have known I would be here at this time? Not wasting another second, I head over to the car and bang on his window. As it lowers I can see he knows he's busted.

CHAPTER SEVENTY-SIX

Finn carried the mugs through to the living room, and rested Kate's on the coaster on the coffee table. 'What is it? You look like you've just seen a ghost.'

Kate glanced up with a mad look in her eyes. 'I figured out what was wrong with the re-enactment: make-up!'

'Make-up? I don't understand.'

She pointed at the screen. 'Amy was found naked at the scene, right? So the director had to craftily shoot the crime scene for the re-enactment, so as not to show any nudity on the screen. But look at the actress's face. What do you notice?'

He studied the screen, before sighing. 'I give up. Apart from the fact she doesn't look much like Amy.'

'It's the make-up. The actress is wearing eyeliner and dark lipstick, which is how we know Amy was dressed up on that night, from the footage we have of her in Waterloo station.'

'And?'

She handed Finn the crime-scene photograph. 'When we found her, she wasn't wearing any make-up.'

'So? Maybe she took it off.'

Kate clapped her hands together excitedly. 'Exactly!'

Finn still wasn't sure what she was getting at.

Kate rolled her eyes. 'The scene of crime officers suggested there might have been a struggle inside the flat before Amy was killed, but they couldn't say conclusively that the mess they found was as a result of the killer attacking Amy. You said yourself, she wasn't the neatest of homemakers.'

He smiled at the memory. 'Yeah, her place was usually a bit of a pigsty.'

'But the fact that she removed her make-up before she was killed tells us that she was in her flat for an extended period before he struck.'

His eyes wrinkled with confusion. 'How does that help us figure out who did it?'

She took a large gulp of coffee. 'It means she was with the killer before he struck. I believe she invited him in, and she must have felt comfortable enough with him being there to remove her make-up.'

'So, because she removed her lippy, you think that means she knew her killer? How do you know the killer didn't wipe it off afterwards? He cleaned his DNA off the other victims with some kind of cleansing wipes, right? Maybe he did the same to Amy?'

'Although traces of ammonia were found on Amy's body, none was found on her face. It's in the pathologist's report. In fact, it even mentions the presence of a moisturising cream on her cheeks.'

Finn perched on the arm of the chair. 'But if you're right, then it means Brookes definitely wasn't the killer.'

She nodded grimly. 'Just stick with me for now. I don't think she would have invited someone like Brookes up. You've seen his picture.'

'Maybe that's why she removed her make-up: to make him feel more comfortable with his own appearance?' Finn was growing increasingly agitated. 'Or maybe Brookes was wearing a wig and make-up himself, to look more normal.'

Kate tilted her head. 'I know this is difficult for you to hear, but I think Armitage's team are right. I think whoever killed Amy dressed the scene to mirror Brookes's MO.' She paused. 'I need to go back to the beginning. If Amy knew her killer, then maybe she'd been on a date with him before. I need to find the original list of suspects.'

She reached down into the pile of papers at her feet.

Finn stood and picked up his coat and scarf.

She took another swig from the mug. 'Where are you going?'

He looked solemnly at her. 'I should get back. My dad will be wondering where the hell I am. You need to focus anyway, and I'd only be a distraction.'

'Please, Finn, don't be despondent. I know that separating this crime from the other three was a blow, but actually I think it puts us a step closer to finding out the truth.' Kate was filled with renewed energy. 'It might take us a bit of time, but we'll find him. I promise you that. You don't need to take off. In fact, you could really help me if you stick around. I have a ton of questions that need answering. For example, where did the killer get the murder weapon from? Did he bring the knife with him? If so, was he always planning to kill her? Also, how did he manage to find out so much about Brookes's MO? How did he know to wipe her body down with wipes? That bit never made the press…' Her words trailed off.

Finn blurred as thoughts raced through Kate's mind.

Someone Amy felt comfortable getting a lift from – comfortable enough to invite them into her flat.

Someone who knew enough about the previous murders to dress the scene in the same way.

Someone who left no DNA in the flat, or whose DNA presence would be dismissed.

Finn's face came into focus as her blood ran cold. 'When we spoke in London on Saturday, you said Amy didn't tell you anything about the investigation. How did you know that Brookes wiped down his victims with an ammonia-based product?'

He stared down at his feet as he reached into the inner pocket of his coat.

Kate's heart skipped a beat as she saw the blade.

CHAPTER SEVENTY-SEVEN

1 HOUR UNTIL I DIE

Finn stares back at me from the driver's side, and I can see he's been crying. Without a second's thought I pull open the passenger door and dive in. It's good to be out of the cold air and heavy rain. The engine is still running, but the windows and windscreen are misted over.

'What are you doing here?'

He doesn't answer as fresh tears fall.

I gently rub his arm. 'What's going on, Finn? Why are you so upset?'

He wipes his nose with the back of his hand. 'I think she wants a divorce.'

I'm aware that things have been tense between Finn and his wife for a while. Mum still thinks they're the perfect couple, but she doesn't realise the strain that trying for a baby has been having on their marriage.

'I'm sure she doesn't,' I say, eager to console him.

But he shakes his head. 'It's what she said. She's buggered off down to her parents' place in Devon. I'm going to have to explain to Erin why she's not coming for this family gathering. She says if I want our marriage to work, I have to move down to Devon permanently.'

My heart goes out to him. I can't begin to understand everything that has occurred between them, but why do some women not appreciate what they've got?

'Let's go somewhere for a drink,' I tell him. 'I'll help you come up with an excuse you can feed the others. If there's one thing I've mastered down the years, it's lying to my mum.'

He wipes his eyes. 'Where?'

'Can you take me to my place? I need to change before we rock up at theirs. We can chat and then you can drive us over there, and we can both pretend we're content with our lives.'

I invite Finn up to the flat and tell him to open some wine, but it's as I'm changing in my room that I remember he never did explain why he was at the theatre.

'Erin called me this morning,' he explains. 'Said you'd had a fight and asked if I'd check you were okay. I arrived here just as you were heading out. I called out to you, but you were on the phone to someone. I heard you tell them you were heading to the theatre, so I drove there, hoping to catch up with you.'

I think back to when I left the flat earlier, but I know I phoned the DI from inside, and I definitely didn't hear anyone call my name. And then it dawns on me. I open my door wider so I can watch him from my mirror. He's sat on the sofa, and his hand is trembling as he drinks his wine.

'How long have you been watching me for, Finn?'

He looks up and our eyes meet in the reflection. 'Wh-what? I don't know what you—'

'I'm not angry, but you really shouldn't be putting yourself at risk like that. I'm a big girl and I can look after myself.'

He stands, lowering his glass to the table. 'I'm just worried about you, that's all.'

He's sweet, but I feel a little patronised by his response. I'm struggling with the strap on my top and he steps into the room and offers to adjust it for me. But as his warm fingers linger for too long on my bare shoulder I suddenly realise that his attention is more than sibling concern. And that's when I feel his hot and sticky breath on my neck.

CHAPTER SEVENTY-EIGHT

Turning the blade over in his hands, Finn's face was a tangle of emotions. As tears slid down his cheeks, he continued to stare at the blade.

Kate remained frozen to the spot. Her mind had been connecting dots without realising what the final picture was supposed to be. In every subsequent conversation Finn had spoken of his love for Amy and how he felt guilty about failing to protect her. How had she fallen for his lies?

He'd made no movement towards her, but the threat of the weapon in his hands quelled Kate's urge to rush at him.

She jumped as he finally spoke. 'I didn't mean for it to happen.' His words were barely discernible beneath the weight of anguish. 'I didn't know what else to do.'

Kate's breathing had quickened, but the rise and fall of her chest was steady. Trying not to draw attention to any sudden movement, her fingers slowly reached into her trouser pocket and slid her phone out and onto the sofa. Delicately brushing her finger over the print sensor, she unlocked the screen and tried to call the first name in her contacts without looking.

'Tell me what happened? I'm sure—'

His head snapped up. 'Shut up!' His eyes were still filled with tears, but there was confusion in the darting movements of the pupils. 'I killed her… I killed Amy…' His shoulders seemed to relax as the pressure of the burden he'd been carrying for the past year lifted.

'Finn? Look at me,' she said, fixing him with a stare, the phone hidden by her hand. 'It's okay. I'm your friend, remember? Just tell me what happened.'

He thrust the blade forwards defensively, but there was still a six-foot space between them. The light overhead glistened off the blade. 'You won't understand. It wasn't my fault… not really. It was an accident… she… Oh God, what have I done?'

Kate gently flapped her free hand in an effort to calm him. 'Please, Finn, sit down and tell me what happened. If it was an accident, then I'm sure we can—'

His eyes darted left and right, but his knife arm remained flexed, ready to strike if threatened.

'Amy called me from the theatre,' he began, his eyes fixed on the wall as the memory played out in his mind. 'She said she'd had a tough week and was looking forward to the family catch-up at the weekend. She asked if I'd pick her up and drive her to my dad's that night. I didn't feel great, but I'd have done anything for her. She knew that. I loved her. She was more than my sister. I collected her from a car park near the Southbank. She said she needed to pick up a few bits and pieces from home, so I drove us to her flat. She told me to come up while she packed. She opened some wine and…'

Kate couldn't tell how much of the conversation her phone was capturing. She needed to get him closer to the microphone.

'I could see her changing from the mirror in her bedroom. She never realised just how beautiful she was. I don't know if it was the wine, but I couldn't stop watching her. She caught me looking and asked me to come into her room and adjust the straps on her top. My fingers trembled as they brushed the skin of her back, and I leaned down and kissed the nape of her neck. Her hand brushed my cheek, and she turned and we couldn't keep our hands off each other. She pulled my shirt off and undid my trousers, but suddenly freaked out.

'She wanted me, I'm certain of it, but as I tried to kiss her again, she pushed me away. I knew she was scared of what it could do to our family, but I'd never wanted her so much. It's not like we were related by blood.

'I told her to calm down, but she started calling me names. She was trying to make me angry, but I could never be angry with her. She stormed out of the bedroom, but tripped on something and caught the back of her head on the corner of the coffee table. There was no blood, no sound. She just lay there, her eyes closed.'

Kate pictured the post-mortem photographs. 'You tried to rape her, Finn.'

'No! She wanted me, but then she freaked out.'

'The pathologist found bruising around her thighs.'

'It wasn't like that. She wanted me to…'

She could see in his face that he'd been telling himself the same lie for so long that he was now almost convinced it was true.

His head dropped once more. 'I thought she was play-acting at first. But as I felt for a pulse, I couldn't find one. I didn't mean to kill her, but I was the only one there and I knew nobody would believe my story. I panicked. I couldn't face jail for something I hadn't done. And then I spotted the knife in a box near the computer. There was a packet of cleansing wipes too, and photographs of the other crime scenes. Suddenly the answer was so clear. She'd left me the tools to save myself.

'I carried her down to the alley and removed her underwear. She'd told me how the killer wiped his victims down, and slashed them with the knife. I knew that if I could make it look like he'd done it, then nobody would suspect me. It was so difficult to cut her up like that. I had to finish the bottle of wine to get the courage to do it.'

Finn looked back up at her. 'I was ill for days. I was convinced you lot would see through what I'd done and come and arrest me, but you seemed so keen to go along with her being another of the serial killer's victims that I thought it would be okay. I made a promise that I would do whatever it took to find the monster she'd been hunting and ensure he paid for all the pain he'd caused. And now, now we have!'

Trying to keep him calm, Kate raised the phone. 'I can call one of my colleagues to come and take a formal statement from you. I will explain the situation and—'

He dived forward, striking her hand with his own, sending the phone crashing across the room and into the wall. 'I can't go to prison for what happened. It wasn't my fault.'

Kate's eyes widened, the blade only inches from her face. 'You don't want to make things worse, Finn. Let me take you in. It's what Amy would have wanted—'

His face flashed with anger. 'How would you know what *she* wanted? You're just as responsible for what happened to her. And now – now you've left me with no choice…'

CHAPTER SEVENTY-NINE

Kate dodged as he swung the blade towards her. 'You're not thinking straight, Finn. Killing me isn't the answer. People know you're here…' Her eyes darted as she tried to think of anything else that would stall him while she tried to find something to defend herself with. Her eyes fell on his phone. 'And your phone is here too. Laura knows you're here and your phone's signal will validate the fact; they'll soon come looking for you.'

'It doesn't matter anymore. I'll go on the run.'

'No, Finn. Life on the run isn't easy. Always looking over your shoulder to see who's chasing you. And believe me, killing a police officer will mean you *always* have someone on your back.'

He sneered. 'You lot didn't find me for a whole year.'

'But think about how that secret has haunted you. You said you weren't sleeping properly, the farm is struggling financially and your marriage is on the rocks. You're not coping, Finn. You know you have to do the right thing and come clean. I can help you; I can make sure you get a fair hearing. You'll be able to explain your side of the story.'

He took a step closer. 'It's too late for all that. I don't want prison, and I don't want my parents disowning me for what I've done. This is the only way.'

Finn gripped the knife, blocking Kate's only way out. She was trapped.

'You're not a killer, Finn. You said Amy's death was an accident. It's different.'

'You said yourself: desperate people are capable of so much more.'

'You're not thinking clearly, Finn. There isn't another suspect you can pin this on. Brookes and Nicola Isbitt are gone. There isn't another psycho out there who'd try and kill me. This will be examined over and over until they arrest you. Go now and you can do your best to get away before I call it in.'

He saw his phone on the sofa next to her and grabbed it. 'You won't be phoning anybody.' Then racing to where her phone had landed, he stamped on it until the screen cracked and dimmed. 'There we go.'

Kate scanned the room again. Her crutches were on the floor where they'd fallen earlier. If she could stretch her right foot out, she might just be able to hook one of the handles with her toes. It wouldn't do much to scare him off, but it could provide some protection, even if just to keep him a short distance away.

He turned and moved back to the window that looked down on the communal garden. 'You were right earlier… things did go a bit further with Amy. She seduced *me* though. She wanted me to watch her changing, that's why she left her bedroom door open and stood in view of the mirror.'

Stretching her foot out, Kate couldn't shake the feeling of light-headedness washing over her.

'I knew she wanted me. She lived for danger and sought it wherever she could find it. Coming after me was the ultimate temptation. If our parents weren't married she wouldn't have looked twice at me. But the thing was, I wanted her just as much.'

The loophole of Kate's crutch was just out of reach. She tried to shuffle herself down the sofa cushion. Her toes were barely an inch from touching the grey plastic.

'I let her seduce me. I'd have done anything for her, and she knew how to wrap me around her finger. But she got cold feet and pushed me away. I fell off the edge of the bed. She raced out of the room, but I chased after her. I was still aroused and wanted her to explain what was wrong. I could see she still wanted me, but she was denying it. We crashed into the shelving unit in the lounge, and we fought, but she drove her knee into my privates, and as she clambered up, I reached for her foot, and it was *that* trip that caused her to fall and bang her head.' He turned and saw Kate's right leg straining to reach the crutch. He moved quickly towards it and kicked the crutch further away.

Kate's shoulders slumped, and she shuffled back up the cushion, anticipating what he planned next. 'Don't do this.'

He tilted his head as a sickening smile spread across his face. 'How's your head, Kate?'

Her face wrinkled with confusion. 'My head?' A wave of nausea swept through her, and the feeling of light-headedness grew. 'What did you…?' She glanced back at the mug of coffee.

'I'll phone Laura when I'm done here and tell her how worried I am about you. I'll tell her you're devastated by your failure to find the real culprit, and that I'm concerned about your health. I know your colleagues have been worried about your mental state in recent weeks. Laura will turn up here and find you in a bath of water, both wrists slit, and your death will be ruled a suicide. Nobody will be looking for me, because you'll have killed yourself.'

Her vision was blurring and lethargy made her limbs sluggish. 'What did you do?'

Finn's manic grin grew wider. 'I crushed and mixed some of the painkillers I found in the kitchen into your drink. Your death will be a tragic tale of how far you pushed yourself to solve Amy's murder. Right. Over. The. Edge.'

Two blurred images of his face smiled down on her as he pocketed the knife, and bent to scoop her up. She tried to flap a fist towards him, but her arm barely registered the movement. As Kate tried to speak, her face felt like it had dropped and the words that came out were slurred.

*

By the time he had lowered her into the tub, she'd lost feeling in both arms and legs. But her hearing remained strong. The plug chain echoed off the edges of the bathtub as he fitted the plug and turned on both taps. The water rushed out of the tap and she could just about sense it lapping against her. Kate made one further attempt to reason with him, but the words that came out were incoherent.

CHAPTER EIGHTY

Water splashed against Kate's cheeks as she battled to stay conscious. Her eyes were too heavy to remain open, but if she could just stay focused, she was certain she would think of something. Her body felt warm, but she couldn't tell if that was the temperature of the bath water or whatever he'd drugged her with.

She felt him lift her right hand out of the bath. Although she couldn't control her hand, she could feel his fingers around her palm.

If only she could scratch him, or somehow leave a trace of his DNA on her body where it couldn't be cleaned off. If these were to be her final moments, she didn't want Chloe growing up thinking she'd simply given up. She'd always been a fighter.

He still hadn't pressed the blade into her skin. With all her effort, she marginally opened her left eye. Finn's profile came into view, but he was no longer looking at her. He was staring at something beyond the bathroom door.

Was someone else here?

Kate allowed the eye to close again, and focused on what she could hear. The taps were still running, and the water was lapping against her earlobes. She tilted her head ever so slightly to the right, submerging the left side of her face, and allowing her right ear to focus on indistinct sounds.

Banging? Was that what she could hear?

Her hand plunged back into the water as Finn dropped it and went off to investigate.

Had someone come to check on her? Was Laura downstairs buzzing? She needed to warn her.

Focusing on her arms, she commanded them to lift her body out of the water, but they refused to cooperate. The water level continued to rise, and suddenly water was billowing up her nostrils. With the last of her strength she sniffed, drawing the water in quicker, and then roared out in pain. She couldn't tell how loud she sounded, but the intense pain remained in her head as the water continued to flow over her face.

It would all be over in seconds. She'd heard that drowning was one of the most painful ways to die. That thought terrified her.

The water reached her right eardrum, and the rest of the room fell into silence. The last of her oxygen was running out. Her chest felt like it would implode if she couldn't get a fresh breath. The pain stretched out to her shoulders, and she began to pray that death would come for her sooner rather than later, when suddenly there was a large commotion somewhere nearby.

And then the metal chain of the plug clanged against the side of the bath, and an arm was beneath her neck, lifting her out of the water. Was this Finn checking if she was dead? She made no effort to open her eyes, not wanting to give him the satisfaction.

Trembling fingers brushed matted hair from her cheeks, and gently tapped against her skin.

A voice broke through the deathly silence. 'Can you hear me? Kate, I said, can you hear me?'

She felt weightless as she was lifted from the water and carried like a cloud through air, before being laid down on something soft.

'Wake up. Come on, Goddamn you!'

Did angels swear?

Her nose pinched and suddenly someone was blowing into her mouth. The breath tasted fishy and repulsive. It tasted like when Ben kissed her after he'd been eating a tuna sandwich.

Kate could feel the nausea building from inside her, and then a mixture of bile and water erupted out of her mouth, and she was leaned to the side as the liquid escaped.

'Oh, thank God,' the angel said. 'Kate? Kate? Can you hear me? You're going to be okay. Everything's going to be okay. Just stay with me.'

That's funny, she thought, the angel even sounded like Ben.

CHAPTER EIGHTY-ONE

When Kate woke, she was surprised to find herself in fresh pyjamas, lying on a firm mattress. She opened her eyes, and was relieved to be able to wriggle her fingers. She'd never been so thankful to feel the throbbing in her left ankle. The room looked familiar, but it wasn't her own. The whirring machines behind her head, the door at the far side of the room, and the small bathroom off to the left could only mean one thing: hospital.

A voice shouted. 'She's awake.' Ben's face filled her vision a moment later. 'How are you feeling?'

She considered the question. 'Like shit.'

He helped her sit up, and passed her a glass of water. 'Best if you sip it. You've probably swallowed enough water for one day.'

The memory of Finn's confession and actions crashed into her mind like a train. 'Ben, Finn's in the flat, you need to—'

'Shh-sh-sh, it's okay, he is in custody. You don't need to worry about him now.'

'I don't…What happened?'

'You're lucky that you've got people who care about you. You called me and I could hear muffed voices. I thought you'd dialled me by accident, but when I tried to phone back, you didn't answer. I got here as soon as I could, and I called out to you as I came through the front door, but all I could hear was the bath running. I looked towards the bathroom and saw Finn standing in the doorway, holding a knife. My instinct was to get out of the flat, but then I saw that you were in the bathtub. I don't know what came over me, but I lunged towards him, and we crashed through the door and into the medicine cabinet above the toilet.

'I saw you in the bath and wanted to lift you out of the water, but he caught me off-guard and sent me crashing back out into the hallway. He still had the knife, and kept thrusting it towards me. I thought he'd kill me, but somehow, I managed to get a couple of lucky punches in, and knocked him out.

'When I lifted you out of the bath, I was convinced I was too late. I managed to resuscitate you, before securing him and calling Laura. SSD are currently collecting evidence in the rest of the flat. I had to give them your wet clothing, I'm afraid.'

Kate blinked several times. 'You knocked him out?'

An embarrassed grin broke out across Ben's face. 'I never knew I had it in me.'

She didn't want to hide the fact that she was impressed. It was his humour and inner strength that had first attracted her to him, but there was more to him than she'd given credit for. 'I'll have to watch my step next time we argue then,' she teased.

'Your ankle is still the size of a rugby ball. You're going to have it X-rayed and I'm not going to take no for an answer.'

Kate leaned forwards and wrapped her arms around Ben's shoulders. 'For once, I'm not going to argue with you.'

CHAPTER EIGHTY-TWO

Taking her seat in the public gallery, Kate watched as Finn was led up from the cells beneath the court. Behind the glass, two prison officers escorted him into the dock and removed his handcuffs.

Finn's father was seated in the front row of the gallery, but he'd made no effort to acknowledge Kate. Amy's mum had been too distraught to attend court, and now that the jury had confirmed they'd reached a verdict, they were only minutes away from learning the outcome.

Despite the extensive swelling of Kate's ankle following Nicola Isbitt's attack, the X-ray confirmed no permanent damage, and she'd attended the office a few days later, receiving full clearance from the Professional Standards board following the high-speed pursuit. The supe had looked neither pleased nor disappointed. Armitage's positive feedback to the supe had probably aided that.

In the days that had followed the raid on Brookes's flat, they'd discovered letters he'd written to his dead sister, vowing that he would avenge her pain and suffering. Somewhere in his warped view, he'd held those in social services accountable for the continued abuse she'd suffered at the hands of their father. Mrs Graham had confirmed Steph had originally been born to the Olufabe family, and in the days before his death, Brookes had been planning a trip to Holland where the fourth care worker's son had moved to. Brookes had planned to use the £2,000 he'd withdrawn in the week prior to Amy's murder to buy a ticket to Holland, and probably to kill his fourth intended victim. But what he would have done after that was anybody's guess. Kate knew he would have struggled to return to any kind of normal life.

Despite Finn's confession to Kate in the flat, he'd taken his solicitor's guidance and refused to answer a single one of her colleagues' questions. Armitage's team had had him transferred back to London, but his silence had endured. Kate watched him now, his head bowed, staring at the floor.

There'd been no sign of his wife in court either, though Kate had heard a rumour that she had filed for divorce in light of what had happened.

Kate had expected to feel a huge weight lifted from her shoulders, now that she knew nothing she'd done had led to Amy's murder, but when she closed her eyes, rather than seeing Amy's still face on the pavement, she imagined Finn's face staring down at her through the water. She remembered the overwhelming sense of dread as the water filled her lungs and the devastating knowledge that Chloe would never see her again. And she would never see Chloe.

She'd trusted Finn, and at no point had she questioned his motives for wanting Amy's murder blamed on someone else. The supe had been right to warn her that she was too close to see what was really going on. But it had been her responsibility to learn the truth. Even though Amy had acted out of character by going to the theatre that night, Kate should never have allowed her to be in that position in the first place. It was her responsibility to protect all of the officers in her team. Whilst she hadn't fallen naturally into motherhood when Chloe had arrived, she had to embrace a maternal role with her team.

The head juror passed the piece of paper towards the usher, who in turn passed it to the clerk to examine, before the judge commanded Finn to stand. Finn's head remained bowed, and as the judge confirmed the guilty verdict, he looked up and stared at Kate, and she was sure she saw relief in his eyes.

To this day she couldn't be certain that he would have cut her wrists had Ben not arrived. Although he'd said he would, and he'd started filling the bath, she couldn't escape the possibility that he would have changed his mind and pulled her free. Ultimately, he'd struggled with the guilt of what had happened to Amy, and he probably would have confessed the truth at some point. Although he would now spend the best part of his life incarcerated, he would do so knowing he'd shared his dark secret.

Kate had seen enough. She stood, left the gallery and headed down the stairs out into the cool breeze. She didn't expect gratitude or congratulations. But she'd achieved justice for Amy. She had done her job.

A LETTER FROM STEPHEN

Yay, you've made it to the end of *Dying Day*. I was pulling my hair out towards the end, were you? If you want to be kept updated on my other Kate Matthews novels, join the mailing list here: www.bookouture.com/stephen-edger. You can also get in touch via Facebook or Twitter. Nothing thrills me more than hearing from a reader who has enjoyed my books; I promise, I won't bite!

I want to thank you for reading the novel. If you enjoyed it, I would be so grateful if you could leave a review. It doesn't need to be long, just a few words, but it makes such a difference. It will help new readers discover one of my books for the first time. I cannot understate the importance that book reviews play for authors. Every review has the potential to lead to an extra sale, and every extra sale encourages a writer to work on their next story.

I am busy working on the third instalment in this series, and I promise you're in for a treat. Kate Matthews' journey will continue in the New Year. Thank you again for reading my book. I hope to hear from you soon.

Stephen Edger

: www.stephenedger.com/

: AuthorStephenEdger

: @stephenedger.

ACKNOWLEDGEMENTS

I'd like to say special thanks to the following people, without whom *Dying Day* wouldn't be in existence today:

Parashar Ramanuj, my best friend for more than twenty years and my first port of call whenever I have strange questions about medical procedures and body parts; Joanne Taylor, who has been reading and providing feedback on my novels since the beginning; Elaine Emmerick for reading and championing my work; and my incredibly supportive family, in particular my wife Hannah, who puts up with my mind wandering mid-conversation as a new plot twist strikes.

I'd like to thank my eagle-eyed editor Jessie Botterill and the incredible team of editors, cover designers and marketers at my publishers Bookouture. I've learned so much and everyone has made me feel so welcome. I'd also like to give a shout out to the other Bookouture authors who are massively supportive and super talented.

Final thanks must go to every reader of my books for encouraging me to follow my dream and not to give up.

Ingram Content Group UK Ltd.
Milton Keynes UK
UKHW021834060723
424684UK00011B/722